Tower

of

Vengeance

by

Samantha Ward-Smith

published by

Mabel and Stanley Publishing – Jan 2025

©Samantha Ward-Smith - All Rights Reserved

Tower of Vengeance

Disclaimer

This is a work of fiction. Unless otherwise indicated, all the names, characters, businesses, places, events and incidents in this book are either the product of the author's imagination or used in a fictitious manner. Any resemblance to actual persons, living or dead, or actual events is purely coincidental.

Trigger Warning

This work contains a brief depiction of sexual violence, which some readers may find distressing. The content has been kept to a minimum and is included to reflect the historical context of the period in which the story is set. Reader discretion is advised.

Tower of Vengeance

For Howie

Prologue

1214

The smell of roses is sweet and heady. My hand caresses a soft, velvet petal and I luxuriate in the intoxicating perfume. My garden is a tapestry of colour – vivid reds, delicate pinks, pure whites, and sunshine yellows. The summer's breeze warms my face, and I feel the silk of my gown caress my glowing body. I watch my young son running ahead as I pause. He turns and urges me to follow, and I laugh as my small lapdog jumps up at him, causing him to tumble. They are a tangle of limbs with shrieks of joy and yaps of excitement.

'Maude.' My name is whispered, and I feel my husband's arms around me. I close my eyes and sink into his strong embrace. A masculine smell of horse, leather, and sweat. His lips in my hair. A murmur of desire.

Suddenly, a door slams.

I open my one good eye. The other is swollen shut, encrusted with blood. The dream fades. Through the bars of the cage, I see the grim walls of the turret. I feel the cold wind as it chases through the thin arrow slits which encircle me in my prison. I hear footsteps coming up the stairs and I attempt to shrink back to protect myself, but the cage is small and I can

Tower of Vengeance

only crouch in my filth, my gown torn and my body weak from the days I have already passed here.

I watch as the King's man enters. That same familiar sneer on his ugly face. He is the man who brought me here, the one who keeps asking me to submit to his master. In his hands are a tankard and a covered plate. My stomach betrays me as it groans with hunger, for I cannot remember when I last ate. He beckons me with a smile, and I shuffle forward on hands and knees which catch on rotten straw.

My cracked lips sip from the proffered ale. It is glorious in its wetness and helps soothe my dry throat. He allows me only one sip before he uncovers the plate. My mouth salivates with desire at the plump white egg that he now offers. He picks it up and holds it to my mouth. My teeth bite down on exquisite softness. But hunger is a false friend. A bitter taste explodes on my tongue and as I hesitate, his smile is replaced with a smirk as he forces the egg into my mouth, clamping it shut, holding my head as I struggle. It is too late. In that split second, I recognise the belladonna berry that was pushed into that deceitful egg. I know from my own experience of growing the plant that just one berry can be deadly, and my fate is sealed.

He releases his hand and laughs at his betrayal. I spit out what I can and my body retches, trying desperately to expel the poison that is now coursing through me. My heart is beating faster at the realisation that within a short while I, Maude de Mandeville, will be dead.

Tower of Vengeance

Everything I love has been taken from me. All because of the King's desire and power, and my own stubbornness not to submit to his will. He has won and I am defeated. The Wheel of Fortune has turned against me.

My murderer leaves me to be alone in my despair at my fate. Too soon, death will come for me. I will never see or hold my husband and son again. I could weep if I only had the strength. I shiver from the cold although my face burns, flushed with this wretched poison. Even the sound of the ravens circling the turret, calling loudly, cannot keep me from the grip of death which tightens in these final moments.

But a voice whispers to me…*There is a choice to be made.*

Tower of Vengeance

PART ONE

Maude

Tower of London

As my life drained out of me, I found my shadow self at the crossroads with Death. He was a silent figure, shrouded by a cloak, face concealed until the moment you die. Behind me was the cold turret where I could see my mortal body struggling with my last breaths. A pointless task, as poison such as this has no cure. I could feel the hopelessness of it all, of a life taken too soon, but as I despaired, a figure appeared from behind Death. For a moment, I thought it was my husband, Geoffrey, with his dark hair curling down his long, white neck, and with his ready, charming smile. But I knew it could not be him for this figure was no mortal. The man before me had skin that shone like alabaster, contrasting with the darkness of his hair. His clothes were a fire of red silk that shimmered as he walked.

    As the handsome young man approached me, he held out his hands towards mine and, clasping me to him, I could see such kindness and understanding in his deep blue eyes. I broke down sobbing and begged him to help me, to let me live, for surely he was an angel sent to save me after I had been so unfairly wronged.

    'Death has claimed your mortal body already and I cannot cheat him of that, but I can offer your soul a choice,' he said softly in his beguiling voice.

Tower of Vengeance

'But first I will show you three paths and down one of them Death will lead you unless you take what I offer you.' We turned towards the first path.

'Behold Purgatory, the waiting place for most of the dead before they are allowed in Heaven. Where sins are tallied, confessions counted, and funeral masses accrued.' He paused to look at me. 'However, you will die unshriven. You cannot confess your sins; murder has taken that from you. Your family, scared and forbidden to even mention your name, will be unable to say enough masses and prayers to help you. How long do you think it would take you to escape Purgatory? You could be in this limbo for eternity,' he warned me.

The path he showed me was shadowy, but although I was unable to see what lay ahead, I could feel the weight of expectation, of desperation, and an impatience to be gone from the poor souls within. We turned from it as I was led along to the second path that sparkled with a golden glow. The dread I had felt on that previous path lifted and was replaced with a sense of peace and happiness, as if all my cares had dissipated.

'This second path is Heaven,' the man whispered, as if he too was in awe at the sight in front of him, 'that beautiful, wondrous place where all is harmony and love. To go straight there, however, you must be truly good, a saint rather than a sinner. You can pay the pardoner all you can afford from your earthly riches, but he gives you false hope. God sees all; he sets your time in Purgatory, controls your access to Heaven. It is a difficult path to be allowed to travel, especially for those who die without penance or absolution such as you.' He sighed and I once again felt a hopelessness, knowing without doubt that this path was blocked to me until such time as God might allow. This man was right – how could I be absolved of my sins when I had been unable to confess? Would God be merciful to a poor murdered soul? I remembered that the priests had always told us that He would not give mercy to the unshriven, so I realised entering Heaven was unlikely.

'Come, let us see the final path.' The man gestured, pulling me away to see what lay ahead, but I already knew. The final path could only lead to damnation, to fiery Hell from whence I could hear the cries of despair and agony. Punishment for the greatest of sins. The Devil's kingdom. I wondered if I truly deserved Hell and if instead it should be my murderer in my place. Why was this man, my angel, tormenting me so?

'Down which path does your life deserve to take you, do you think? Shall we look?' The man clicked his fingers and the scene changed.

My blessed childhood played out before me as I stood before Death. Cosseted by my loving father, Robert Fitzwalter, and my handsome older brother, Walter, it brought back happy memories, for we were a rich and powerful family. My life was one of comfort without care. Then came my marriage to Geoffrey de Mandeville, the Earl of Essex, and a worthy match for one such as me. He was also my father's strongest ally. He was a handsome, good, kind man. It wasn't difficult to love him. I was the

Tower of Vengeance

luckiest of women and grateful for my good fortune at securing such a match.

I was in my sunlit home, filled with happiness and laughter. I saw my stillroom with my servant, Maria, helping me as we made cures and potions for the household. The smell of the rose garden gently wafted through the windows, and I could hear my young son playing. And then I was dancing in the great halls of my father and of my husband. Endless nights of pleasure at a dazzling court. I felt the admiration amongst the men for I was regarded as beautiful and, knowing the value of that beauty, I basked in their attention while remaining loyal to my husband, who also took delight in his captivating wife. There was such pride in my face as I saw them coveting me, for youth makes us brave and we are careless with our vanity.

Before I could stop it, I was once again reliving that dreadful, fateful night at Baynard's Castle, my father's London home a short ride from the formidable Tower of London. The candles were flickering, the noise of the guests was so loud, and there was an underlying tension in the Great Hall. I wanted to turn from the scene that had led me here to my death. The King was seated next to me, stroking my arm as he leant towards me. I retreated from him, a look of revulsion on my face, unable to conceal my disgust of the man who was an enemy of my family. He came with false promises because he did not want peace after all; he wanted to gain a mistress. Too late had we understood his purpose, and now I was trapped. He seized my arm and pulled me up from my

Tower of Vengeance

chair. I screamed and the world went black.

Another click of the man's fingers, and I regained myself as I saw the familiar stone walls of my prison again. I had been brought here in the dark of night, dragged up the winding staircase of the Stone Tower and thrown into this small square cage within the round turret. I was trying to ease my battered body off the floor, but I was too weak. That cruel wind was dancing through the small windows, and I shivered in my once beautiful green gown now torn. I fell back onto the filthy straw which had been hastily scattered on the floor of the cage. Then the door opened, and the King's man had returned to ask me once again:

'King John wants to know if you will submit.'

I used all my strength and spat at him. Defiance was all I had left after everything had been taken from me. I no longer cared what would happen to me. There could be no way back after I had rejected the King.

'We'll see how long you last without food and ale. The King wins. He always does.' He laughed, enjoying watching my torment.

'On my son's life, I will never submit. I curse your wretched King.' I could never betray my marriage vows to the man I loved; or betray my family, who were sworn enemies of the King. I would not submit to the very man they hated. I would not be able to look my son in the eyes if I let King John bed me. Even if it spared me my life, it was not a fate that I could live with.

Tower of Vengeance

'Bleeding witch,' the man hissed, as he recoiled from my words. 'Your son is as good as dead.' And he left the room as quickly as he had entered.

Reliving that moment again made me worry about the future of my beloved son, as I found myself back at the crossroads. My guide looked at me quizzically. 'How important is your son's life? Your wish for revenge? Does the path Death will choose for you give you what you most desire?'

My entire being willed revenge on King John, the man who ordered my murder, who tore me away from my life, my family, my little boy. I could only hope my son was still safe. I worried about his fate if the King had found him. I was certain that monster would order my son's death, and the thought broke my heart, for I would do anything to protect my family.

'I can give you such power,' the man whispered in my ear.

'Who are you?' I summoned the courage to ask.

'I am the Devil of course, and I come to offer you a pact.' He laughed softly, caressing my hands.

I gasped. He looked nothing like the devils who cover the church walls, for he had no horns, forked tail, or cloven hooves, no burning fires dancing around him. But even though I had been taught that the Devil is evil, I found that he had such a charisma that I could not pull away from him. I had

Tower of Vengeance

to hear what he had to say, for I had nothing left and the paths shown me would not bring me peace.

'I see you falter, my dear. But come, do you truly want to spend an eternity in Purgatory whilst your death goes unavenged? King John will be joining me soon in the depths of Hell. He has an appointment with Death that grows ever closer. But he has children who prosper in palaces, surrounded by luxury, destined to marry, to have children themselves and continue his line. The son who will wear the golden crown next is no better than his father, for he too will wish to destroy your family. Your own son, although safe for now, is destined to a short, unhappy life if you do nothing, for men will search for him. Despite his young years, he has enemies in high places who want him dead. Your son will die on the London road sixteen years from now if you do not take my deal. King John's son will take his own revenge on your family. Is that what you want? Another life to be unjustly cut short?'

'What can I do?' I asked, determined to save my son.

'In return for your soul, I will give you the gift of the afterlife, where you can stay here within these walls as a spirit with the opportunity to avenge your death and to protect your son. But I will not allow you to kill those of royal blood, that is my one condition. If you break this rule, your son or his family will die too.' The Devil laughed before continuing, 'But there are other forms of revenge that you can use. After all, you were born with the power of magic as the daughter of witches.'

Tower of Vengeance

'My mother.' I smiled remembering her. I had long known of her powers whispered to me by her old servant Maria, who had cared for me after my mother's untimely death. But I had dared not believe that I had inherited her abilities.

'Trust in your inheritance and your magic will come,' he said, reading my thoughts. 'Use your emotions, as these are a great tool to harness your power. Test your strength, for you will have the capacity to kill if it aids both your son and your revenge…unless of course they are royal – remember my stipulation. Real revenge comes not from Death but from emotional suffering, anguish, a love destroyed, a life changed; there are so many ways to hurt a person without killing them. Nevertheless, be careful of your desire for vengeance, for it can change not just you but your family too. Every life you take could have consequences on who you become and how it affects your own son.'

'Can I leave the Tower? Can I see my son?' I was eager to know.

'No, you cannot leave these walls. They are your strength and will tether your spirit after your death. And you will need to wait for your son. However, you can use the time wisely to forge your ties, to gain your power, to be ready to protect him. But come, you must decide, for soon your mortal body succumbs and your soul will be ready to depart. Will you take my kind offer and stay here as a ghost avenging your murder, protecting your poor helpless son, or let Death decide your fate? Only I doubt you will leave Purgatory for a very long time if that is what Death chooses for you,' he warned with a chuckle.

    I looked in Death's dark eyes as I gave my soul to the Devil, replacing one eternity with another more dangerous path. It was the only choice I could make to protect my son and seek revenge. I watched my body slumped on the turret floor, the last breath of life extinguished. I began my existence on the edge of death, with just the ravens for company. Creatures of darkness who sensed my loss, my anger, and who would help when the time came to bring my son to me for his own protection and save his life from the fate that would otherwise await him.

The Stranger

Sixteen Years Later

The raven stopped pecking the eyeball in the severed head it had been enjoying and listened to the voice carried by the wind. As it spoke to her, the raven spread her tattered wings and flew into the winter sky. She soared above the London skyline, beyond the smoking chimneys where they met the grey clouds. She followed the road leading out of the city, where carts filled with valuable goods trundled back and forth, taking no notice of the peddlers, the farmers, and the soldiers on their own journeys. The breeze lifted her over the green fields of Essex until finally the raven came to a small village where the daily market had finished for the day. She swooped down and settled on the ale-stake swinging gently over the decrepit old alehouse. The establishment was gradually filling up with people eager to spend their meagre earnings on a much-needed pot of ale. The raven waited and watched the road as the pink afternoon sky slowly faded into dusk.

William de Mandeville was cold and hungry as he walked along the path. He was covered in mud, his clothes soaked by the unrelenting rain, and his legs ached from being on the road for two days now. He had not dared stop since he left the Priory. To avoid being discovered, he had trudged through the woods rather than risk the easier route of the road. His mouth was dry from lack of fluid and his body faint as the last meagre piece of bread he had snatched before he fled was now a distant memory. He needed to rest awhile and have something to sustain him if he was to have the strength to continue his journey to safety. He shivered from the chill of the evening as the rain continued to fall. When he spotted the alehouse, he wondered if he could take such a risk. Deciding he was in desperate need of refreshment, he pushed open the door, but didn't notice the raven looking down at him from the ale-stake.

The room was crowded, and he was immediately cheered by the warmth of the fire. Will savoured the comfort it brought after his dangerous journey, which had left him weary. He made his way to a table in the furthest corner, tucked away in the shadows so as not to attract attention, and handed over a few precious coins for a pot of ale and a bowl of hot pottage. He greedily ate the tasteless stodge and guzzled down the weak ale, relieved to sate his hunger and thirst. So intent was he on finishing his meal that he did not notice the old woman who had slipped onto the bench beside him.

No sooner had he ate than the door swung open and a group of armed men marched in. The lively chatter hushed to silence. Will could feel his own heart pounding so loudly he thought it might beat out of his chest. He pulled his cloak over his head, shrinking back as much as he could in a desperate attempt to avoid being recognised, but knowing it was unlikely he would escape.

Tower of Vengeance

'We are looking for William de Mandeville, wanted on the orders of King Henry. He was seen in this area. Death comes to anyone who shields him and a reward to anyone who gives him up!' barked a tall man with a scarred face, his cloak displaying the King's insignia. He gestured to his men to search the room. Roughly, they started to pull men from their seats, demanding to know their business in the village before throwing them back down once they realised they were not the man they sought. Will, gripping the ale pot, knew it was over. It had been a risk to come here and one he felt foolish for taking now that he would be caught. These were the same men who had pursued him from the Priory; they would know him by sight and even in the unlikely case they didn't, he had no business here nor anyone to vouch for him. Despite his best efforts, the chase was over and soon he would be the prisoner of the King who had long wanted him dead, the same fate that had befallen his mother.

As one of the guards approached his table, the old woman beside Will grabbed his arm. He flinched at the stranger's touch, but she held firm as if to calm his trembling body and steady him.

'Me and my son have come from market,' she explained to the man, her milky grey eyes appearing to mesmerise him. 'He's a simple boy and easily scared. We are merely resting awhile and will soon be on our way.' The man hesitated, but the woman held his gaze. Will waited breathlessly to see what the man would do.

'Anything over there?' the scarred man yelled over to his charge. Will looked down as the woman gripped his arm tighter.

'No, nothing but an old woman and her fool,' the guard replied. Will nearly collapsed with relief as the man turned away from the table, leaving them alone in the gloom. The men, unsuccessful in their quest, left the alehouse; the other customers quickly departed too, keen to avoid further trouble that evening.

Will and the old woman stayed in the shadows for a few moments. He whispered to her, 'Who are you? Why did you save me? I owe you my life.'

She leant towards him, and he could smell the stale ale as she answered in a low voice, 'I am Maria, an old friend of your mother's. I took you to the Priory when you were three. I have never stopped watching you these past sixteen years. I had word you had fled here.'

He gasped at the mention of his mother, as her death was a distant memory. He had been a young child when she passed, but he knew it was one of the reasons his life was now in danger. He wondered how this old crone had known such a lady as his mother, but then there was something familiar about her face even now she had aged. Her once smooth skin had wrinkled, yet there was still a twinkle in her once vibrant eyes. He tried to capture the fleeting memory of his beloved mother with another woman laughing in a sunlit room. Maria – the name was indeed known to him.

'We have little time,' she warned him. 'Those men will not give up, and I cannot always save you. Heed my advice and then be gone. Continue on this road and make for London. I know you plan to seek out your grandfather, but his house is being watched and it is a trap in waiting. If you try to go to him, you will be caught. Instead, travel to the Stone Tower which lies at London's heart. Ask at the gatehouse for a woman called Jane Lund. She runs the Tower's alehouse known as The Stone Kitchen. Tell her you are the son of her sister, Alice, who married Peter the Tanner.' She spoke with haste, eager to aid his safe passage.

Will was perplexed. 'But what of this woman and her husband? Where are they now? Why would she believe I am their son?'

'They are dead of the flux along with their only son, Will. A strapping lad of nineteen like you,' she explained, and he felt a shiver at sharing a name with the dead boy. 'Jane Lund is in need of a lad like you. Her husband has recently passed and, in her grief, she will hardly question you. There is a daughter, Emma; she is young and full of dreams. Give Jane this. She will know it.' She placed an old poppet doll in his hand.

'This seems a cruel charade. Why should I listen to you?' he stuttered, uneasy at the thought of such deception.

Tower of Vengeance

She made to leave but not before pleading with him a final time. 'Because you have nothing else. I know who you are and what you have done. The Tower will hide you but be careful, as it also has its temptations, and she awaits you.' With those parting words she left, and Will was all alone apart from the alewife clearing the room. The old woman had disappeared so hastily it was as if she had never been there. But as he looked down, he saw the poppet in his hand, so assured himself she must have been real. He needed to heed her advice and leave at once before the men returned, and get as far away from Essex, to seek sanctuary in the city.

The woman's plan seemed foolhardy, but he felt he had little other choice if his grandfather's house was indeed being watched as she claimed. He had heard of the great Tower in London, the castle similar in some ways to that in Colchester. There had been gossip amongst the women in the Priory kitchen that his mother had died there. He left the alehouse and started walking, wondering if he could be so bold as to hide in the fortress of the King himself.

He panicked that more men were hunting him when he heard horses thundering along the London road behind him. He crouched behind a tree and, as they passed within inches of their quarry, he realised making for the Tower and Jane Lund was his only choice.

The raven had flown up from the ale-stake and covertly followed Will from above as he made his way to the city. Will was careful to keep off the road now, walking through the cold night, not daring

Tower of Vengeance

to venture into the numerous hamlets and villages that he could oftentimes glimpse through the trees that shielded him. He became ever wearier as the chill set in his body, but he remained determined to reach the safety of the city. After another long, arduous day, London came into sight as night once again threw its mantle over the sky. Will settled down in one of the many ditches to await the opening of the city gates, relieved to rest awhile.

The raven left Will and flew to the Stone Tower, where she knew Maude, her mistress, waited for the safe arrival of her son. And as the sun rose on a new morning, the bakers, the butchers, the pie-men all readied themselves for a busy day. The skilled labourers bustled on their journeys to start their work. The street whores returned to their wretched beds after a night's trade. The merchants and bankers stepped around the beggars hurrying to make their money. The children raced through the streets – playing, begging, stealing. No one could see the ghost of the woman as she watched from above; they would simply see the raven, feathers ruffling in the breeze.

Unaware that he was being watched, Will opened his eyes as the bells rang out to indicate the city gates had finally opened. He was cold and covered in mud from the dark, damp ditch he had sheltered in last night. He clambered out, brushing off what dirt he could to make himself more presentable, and joined the throng of people making their way to one of London's great gates. He had been told to enter by the Aldgate and could see the imposing Tower of London shimmering in the distance, its four turrets standing out against the city skyline.

After the days on the road with only his own company, Will was unprepared for the noise and the large volume of people pushing their way into the city alongside him. It felt as if a thousand bells rang out across the rooftops calling the people to their various destinations. As he entered the city, Will encountered the tradesmen selling their wares, tempting the travellers with hot pies and lumps of bread. Their cries merged with those begging for coins or food, over the moans of the sick who huddled in the cramped busy streets. The odour of the city was one of decay, rotten food, and the bitter smoke coming from the many fires and chimneys. London was unlike anywhere Will had ever been. It overwhelmed him and he almost regretted that meeting with the old woman who had sent him to the city, not sure how he would find his way here.

But somewhere within these city walls was his grandfather's house. He would need to see if it was indeed being watched. If not, Will could make contact with his grandfather and he would be safe; his birthright could be fought for and a supplication made to the King to show clemency. Failing that, his grandfather had the resources to send him back into hiding, perhaps this time despatching him overseas to one of his households there. Will had to believe he could be reunited with his family and regain his status, otherwise he would have nothing left. It had been the thing he had dreamed of when he was in the Priory and he couldn't face the thought of being alone in the world.

Tower of Vengeance

Lost in his thoughts, Will had not noticed how far he had walked through the city, as he was unexpectedly confronted with the Tower walls. In front of them lay the moat – a foul, dank ribbon of water that snaked around the castle. Will could see that it would undeniably be effective for prisoners or invaders, as few would choose to jump into its murky depths, which contained all manner of waste and dead animals. The smell mingled with that of the city, and the breeze that gusted from the river gave the air a saltiness and a tang of fish.

The Tower's high, forbidding walls encompassed a large area of land, making it appear like a separate city within the walls of London. Will could make out the wooden drawbridge and gatehouse on the west side, and he strode assuredly towards it. Already there appeared to be a crowd of people entering through the gate. Wagons with supplies trundled over the drawbridge waiting for their orders to proceed, granted by the soldiers in charge. The Tower was busier than he could have imagined. The old woman had been right after all; it would be a good place to hide in plain sight with all its comings and goings.

As he grew closer to the soldiers, he felt some trepidation at how to get past them. Most of the people in the queue to enter appeared to be men who had been sent to work on the building itself, and Will heard the sound of hammers and axes already coming from within the walls.

'Name and business?' the soldier demanded.

Tower of Vengeance

'Will Lund – nephew of Jane Lund, the alewife. She runs The Stone Kitchen.' Will spoke confidently and stood tall, hoping it would be enough to be granted entry. He had no idea what he would do if the soldier refused him. He had little money left and was already exhausted, cold, and hungry. He thought of the beggars he had passed and shuddered at the thought of joining them on the merciless streets.

'About time she got some help,' the soldier grunted, and waved him through, his desire for ale outweighing any qualms he may have had about admitting a stranger into the Tower. 'Look out for the ale-stake and you will find her soon enough.'

Will breathed a sigh of relief and quickly followed the other men through the gatehouse, along a stone walkway to another tower which housed more soldiers. Will proceeded on his way without being challenged, being ushered straight through. As he emerged out of the dark interior, his eyes were drawn to the tall, square Tower itself, which dominated all around it. The walls around it shrank in comparison. It was both terrifying and beautiful. Its four turrets would be noticeable to anyone approaching the city from the river, sending out a message of strength and impregnability. Will was awestruck as he gazed up at it.

A raven swooped past as he stood there, breaking him from his reverie, and he looked around for The Stone Kitchen. To his left, in front of the Tower, stood two small buildings. The rear building was a storehouse with men unloading heavy sacks into it. At the front was a two-storeyed building. It was made of a similar stone to the surrounding walls. Its pointed tiled roof had two chimneys – one currently had a wisp of smoke snaking out of it – and it had just a few windows currently shuttered against the cold. There was one door at the end of the building, reached by a couple of steps up and facing towards the entrance tower Will had just walked through. An ale-stake was suspended over it exactly as the soldier had told him. Gathering his courage, Will entered the alehouse and hoped Jane Lund would accept him as the crone had predicted.

    Jane wearily turned towards the door as the stranger entered. It was early, and she was readying the ale for the morning service, which had not yet begun. She was surprised to see a young man enter at this hour. Although his cloak was dishevelled and splattered with mud, he did not look like one of the workmen or soldiers that usually frequented the place. As he moved closer, she could see a sharpness about the face as his dark eyes took in his surroundings, suggesting he was new here. She noticed his smooth-looking hands, which indicated he was not a labourer from the countryside or a builder who handled tools. His clothes – a black cloak, dark tunic, and sturdy footwear – were clearly of good quality even underneath the dirt.

    'I'm looking for Jane Lund,' he said. His voice was deep, with a calmness to it.

    'You've found her. And who may you be?' she enquired gruffly.

Reciting the story the old woman had told him, he replied, 'My name is Will. My mother was your sister, Alice, and my father Peter the Tanner. They both died of the flux, and I believe you are all the family I have left.' He had seen her carefully scrutinising him and he was anxious for her to accept his account, even if he also felt guilt at lying to her for his own means.

Jane was stunned by the appearance of her nephew. He had dark curly hair like Alice, and the short sturdy build of Peter, but she was hesitant to believe this refined young man was their son. Will saw the hesitation and he strengthened his resolve – she had to believe him and let him stay here, otherwise he did not know where he would go next.

'My mother told me to find you here at the Tower and to give you this so you would know that I am who I claim.' Will held out the poppet that he had been given.

Tears pricked her eyes as Jane immediately recognised her sister's childhood doll. Jane had sewn it herself and she knew every stitch, having had made it for her sister's fifth birthday. It was a simple doll made from discarded sacking; she had made the black eyes with scraps from an old cloak. The mouth was stitched with rough wool; she ran a finger over the wonky smile her nine-year-old self had made. She turned the poppet in her hand and could see her sister as clear as day in her mind's eye. Overcome with a sudden sorrow at the revelation her sister had passed, she sat down on the nearest bench to compose herself.

Tower of Vengeance

Will sat down beside her, not knowing what to do next. He felt awkward for the lie he had told and was now trapped by, but most of all he felt a keen sadness that he had brought news of the death of a clearly beloved sister. He glanced at Jane and noted the exhaustion in her drawn face, the streaks of grey in the brown hair prematurely aging her, the blue eyes faded with a deep grief, and the stooped, weary shoulders of a hard life lived. Yet if he was to survive here, Jane had to believe him and give him a place to stay, at least until he could get to his grandfather.

'Well, you could be useful to me. My husband Mark fell to his death on the north wall three nights ago in a nasty accident, and I have need of a strong pair of hands to help me.' She stuttered over her husband's name, her loss still raw. 'With all the building work and the soldiers, we are more popular than ever. You will have to sleep downstairs as my daughter Emma and I have the rooms upstairs. But you don't look like a tanner's son? Didn't you learn your father's trade?' she asked, puzzled at why he didn't look like he had known that work.

Will had been turning this over in his mind since his encounter on the road, knowing that even the simplest of souls would realise he had never been a tanner. 'I had shown some aptitude in our local church, and the parson there was frail and needed help. My father already had an apprentice, so my parents agreed that I would be tutored by him and later perhaps enter the Church myself,' he explained. 'My mother thought it would be a better life for me, but when the flux spread through the village, the parson died too. My mother, as she lay dying, implored me to come to you. She said you were the kindest of sisters and would be sure to help me. I am willing to do anything to assist you. I am strong and healthy and have some education, which may or may not be of some use to you.' There was some truth to what he told her, as he had been educated in the Priory. He just hoped he had said enough to convince her.

Jane reasoned her sister had been the clever one, and she would have wanted the best for her boy. It was their father who had pushed Alice to marry a tanner, whereas her sister always had more romantic notions. It made sense that a role for her son in the Church would have been just what Alice would have wanted. Of course, she would ensure Alice's son had a roof over his head. At such a time of loss, the rest of the family needed to stick together, and having a strong young man to help her solved the problem of how she would get by without Mark by her side.

'Come on then, let's get you settled and ready for the morning service. You need to get the dirt off those clothes and some breakfast inside you,' she ordered him, before calling to her daughter, 'Emma, bring bread and a mug of ale for your cousin as quick as you can, girl.'

As Jane turned away, calling her daughter's name, Will felt a curious sense of being watched, and his skin prickled. Something moved slowly in the gloom of the room, deep in the shadows. His heart started to race as he feared he was about to be discovered, that the ruse had not worked and a guard lay in wait for him. He shivered trying to see who was there, and he felt the sensation of someone trying to reach out to him. But as the girl entered the room, disturbing the shadows, the mood shifted. There was nothing present but a feeling of loss.

The Alewife's Daughter

As Emma brought through a tray, Will saw a girl not much younger than him, pale and as tired-looking as Jane. There was the same sorrow about her face. A face that was framed by dull brown hair and made unfriendlier by her downturned mouth. As she looked at him, he was startled by her grey eyes, which were speckled with green. Her eyes transformed her, and perhaps there were hidden depths to the plain girl after all. As she offered him the food and ale, he vaguely smelt the sweet scent of roses.

He could see her looking warily at him at first, but then he sensed a fascination and worried for a moment if he seemed too different from the usual inhabitants of the Stone Tower. He held her gaze and watched as she blushed furiously, turning hurriedly from his dark eyes. She snatched the dirty cloak from him and scurried back to the kitchen to clean it, closely followed by her mother. Will finished his ale and quietly followed, but paused at the door to listen to the two women.

He could hear Jane whispering, 'It seems so odd him turning up like this, but he had this.' She must have been showing Emma the poppet, which she had not let go of since he handed it to her. 'I know this was my sister's. And we need the help. It's hard without your father.' Her voice was tinged with sorrow.

'Yes, Ma, it'll be good to have a man to help us.' Will could hear her voice falter, as her father's recent death still stung. 'You've been so tired, and there seems to be more and more customers recently with all the work going on. But he doesn't seem like one of us. He looks like one of them who sometimes stay in the Stone Tower, with his smooth hands and skin. Has he ever done a day's work? And Ma,' she said tentatively. 'Did you smell roses?'

Will caught his breath.

'What do you mean? Roses? Are you out of your senses? He smells of the road like most travellers do, and he needs to get clean before we start serving. And such nonsense about him being like them in the palace.' Jane tutted, brushing aside Emma's words. 'Now clean that cloak, and we need to heat some water for him to scrub the dirt off. I wonder if your father's clothes will fit him?'

Will entered the kitchen as Jane climbed the stairs to the upper bedchamber, where he presumed the clothes were stored. Emma had set a large pot on the kitchen fire and was startled to see him. 'I am heating water for you to wash with, and Ma has gone to find you some clean clothes,' she explained. He could see that his presence unnerved her slightly, and she moved away from him, creating a respectable distance between them. Emma's voice was oddly soothing, and a sense of peace washed over Will. He almost laughed at the effect that this young girl had on him. Yet he quickly dismissed it as tiredness from the road, as Jane came down the stairs with a bundle of clothes.

Tower of Vengeance

'These should fit you, and you can use the old storeroom next door to wash and change. We will need to clear that room to give you a proper place to sleep, but in the meantime, you can sleep by the kitchen fire tonight. It will be warm, at least, and I'll bring down a blanket for you.' It would be odd to see him in her husband's clothes, but needs must until the boy's own clothes were clean and dry.

* * *

In the days that followed, Will learned the routine of The Stone Kitchen. The day began early, brewing the ale in the small cellar below the kitchen, with Jane explaining the types of ale for the different customers. The small ale for the consumption of the workers, and the stronger ale for the evening when the soldiers of the Constable came in. The midday service which began at ten in the morning saw one of the busiest times of the day, with the workmen coming in to partake of their daily allowance of ale, which formed part of their wages. Although they were busy then, it was an easy task handing out the pots of ale to the men and women who were momentarily breaking their long working day. It was the evening which was the hardest part of the day for the alehouse. How Jane had managed for even a few days without her husband, Will could not imagine. He soon realised why Jane had been quick to believe his story and had eagerly accepted his help. The soldiers drank hard, gambled what little money they had, and inevitably fought with each other as tempers flared. Will had to quickly learn how to break up a fight.

When new soldiers arrived or the alehouse door slammed open, Will would recall the panic of his escape, sweat breaking out on his body, and he would have to stop his hands from trembling. The nights would often bring nightmares. He dreamt of the flight from the Priory, that fateful moment he ran away haunted by the face of the man who had betrayed him. Then he would wake in the early hours, hoping he hadn't cried out in his sleep to give himself away, and would long for the day to break when he could distract himself with work.

Two months passed and there had been no discovery, so he began to feel more at ease and settle. He had begun to realise that no one really noticed the alehouse inhabitants unless they needed ale, or if he was required to step in to break up one of the numerous fights. Despite his apprehension, no one questioned him — after all, who would believe that the fugitive William de Mandeville, heir to the Earldom of Essex, was working in The Stone Kitchen?

One evening a few days later, however, he noticed a change in the customers. There was an edge to their demeanour which made him anxious. He was moving amongst the tables, collecting empty pots and jugs, refilling the ale, accepting coins, and listening to the snippets of conversation. It was late, and there were only a few men left as the fire crackled quietly and rain lightly tapped on the roof. Will went unnoticed by a group of men discussing the latest news from the city.

'I was in his lodgings today when a messenger came in with the news,' said one of the soldiers, who Will recognised as one of the Constable's more senior men, 'and he was not best pleased, I can tell you.'

'Is it true then? Is old Fitzwalter actually back?' asked another.

Will was startled at the sound of his grandfather's name, but he continued to wipe the empty table next to the men, trying not to draw attention to himself. If his grandfather was definitely back in London, he might finally have the chance to make contact with him.

'That's what the messenger said. Made his peace with the King, it seems. Denies any existence of the boy. Says it must be one of those imposters who want the de Mandeville inheritance and the title.' Will froze; the words were like a dagger to his heart. It would seem that his family had abandoned him and all could now be lost, with him resigned to a future hiding within the Tower walls and having nowhere else to turn.

'So, they were chasing a fool around Essex then?' asked one of the men, and they all laughed at the thought of their fellow soldiers chasing an imposter in the wet winter months.

'The King doesn't believe him though, so the reward still stands, and Baynard's Castle remains guarded by the King's men. A man died and the Prior disappeared. Seems odd if the boy was an imposter after all.' Will's heart sank as he realised there was no way of getting past the King's men watching his grandfather's house, and the truth about the night at the Priory was now known.

'How would they prove the boy was the de Mandeville heir? I mean, I could say it was me – what proof would I need?' The men chuckled at the idea of the grubby old soldier being a young nobleman.

The senior man lowered his voice slightly, before confiding, 'It is said he has the witch's mark. He was born with webbing between the toes of his left foot. He got it from his mother, and she was killed in this very place because she cursed old King John.' The men gasped and the fire suddenly sparked, making them jump. The word 'witch' had shocked them, and a couple of the men had made the old sign of protection, still as fearful as ever at the idea of unnatural powers at play. Will's foot tingled as if to betray the webbing that his shoe concealed, although he was stunned at the accusation his mother had been a witch and that he may well be one himself.

'I thought she had rejected the King?' the old soldier remembered. 'Wasn't there some gossip all those years ago when Fitzwalter and de Mandeville fled the country, only to return to curb the King's power with the great Carta?'

'That's what the family would have you believe. That she was a victim. But I was told by one

Tower of Vengeance

of Hubert de Burgh's men that she was born of a witch and had cursed the King. And didn't he die a year later after yielding all his power to her father and husband? Cursed, I reckon!' he muttered.

The men recoiled in shock, and this time all of them genuflected to ward away any evil power. The room felt oppressive and gloomier; the candles seemed to have dimmed. If the King's high councillor had said she was a witch, who were they to dispute it? No wonder the current King was looking for the boy. Will could only listen to their gossip and wild theories.

'The Constable is not happy. Thinks Fitzwalter is trouble, that him being in London means the problem is his, and you know how he hates to dirty his lily-white hands.' They laughed, breaking the tension as Will remained rooted to the spot. He wanted to get away from them after the claims they had made about his mother, but he hoped that they might reveal something else of value. After all, it was the first time he'd had word of his grandfather's return.

'Oi, Lund, stop wiping that bloody table and bring us more ale,' one of the men shouted, and Will, brought back to the present, hurried back to the ale barrel to fill a jug for them.

Will carried on moving around the room, dealing with a few last requests for ale while listening carefully for more news, but it seemed the men had moved on from his grandfather and were now discussing the best whores in the city. The dice money was being counted up as the evening was drawing to a close. Even though Will learned his grandfather was in London, scarcely a stone's throw from him, he had denied Will's existence. Will hoped he had done it to protect him, to keep him safe, but still it hurt to hear himself rejected by the only family he had left. Fitzwalter was so close, but Will was unable to get to him with the King's men guarding his house. If he got caught, his grandfather would be unable to save him from certain death as punishment for his own deeds, and furthermore, the revelation of Fitzwalter's own lie would destroy his peace with the King. Will needed to get a message to him so his grandfather at least knew where he was hiding, but Will wasn't sure how he would manage that as there was no one he could trust.

Emma returned from the kitchen and noticed Will's flushed face.

'Are you alright? Men not causing any trouble?'

'No, I'm fine, just hot from the fire.'

She watched him go back over to the men and saw him straining to hear what they were saying. Will had an unsettling effect on her even after these months had passed – as if there was something she should know that he was hiding from them. She was sure he was not her cousin. Her mother was quick to accept his claim, with her grief consuming her, and she had been in such a daze since her husband's death. But Emma noticed how nervous Will was of new people, as if he was worried they would recognise him. Each new group of soldiers seemed to unsettle him for a few moments. She needed to confront him but she was worried about what she might discover. She questioned who he could be and why he had entered their lives, and more importantly, why she didn't want him to leave.

Will looked over at Emma working quietly at the bar, and once again he felt a sense of peace. He walked over to her, wanting to hear her gentle, soothing voice, but then he felt something brush past him. Startled, he looked around, and asked her, 'Can you smell roses?'

Emma dropped the pot she was holding and whispered, 'You can smell them too?'

'I often smell them, and I keep wondering what causes it as we have no roses in the Tower, do we?'

'No, we don't. I keep smelling them, and at the same time I feel like I am being watched,' she admitted.

'Like there is something in the shadows?' he suggested, as he looked furtively around him. Ever since that night in the Priory, he had spent his life looking over his shoulder for soldiers, for someone coming to betray him. The feeling of being watched only heightened his fears. He thought it had just been him imagining things, but if Emma could smell the roses too, what could that mean? He wanted to question her further, to seek reassurance that it wasn't his past come to haunt him.

'What are you two fools talking about?' Jane grumbled, as she came in from the kitchen. 'There are customers who need to leave now; it's late and I want my bed, yet you two are standing there talking about bloody shadows.'

As Will bolted the alehouse door behind the last of the soldiers, he took one last look around the room, checking the fire was out and the pots were all cleared away. The shadows shifted and once again he felt something trying to reach out to him. Part of him wanted whatever it was to reveal itself, but the other part of him pushed it away, wanting it gone as he left the room for the warmth of the kitchen.

Tower of Vengeance

Maude

I continue to watch my son from the darkness, and how I long to reach out and touch him. But here I am – cursed as a phantom who cannot speak, and unable to touch my own boy who I have longed to see over the years that have kept us apart. A moth burnt by a royal flame when I danced too close. A moth who thought she was a beautiful butterfly who would dance forever surrounded by love, her children, and her roses. Maria had warned me, whispered of darkness, of pride, of revenge, and of fury within the Tarot deck. The hanged man, the falling tower, and the destruction of all that you hold dear. But yet I laughed and tossed my long black hair as I always did when I wanted to ignore something, to push away darkness with my beauty and my youth. The clinging scent of the roses I have lost haunt my despair, but their smell at least allows me to signify my presence, otherwise I would be no more than a shadow in a room. It is a curse and a gift.

    My only constant has been Maria, my faithful servant, who found Will on the London road and sent him to me. She had remained in Essex after my death and had moved to the village of Binham under a new identity to remain close to Will. She had alerted me to the commotion at the Priory after she had discovered Will's escape, when she had aided Abbot Thomas' own flight to my father. I had quickly dispatched my raven to find my son. I know not how Maria got to that alehouse so quickly when I communicated with her his whereabouts, but she has her own magical powers and she was able to guide my son on his path to me.

 It was also Maria's knowledge and experience that helped me embrace my own witch's power that I had long suppressed, and which had lain dormant throughout my mortal life. After my death she had felt the pain of my passing, had known that I had not crossed over, for it seems that she too is the Devil's creature. Slowly, she had managed to push her way through to my spirit, as if she was parting the curtains of my death chamber. I found that by focusing on the memory of her, a channel between us opened. The link between us grew stronger. She shared her knowledge and my power grew. The moving of objects, the glancing touch of my presence, the shifting of the dust in the shadows, and the power to push into someone else's mind, to sometimes communicate, but mainly to discover what they are thinking. This does not always work – the subject must be weak, and I have now discovered it does not work with Will or with those of royal blood – but when it does it can be a useful skill.

 I use it on my raven, Erin, to some effect, but as with all such creatures, she has a will of her own. My raven found me shortly after I emerged from the shadows of Death. These clever black birds are friends of the dead. Erin is my constant companion, my familiar. She can raise the dead, my clever, canny bird, but she trusts not the Devil and they avoid each other. It seems he cannot control her, which unsettles him.

Tower of Vengeance

But the years have passed. I remain a ghost within the Tower's stone walls. My murderer is dead, although his son, Henry, wears the tarnished crown. My husband, too, is dead. My father an exile. But my son has returned, and I finally have some much longed for happiness.

The Devil touches my shoulder, and we leave the alehouse for my stone turret. I feel a shock as I notice him shuffling a set of tarot cards and, remembering Maria's warnings all those years ago when I was a mere mortal, I wonder what he means to do with them. They were not mentioned as part of our sinister pact. I feel unease for the first time since I made my choice – perhaps there is a more dangerous game to be played.

'I have fulfilled part of my bargain, have I not?' He smiles and casually pulls out a card – the Wheel of Fortune – and sets it spinning. 'Your son was saved on the London road from a certain death because you and your wretched raven could tell Maria where he was, and now here he is under your loving protection.'

He is right; my son is here at last. My unease disappears and I am full of ecstasy.

'You have had sixteen years to prepare for this moment. You have gathered your strength and power, which you will need to protect your son and avenge your death.' The Devil smiles.

'I long to talk to him, to let him know I am here.' I feel such joy at the thought of building a relationship of sorts with my son, but the Devil laughs.

'You will find that difficult, my dear, for you will need much strength for that. Just one word will sap your energy, because do you really think that death is that easy?' He finally stops shuffling his cards and casually hands me Temperance.

'Patience and self-control are what you need. Use your power wisely, for you are still a mere beginner at this game. Don't overwhelm the boy either, for that will only scare him. Be subtle if you can.' He sniggers and is gone.

The card mocks me and I throw it away, watching it dissolve into the stone walls.

I want to savour my delight at seeing my son again, and I have no time for the Devil's warnings and games. I go to find my son once more, ignoring the sound of the Wheel turning.

The Prisoner

Early the next morning, Emma and Will started brewing the ale for the day ahead. Jane was asleep in the upper bedchamber, tired from the busy service the evening before. 'What did you mean about the roses?' Will asked, now that they were alone together. His dreams had been full of roses and a memory he couldn't quite hold onto. Brief, fleeting moments at the edge of his sleep, but now he remembered a woman's voice, laughter, and the touch of a kiss.

'It's a funny thing,' Emma whispered. 'I first started to notice the scent when my father told me the story of a prisoner who was here just before I was born.'

'What prisoner?' Will asked, feeling ice cold even though the room was warm from the freshly fermented ale.

'A lady called Maude, who was imprisoned in a cage within the circular turret of the Stone Tower. Father said she had upset the old King.' Emma glanced around the cellar, as if expecting King John's spies to come out of the shadows. Even though he was long dead, people were still wary about their talk being overheard by the wrong person. 'He was an evil man according to my father, especially for what he did to the lady in the turret.'

Tower of Vengeance

'Did your father know her then?' He watched her stirring the ale, looking at her determined face as she recounted her tale.

'Oh yes, he was one of her guards. He said she was the most beautiful woman he had ever seen. They were told to starve her on King John's orders, and my father hated himself for it. So, he smuggled in a piece of bread one day despite the danger to himself if he was found out. Ma was so scared that he would get caught that he promised her he wouldn't do it again. You see, Ma was pregnant at the time and worried about being left alone with the baby. My father would certainly have been killed if King John had found out. They never spoke about it after that out of fear of what would happen to us for helping one of the old King's prisoners.' Emma glanced around nervously to check the cellar was still empty.

'What happened to her then, this lady?' Will enquired, feeling his world closing in on him. His heart was hammering so loudly that she must hear it, but she was intent on her story, the link to her father and the closeness they had shared over the secret of the doomed prisoner's fate.

'It was awful, and my father was so upset. The King had her poisoned!' Emma shuddered. 'You must never tell anyone I have told you this, for we'll all be in danger.'

Will felt nauseous as he listened to her words. It was the final confirmation of the rumour that had marked his life. A whisper in a corner from the monks who had sheltered him, and the tittle-tattle in the Priory kitchens of the women from the village. Now the memory that eluded him in his sleep pushed its way into the forefront of his mind and he was transported back to another room, filled with light, flowers, and the heady smell of herbs. There was a laughing lady with long black hair, which danced down her back as she lifted him in her arms and swung him around, kissing his face over and over, playfully making him giggle. And the smell of roses, such colourful roses that grew in the garden he could see beyond the window.

'Will, are you alright? You have gone so pale.' Emma looked at him anxiously as his eyes glazed over.

He turned to her at the sound of his name, remembering where he was.

'Sorry, Emma, it's such a horrible story. Poisoned?' He could hear the tremble in his own voice, choking on that word.

'My father told me that she kept refusing to submit to the King, but she was getting weaker and weaker. The King got fed up with waiting and sent one of his men with a gift for her. He made my father and the other guards wait outside whilst he went in alone. When he left, he told them to dispose of the body and to tell no one what had happened to her. She was never here, he said. They went into the room, and she was lying on the floor dead, with an empty plate by the cage. She hadn't eaten or drunk anything else that day. Whatever the man had on that plate must have been poisoned. She was alive before the man entered the room.'

Emma paused for a moment, remembering what had troubled her most about when her father had confided in her. 'He cried when he told me and warned me to be wary of Kings and those who have power, as they care not what they do to the likes of us. If they can kill a noble woman like her, our lives are worth nothing. Trust not in men such as him or his family.' Emma picked up two of the jugs. 'But we must get this ale upstairs before Ma wakes up. Remember, you must say nothing to anyone about this and especially not to her. She's been through enough.'

'But wait, what about the roses?' Will touched Emma's arm to stop her from leaving, and felt a slight shock as his hand met her soft skin. They looked at each other, feeling a spark of a connection, and then held each other's gaze for a moment.

'I don't know,' she murmured, recovering herself. 'I started smelling them after my father told me about her. I meant to ask him about them, but he died not long after he told me the story, so I never got the chance. If I didn't know better, I would say it's her ghost haunting this place.'

Will removed his hand and Emma, hearing her mother's voice, knew she had to leave, so climbed the stairs carrying the first batch of ale to the kitchen. Now Will knew for certain that his mother had died here, poisoned on the King's orders. The previous night, he had learnt his grandfather was currently unreachable to him, that a reward remained

Tower of Vengeance

on his head, and now it had been confirmed that he was living in the place his mother had been murdered. He felt anger at what had befallen his family, while acknowledging the cruelty and sorrow of the circumstances that found him here. His first impulse was to run away from this cursed place...but he couldn't outrun his memories and his own emotions. He looked around the room to see if he could smell the roses or sense anything in the shadows. There must be a reason behind her presence and why her spirit remained here. The men had called her a witch, and his foot betrayed her mark just as they'd gossiped about. All he knew was that it was more important than ever to conceal his identity.

And then he remembered the old woman on the road who had directed him to the Tower. She had told him that the Stone Tower was his destiny, but how had she known that? It seemed an odd set of circumstances that just as he had fled the Priory, Emma's father had died, opening up a space for him here. He felt a tingle of fear once again.

* * *

Over the next few months, as spring arrived at the Tower and the days bled into one another, Will mulled over what had happened to his mother. The nightmares persisted, as he feared being discovered and was no nearer to getting to his grandfather. The days grew longer, and more workmen arrived to strengthen the Tower's defences and repair the Great

Tower of Vengeance

Hall in the Inner Bailey. He heard through the soldiers' gossip that his grandfather had returned to Essex, to the relief of the Constable, but now that he was further away, it would be even harder to get to him.

There was scarce news of King Henry himself, although there were rumours about marriage alliances and disputes abroad. Will paid scant attention to it all, as he had a hatred for King John's children which he had to disguise. He knew he must not draw attention to himself if he wanted to survive. Many a night when all was quiet in The Stone Kitchen and he was alone in his bed in the old storeroom, he thought about his future, about his mother and if she was looking out for him. He thought he felt her in his dreams, but it was always a fading glimpse. He wondered if life here really was his destiny or if there must be more to it than this. Baynard's Castle stood empty, the Priory was a distant memory, and his new life was built on a lie, a far cry from the life he should have had. The Tower walls seemed to close in on him as his grandfather moved further away from him.

Will and Emma never talked about Maude, and it sometimes felt to both of them that the conversation had not happened. Occasionally, they glanced at each other knowingly when they both smelt the scent of roses or felt the brush of a shadow, but said nothing more. Emma had not thought to question why Will himself could smell the roses and sense the presence in the shadows. She was just relieved she had someone to share the feeling with, a shared experience that brought them closer.

As the year slid away, with summer fading to autumn and then bringing the chill of winter, Will could feel the vestiges of his old life slipping further away. He rarely left the Tower for the teeming, dirty streets of the city, where he worried about being recognised but by whom he did not know. He had walked past his grandfather's house a few times and though it was always heavily guarded, his grandfather's pennant no longer fluttered over its walls, signalling that Fitzwalter had still not returned.

Will shied away from trying to find his mother, having been taught that ghosts meant the Devil's work. Will had yet to find a reason to go inside the principal building of the fortress, which remained empty and locked up, waiting for its King to return. His eyes were always drawn to the circular turret where his mother had been held. Sometimes he heard a raven cry from its roof, as if it was calling to him alone. Fanciful, he knew, as ravens were everywhere in London, and each morning they woke the Tower residents with their loud cries before the morning bell was rung.

Christmas came and went with no visit from the King, much to Will's relief as he had no desire to be too close to the man who denounced him a traitor and a murderer. King Henry had gone to Westminster, to his vast palace further up the river, but not to his fortress. The new royal lodgings were not ready anyway. They were waiting for timber from Essex's large forests to arrive to finish off the Great

Hall roof, but the snow on the roads had delayed them.

    As a year passed since Will first arrived at the Tower, he thought less about the woman on the road, although he secretly mourned his family as Jane and Emma continued to mourn Mark. There was no question now of Will being accepted as part of the Lund family, and no one in the Tower gave it any thought. As long as ale was poured in hearty measures, nobody noticed who served it.

    Emma and Will walked across the Inner Bailey with the ale jugs for the men who had finally arrived from Essex with the timber. The February day was fine and crisp with a chill in the air.

    'Bloody raven!' Will almost dropped one of the jugs as the bird swooped by him, as if trying to distract him from his task.

    'That was close.' Emma laughed, as the raven circled back and flew past him again.

    'What's wrong with that stupid bird?' Will ducked and tried to scare it off. 'Get off, you wretched creature.'

    The men unloading the timber turned and watched as Will and Emma approached, laughing too as the raven continued to dive at Will.

    'Took a fancy to you, mate!' one of the men joked, but Will froze as the raven finally flew off, thwarted in its purpose. He recognised the man, and his heart seemed to stop for fear that the man was sure to know him too.

'Bloody hell! Is that you, Will? Remember me? Harry from Binham. You used to live with the monks at the Priory, didn't you? What the hell are you doing here?' He smiled, glad to see his old friend.

Will looked around to see who had heard, but luckily the other men were either busy unloading the timber or accepting the ale from Emma. He had seen a lot of Harry growing up in the village of Binham. Although Will had been secluded away from royal eyes in the Priory, he had been allowed to play with the village children. Prior Thomas, his grandfather's friend, had believed Will should have some contact with children his own age for his own good.

Will laughed nervously. 'Harry! Good to see you. Oh, you know, I got bored with a load of monks and came to London for a bit of excitement.'

'Well, I can see you have found yourself a girl, but you were always the one the village lasses liked, even though we all thought you would become a monk!' He snorted, glancing towards Emma.

Will pulled Harry to one side, pouring him a pot of ale. 'Yes, and for fear of being mocked, I'm trying to keep that part of my life quiet here, so nobody thinks less of me.'

'Ha, yes, I can imagine you would! Especially with what happened after you left, and Prior Thomas disappearing too. I heard some monk had been murdered about a year ago in strange circumstances. I tried to find out where you were, but it was as if you never existed. And now you turn up here of all places.'

Will tried to remain calm, even though he worried Harry had pieced together the truth of that night, and would know of the reward on his old friend's head that he could claim if he reported Will.

'Who was murdered? I don't know anything about that. If you must know, I fell out with Prior Thomas, so I had to leave. Thought London was as good a place as any to find work,' Will said evenly, hoping Harry believed his lie.

'Oi, Harry! Stop drinking all the bloody ale and get a move on. We have to get on the road before dusk,' Harry's boss yelled at him. Harry shrugged, slapped Will on the back, and hurried over to finish his work.

Will finished distributing the ale, unsure of what to make of the encounter with Harry, and whether he could trust him not to speak up about seeing him.

Emma waited with her empty ale jugs, and after Will had waved goodbye to Harry, they made their way across the Inner Bailey through the gate to the Outer Bailey, toward The Stone Kitchen. Once through the gate and out of sight of the men, Emma stopped him.

'You aren't my cousin, are you? And don't try to lie. I heard every word,' she hissed.

The Secret

The midday rush was about to begin, so Will had promised to tell Emma later in the day when Jane was sleeping. Her mother got so tired in the afternoon and often left them to clear up before the evening rush. Emma had somehow got through the hours until her mother had finally climbed the stairs, leaving them alone together again.

'So, tell me who you are, Will?' she demanded, moving down to sit on a bench opposite him now the tables were cleared. She was scared now about who this stranger really was that they'd let into their home without question.

Will knew there was a reward on his head, and the money would be welcome to both Emma and Jane. But Will knew he had to tell the truth and trust her. He'd noticed her blush when he met her eye, so hoped that the depth of her feelings for him would mean she'd forgive him for the secret he had kept.

'Emma, I am sorry I lied. What I am about to tell you will change everything between us. Can I trust you to keep what I tell you a secret even from your mother?' He looked deep into those still, grey eyes and, taking her hands, his thumbs began to slowly stroke hers. Emma was torn for a moment; she had never kept anything from her mother, but she had grown close to Will. She could not deny that he made her feel special, attractive even, and both being able to smell the sweet roses was a secret that bound them.

Tower of Vengeance

'Of course, Will,' she said, unable to refuse him when he looked at her like that.

Will took a deep breath, and whispered, 'I am the son of Maude and Geoffrey de Mandeville. Maude, the prisoner in the turret, was my mother.'

Emma gripped his hands as if to steady herself from the blow of his words. 'How can that be? There is no son. I am sure I heard the soldiers say that even Robert Fitzwalter himself denied any such thing.'

'He lied to save my life. He has no idea I am here,' Will explained to her. 'I was three when my mother was taken by King John, and I knew nothing about what happened to her or my father for many years. I was hidden away in Binham Priory, which is where Harry met me.' Will was agitated now, as he told her the story of his family's flight abroad and his own life hidden away at the Priory. He could no longer stay seated. He paced up and down, unable to look at the bewildered Emma, who was desperately trying to understand what he was saying.

Will ran his fingers through his thick dark hair. 'All was well,' he continued. 'My grandfather and father made peace with my mother's murderer. My father even married King John's first wife.' The pain of that memory was still capable of hurting the man as much as it had the young boy hearing the laughter of the women who gossiped about it in the kitchen. 'They told the King I was dead. I don't know what they planned to do; perhaps they hoped when King Henry came to the throne, he would be more lenient than his father towards me as Maude's son.'

Tower of Vengeance

He stopped pacing for a moment, looking into the fire and recalling the moment it all changed. 'When I reached the age of fourteen, Prior Thomas explained I was not the orphan I had been told I was. He told me who my father and grandfather were. That there had been trouble with the King and it was best I was kept secret, otherwise they could all be at risk of losing their lives. This was enough to keep me quiet as I didn't want anyone to die, but of course, I wondered about my family and how long I would remain hidden.'

Emma, after hearing how his existence had been denied for his own safety, now felt sympathy for him.

'After my father died in a joust, I was by right the Earl of Essex, but again I heard news of my uncle, Peter de Mandeville, wanting to keep the earldom for himself, and he would sooner kill me than give me what was mine. And then someone, possibly my uncle, stirred King Henry up into believing that there was a de Mandeville traitor ready to join forces with the Fitzwalters again and seize power from a king who had just taken control himself. A bribe here and a bribe there, and finally there was a monk at my Priory, who unbeknownst to me came from a powerful family and told Henry's spies where I was.'

Will poured himself some ale from a jug left on one of the tables into the pot discarded next to it, uncaring whose lips had been on it only a brief while ago. Time felt as if it was standing still, and the shadows flickered as Will drank, fortifying himself to tell Emma the next part of the tale which had haunted him since he left the Priory.

He recalled that hideous night a year earlier when he had been hunted down by the King's men. The bell had begun to ring for evening prayer – a dull, doleful sound which to Will had meant another tedious hour on his knees praising God, his mind wandering on more pleasant matters. As he joined the rest of the community making their way to the church, there was a great sound of horses coming towards the Priory, the thundering of hooves disturbing the quiet night.

'King's men are coming,' the Priory watchman had shouted. 'I see the banner!'

The monks were confused and fearful. Prior Thomas quickly dragged Will away.

'They come for you. Take this cloak and these coins and get away from here as far as you can. Go to the back gate and I will delay them as long as I can.' Will had hesitated, loathe to leave his home and all he had known. But Prior Thomas had insisted, pushing Will towards the kitchen where he could slip out of the Priory into the grounds unseen.

He fled through the empty kitchen, grabbing a stale lump of bread from the table, and then ran across the kitchen garden, through the cemetery, past the mill pond where there was a gate in the precinct wall which led to the main road. He was almost at the gate when the monk stepped out of the shadows – Brother Ignatius. The cousin of the King's closest and most powerful adviser, Hubert de Burgh.

Tower of Vengeance

'Stop in the name of the King!' he screeched at Will; his bony hand stretched out to prevent him. 'I know who you are. You are a traitor, an imposter in God's own house, and you must be brought to justice.'

'I am no traitor. I was three years old when I came here,' Will tried to reason with the agitated monk, but he had already guessed this was the man who had betrayed him.

'Your family would destroy our blessed King. You are a traitor by birth. Your very existence is a blight upon his reign.' The monk spat in Will's face.

'Let me go!' cried Will, as the monk grabbed his arm.

'Here!' the monk raised his voice. 'The boy, the traitor is here!'

Lights were flickering through the cemetery; time was running out and the gate was just ahead of him. Will tried to wrench his arm away but the man would not give up as he gripped Will tighter, his nails digging into Will's flesh in their struggle. Scared, Will swung the stale bread at him, hoping to disarm him, but the monk for all his strength was a slight old man, so much older than the young man he was trying to stop. The monk slipped as he tried to avoid the bread, falling backwards and striking his head on the wall, slumping backwards to the floor.

Will saw the horror on Emma's face as she registered the murder of one of God's own men. 'I didn't mean to kill him! It was an accident and he slipped. He was lying there and I couldn't think clearly what to do. Two men approached, so I had to run into the night and keep running. They had seen my face and would recognise me if we were to meet again, I am sure.' Will sank back down onto the bench, his head in his hands, overwhelmed by the guilt he felt over the events of that night, only the hiss of the fire breaking the painful silence.

Emma got up slowly and walked around the table to sit next to Will. She pulled him towards her and a tear escaped, rolling down his cheek, which he quickly brushed away. She breathed in the scent of him, longing to kiss him, for her feelings for him were only strengthened after hearing of the turmoil he had endured already in his short life. Then faintly the smell of roses and the glimmer of the shadows broke the moment. Emma trembled as realisation dawned that Maude was present somehow. She still did not know how the ghost came to them or what she wanted.

'So, how did you end up here after leaving the Priory?' Emma wanted to know.

Will lifted his head and told Emma about the encounter on the road with the old woman and the poppet.

'Who was she and how did she have the poppet?' Emma whispered, fearful now of strange powers at work.

'It was Maria, my mother's servant. Prior Thomas told me about her bringing me to the Priory and how she had a reputation as a wise woman. I have a vague memory of her with my mother in her stillroom. She told me my destiny lay here at the Tower and encouraged me to come here.'

They stared at each other as Emma tried to make sense of Will's words.

All Will could say was, 'The roses. My mother smelt of roses,' confirming Emma's fears. 'I want to see where she was imprisoned. I need to see inside the turret,' Will pleaded with her.

'We will have to bribe one of the guards to let us in there, but now we must finish our work or my mother will be annoyed with us and wonder what we have been doing.' She moved away to settle herself before her mother returned, so she wouldn't suspect anything. Emma had every intention of keeping her promise to Will and his secret.

'Can I trust you – will you tell your mother?' Will asked anxiously.

She held his hands and looked into those dark eyes. 'I could not burden my mother with this anyway. I believe you, Will, and what you tried to do. You are a victim of King John's, and he was a monster, according to my father. Why does his family live and thrive but you are denied yours? But what of Harry – do you think he will betray you?'

'I don't know,' he admitted. 'But what can I do? I have nowhere to go.'

Emma had not considered the possibility of Will leaving and wanted to dismiss the notion. 'You can't go! You would not be safe outside these walls unless you get a message to your grandfather.'

'His London home is watched by the King's men. I have passed by it a few times. Besides, he is not in residence, and I cannot trust anyone there.' He sighed resignedly.

'We will have to keep watch ourselves, wait for when he returns, and then I could deliver a message for you,' she offered.

'Would you do that for me?' Will looked at her, astonished she would put herself at risk for him when he did not deserve such devotion. She realised, in the gloom of the alehouse, she would do anything for him. Nothing had changed for her – she knew in that instance that she loved him.

'I would do it for you. To give you your life back,' she said simply, before turning away from him and busying herself collecting the dirty pots before he could say any more. She did not want him to see the tears pricking her eyes, no longer trusting her face not to show her love. Her offer was not just good-natured but selfless on her part, too, for she knew that if the opportunity arose, he would leave the alehouse and there would be no place for her in his new life as the Earl of Essex.

Will watched her, grateful that she knew the truth about his identity and relieved that he had found someone to trust. Emma did not seem to know the rumour about Maude being a witch, and that was one secret he hoped to still keep from her, even as the sweet scent of roses enveloped him in a sickly embrace.

Tower of Vengeance

Maude

I was hoping my son would be gone by now – to my father, safe from the King and away from me – as hard as that is to contemplate when he has only just returned to me. I do not want him involved in my revenge, my Devil's pact, but I worry that his soul is already damned after what happened at the Priory with that wretched monk.

I had tried to stop him meeting Harry, a futile attempt by my raven. Maria had spoken to me, her words pushing through into my shadowland, and warned me of the threat when the cart had left Binham. My raven had followed its progress all the way to here, but too late I realised Harry knew about the reward. There was no convenient way to kill him before he left the Tower's walls. I must leave it to Maria to see what she can do, but I fear the threat is real and my son could be betrayed once again.

I worry that now Will has been seen, Mark Lund's death has been in vain and that is too hard to bear. He was the one man who showed me kindness in my prison all those years ago, and he would never know how much that scrap of bread, that taste of ale, meant to me at my lowest point. He risked so much for me, and I repaid him with death. But I had to. Everything I have done since my own death has been done for my cherished son. Maria had warned me Will was in danger, that he needed a place of safety, and that felt like the only solution. If Mark had lived there would have been no need for my son, no sorrow to cloud Jane's judgement, and Mark might also have recognised the dark eyes of a witch's son. A moment's distraction on the unfinished north wall stairs under the deceitful night sky and Mark was dead. It had been so quick, so easy, my first death, but I will always regret having to do it. He was a good man, Mark Lund, and I worry what it will cost me and if ensconcing Will in the alehouse – hiding him in plain sight – has come at too high a price.

And then there is his daughter. So like her father – kind, loving, and helping – a de Mandeville again. She will never betray him. She loves my son, I see it in her face, that softening as she looks at him, the joy when he pays her attention, the brief touches on his arm, and the lust that stirs within her. Poor fool – she will never be good enough for him. But he needs her and now they are bound together with his secret.

I can sense a change in the air. It's close but not yet here.

I am sure Will doesn't remember what Maria told him on the road, but I do. She is waiting, she said, but that woman is not me, and it's not the girl. We cannot see the woman in any of our magic, which worries me further as she is still unknown. Whoever she is, she is part of our destiny, and I will need all my strength when she comes, as she is tied up in my vengeance. I know this. My powers are growing.

Harry may betray us and I must be ready, but how can I stop the King's men if they come? I cannot kill them all. My mind races. The Devil is silent,

Tower of Vengeance

plotting, I am sure. So, we must strengthen the ties which bind us here to each other and the Tower. For we are bound together – Will, the girl, and I – as tight as a lover's knot. A card drops to the floor and as I turn it over The Lovers reach for each other's hands and I feel chilled. That is not what I want and once again I feel helpless.

King's Men

Two weeks later, the door of the alehouse flew open as one of the night watch burst in. 'King's men approaching,' he shouted over the noise. The soldiers who had been enjoying an evening of ale, dice, and singing lewd ballads scrambled to their feet, hastily grabbing cloaks and weapons that had been recently discarded and rushing outside. Behind the bar, Will's heart was pounding and a cold sweat gripped him. He looked around the room and his eyes found Emma, who had been collecting pots. He could see his fear mirrored in her face – wondering if he had indeed been betrayed as he had feared. She rushed over and gripped his arm.

'You must hide,' she gasped. He was numb, unable to move.

'Where's Jane?' he managed to whisper, coming to his senses and knowing he didn't have much time.

'Upstairs. She felt unwell, so I sent her to rest.'

'I have to go,' he exclaimed. 'It may already be too late! Emma, what shall I do?'

They could hear the commotion outside as the Tower's gates were opened on the orders of the King. Will was trapped within the stone walls. There was only one way in and out of the Tower, meaning he could not get past the King's men. The webbing

Tower of Vengeance

between his toes tingled – the betrayer of his mother's kinship which could so easily reveal his true identity.

'They will know I am here in the alehouse; Harry would have told them I served them ale. It won't take long for them to find me here. I need to hide somewhere else and then try and sneak out.' Will was shaking, not able to think straight. Where could he hide with the King's men almost upon him?

'Quick, take your cloak. Here's some money.' Emma, as practical and unflappable as ever, had gathered his cloak, some coin, and even some bread. He went to grab them, ready to rush out into the cold night, to take his chances at least.

'Stop!' The voice was close to his ear, and he dropped the cloak. He looked around to see where the voice had come from.

'Will?' He could hear Emma's anxious voice.

'They are not here for you. You do not need to run. Go outside and listen, but do not run,' the voice whispered – feminine, soft, soothing. Roses. His mother. He was safe.

'Emma,' he whispered, 'did you hear that voice?'

'No, what voice?' She looked around her, still preparing for his flight.

'I need to go outside and see what is happening. I do not think I am in danger.' He picked up the cloak from the floor, wrapped it around him, and – as if in a trance – left the room, leaving a bewildered Emma to hope that the voice had not been false and that Will would return.

Outside, the King's men had now entered the Outer Bailey, and the Constable was waiting with a troop of his own hastily gathered men to see what had brought such company to the Tower at this late hour. A stream of horsemen had clattered through the gatehouse, shielding a covered cart drawn by two horses and surrounded by foot soldiers. Will hid in the shadows to see what was happening.

'Are you the Constable?' the leader of the company barked.

'Yes, I am Sir Hugh Giffard, Constable of the King's Tower. What disturbance is this? I haven't had any messages from the King of your arrival.' The Constable was vexed to be summoned from his warm lodgings, his spiced ale, and his latest whore into the cold February night.

'I have my orders from the King,' the man snarled, brandishing a document with the King's seal, which he handed to the Constable. 'I am Sir Peter de Boisers, and I bring the traitor Hubert de Burgh to be imprisoned here by the King's command. My men will form his guard, and I will take charge of the Stone Tower. All inhabitants now report to me – including you, sir.'

Will was shocked to hear the name of the King's trusted advisor being declared a traitor and a prisoner. The same man who had been such an enemy of Will's family. But his own distress dissipated into

Tower of Vengeance

the cold night air as at least for now he was safe, and whoever had spoken to him had proved right.

The Constable watched helplessly as de Boisers took over, taking his set of keys and shouting orders to the men to open up the Stone Tower, where the prisoner was to be held.

Emma peered out of the door to the alehouse, and from the size of the escort, she knew that no ordinary prisoner had arrived. She watched as the men dismounted from their horses and the garrison's own soldiers were pressed into work to ready the stables. The Outer Bailey was now ablaze with torchlight and a flurry of activity. The Tower's Steward arrived with further men to facilitate the unexpected arrivals. Barely an hour before the great fortress had been in a stale flux, a sleeping giant, but now it was alive with purpose and importance. Will appeared in the doorway, making her jump. He hurried her inside into the warmth of The Stone Kitchen. They hugged each other tightly, feeling the tension releasing in each other's body in relief that they had not come for him, and he did not have to leave.

'I was so scared you wouldn't return.' Emma hugged him tighter.

'I am still shaking,' Will whispered nervously. 'Can you believe that the man imprisoned here is the cousin of the man I told you about at the Priory? He could have been coming for me, but instead he is here as a prisoner.'

'You need to leave here, Will. It's not safe. Tonight proved you are trapped if anyone comes looking.'

'I know, but where can I go? I can feel my mother's presence and I know that she is watching over me. I have to stay here for now,' he insisted.

Emma shivered at the thought of Maude's ghost, and felt sick as the smell of roses once again filled the room. Will's confession had truly changed her life. She now knew she loved him, but with that love and knowledge came fear and uncertainty. They pulled apart as the fire crackled, making them jump, the anxiety of the day not quite gone. They heard Jane calling out to them from the kitchen, sleepily asking what had happened. Emma hurried to her mother to tell her the news as Will started to clear up the abandoned pots and jugs, using the time to calm himself from the turmoil of his thoughts and emotions. Will felt safe but wondered for how long that feeling would last.

Tower of Vengeance

The Lovers

In the coming days the Tower entered a time of greater restrictions, which soured the mood of the inhabitants. Access to and from the Tower was strictly controlled by de Boisers, who was taking no chances on his prisoner escaping. Only his men were allowed inside the Stone Tower, where de Burgh was reportedly being kept in chains. Work had stopped on the Inner Bailey apartments, as no risk was to be taken on outsiders trying to help the fallen minister. The Tower's own garrison quickly found that their own duties were more onerous under the watchful eyes of the King's own man. The Constable was constantly being summoned to de Boisers for orders and complaints, which in turn made him punish his soldiers and anyone else who crossed his path.

It was an uneasy time for the alehouse as there were no longer any workmen, and although the soldiers continued to frequent, the mood was more solemn. The men became ill-tempered with all the restrictions, workload, and punishments. A few evenings later the men had been fractious, and Jane had ended up chucking them out before any of the usual fighting had started. She was exhausted and had felt dizzy.

'Are you feeling ill?' Emma asked worriedly, seeing her mother steady herself against one of the tables as she began to clear the pots.

'Don't fuss me, girl, and get the washing up done so we can all go to bed!' But as she turned, the room seemed to spin, her vision blurred, and she felt herself falling to the ground. Emma screamed, and Will came running from the kitchen. Between them, they managed to lift Jane and sit her on a chair by the fire. Emma got a wet cloth from the kitchen as Will poured some ale into a pot. Jane groaned as she regained consciousness, but her head was fuzzy and she felt so exhausted.

'Let's get you to bed, Ma,' Emma insisted.

'Get your Aunt Joan. She will know what to do. I need her remedies, a drop of tonic to perk me up,' Jane muttered. Joan was Mark's younger sister, with a reputation for healing; and her husband was a powerful alderman known to de Boisers, so would be permitted entry. They got Jane slowly up the stairs and settled her to sleep, Emma watching her all through the night until morning came, when she was allowed to fetch Joan.

'Nothing wrong with you that rest and proper food won't cure, and some of my poultices. You need to get away from this place awhile. You can come and stay with me. Emma and the boy can look after the place.' Joan was adamant, not giving Jane a chance to protest.

'Please, Ma, I just want you to get better, and we'll be fine here running the alehouse until you are recovered,' Emma promised her.

'Now then, my husband won't mind you staying for as long as you need. He will be glad that I have company now most of the children are married and he being so busy. Who would have thought barrel making was so prosperous!' she said with a laugh.

'If you're sure I won't be imposing,' Joan croaked, not having the energy to protest.

'You need a break, otherwise you will run yourself ragged and then what use will you be. I will let you gather up what you need and give your orders to these two – of which I have no doubt there will be many – and I will go and get the cart to carry you to mine.' Joan bustled out of the room before any further objections could be made and swept out of the alehouse to arrange Jane's transport to her own house inside the city.

Emma started to help Jane as her mother told her all the things she would need to know. 'And you listen to me, girl, no funny business with any man while I am gone. You have grown into a comely girl, and I see how those soldiers look at you. Any problems, you send message to me straight away and come and see me if you have the chance. Walter is a good man, so he can help if needs be.'

'I know how to run the place, Ma! And it's not as busy as usual, plus I have Will to protect me from the soldiers.'

'Hmm, well, that's another thing; I need to talk to your cousin alone. Tell him I need to speak to him for a moment.'

Jane looked Will squarely in the eyes when he entered the bedchamber. 'Now, you listen to me. Emma is all I have in this world and no harm is to befall her while I am gone. That includes from you. I want you to promise me not to lay one finger on her.'

'Of course, Aunt Jane! She's my cousin and I will protect her with my life while you are gone,' Will pledged.

The weariness overtook her again and she sank back on the bed. 'Away with you now, there is an alehouse to run.'

* * *

Emma missed her mother, although she knew she was not far away. She felt shy around Will. Even though they had been alone before, it felt different knowing that Jane was not upstairs. They began to be conscious of the physicality of each other. Each time they brushed past each other, the air crackled with an unseen tension. It was as if Jane's absence had created an invisible barrier between them and made them nervous. Will was struggling to keep his promise to Jane as he fought the emotions which had begun to surface since his confession to Emma, an act that had drawn them closer.

She had not judged him and had in fact offered support and help in his darkest hour. She made him feel protected, and he was also conscious of how it had felt to hold her in those moments after they had realised the King's men had not come for him. It had felt so good, so comfortable. He had drawn such strength from her. But now he avoided

Tower of Vengeance

her as much as he could, brooding over not just his mother's death but over the growing feelings he had for Emma. He could not afford to fall in love with her, as he still strived to leave. He could see that his withdrawal hurt Emma, as they both struggled to accept the loss of the familiarity they had so recently felt.

The following week, even the alehouse's walls seemed to be oppressing all of those within it. The soldiers had brought into its warmth the chill of the outside, along with the stress of guarding the high-profile prisoner, and there was a lack of the usual banter and conviviality to them that evening. The garrison's men and the King's men seemed to be in an uneasy stand-off. Will sulked in the background, drawing the ale into jugs as Emma weaved her way through the tables, serving the men just eager for the day to be done.

'Smile, girl!' leered one of the King's soldiers. 'Or shall I give you something to smile about?' He pulled Emma onto his lap, attempting to kiss the struggling girl. His breath was rank and stale on her face. Will, seeing Emma trying to struggle away, rushed from behind the bar, pushed his way through the tables, and pulled Emma from the man. He yanked the surprised man to his feet and punched him in the face, unable to calm the anger that bubbled up inside him. As the man staggered back, his comrades – seemingly stunned at first – jumped up and grabbed Will.

Unwittingly, Will had released the underlying hostility between the men, and fights broke out across the small, enclosed space of the room. Long-held grudges and petty quarrels manifested themselves into thrown punches, and pots and jugs were hurled as they shook off the restraints of the past few weeks. Emma managed to escape behind the bar and hid herself from their anger, as Will took out his own frustrations on any man who got in his way.

The door burst open. 'What the bleedin' hell is going on in here?' An officer of the watch, having heard the commotion on his rounds, stood in the doorway. 'Stop this now, you utter imbeciles, before de Boisers has all your dicks on a platter.' His warning restored order as the men pulled apart from each other, calming down. The officer and his guard ensured that all the soldiers left and returned to their barracks.

'I don't know what happened here, Lund,' he shouted at Will, 'but I don't need any of my men or the King's bloody men fighting right now in this shithole. Do you understand? I can get you kicked out and on the streets at the click of my fingers, so make sure you don't let this happen again.' He took one last look around the wrecked room and left with his escort scurrying in his wake.

Will slumped to the floor, blood running down his face as he surveyed the scene. Emma came out of her hiding place and rushed to his side.

'You're bleeding! Are you hurt?' she cried.

As she took his face in her hands, they both looked into each other's eyes, and she gently wiped the blood from his nose. Despite his promise, he longed for her and pulled her towards him in a kiss. Emma's heart seemed like it might burst as she finally felt Will's arms around her, his lips upon hers, and his hands caressing her. She never wanted to let him go. Desire ran through Will's body as he hungrily kissed the girl in his arms. Even in this moment of fulfilment, as his frustrations melted away, he knew he should stop before they reached the point of no return. In the room, the fire flickered and the light appeared to dim. Will sensed the change and pulled away from Emma, realising he had forgot himself. They smiled at each other and Will drew her into his chest, so he wouldn't have to see the love shining from her beautiful grey eyes, holding her tightly as if this act of closeness would push away the doubts inside him. He wanted her but she was his best friend, and he could not destroy the one friendship he had. He could not give her what she wanted.

Emma snuggled deeper into his arms, burying herself into Will's chest. 'I have never felt so happy. I've wanted you to do that for so long.'

'I know. But I promised your mother I would look after you and not touch you. But seeing that oaf try to kiss you tonight made me so angry and I couldn't stop myself.' He kissed the top of her head protectively.

'I thought the men would kill you! You were protecting me, so you shouldn't worry about Ma. It was a good thing that officer arrived though. Look at the state of this place! Ma would not be happy if she could see it now!' She laughed as she took in the mess, no longer afraid as she had been earlier; after all, the damage could easily be cleared up. And nothing mattered now except for Will's arms around her, which made her feel safe.

'Yes, we better clear this place up and I need to get this blood off.' Will gently released her.

Despite the mess, Emma seemed to be shining with joy, and her eyes were full of love and promise. Will felt uneasy. Oh, he desired her. She made him forget his fears, forget for a moment the eyes of the dead monk who haunted his dreams, forget his situation as a fugitive. But he had to leave. He wanted his birthright and his earldom for his mother as much as anything else. He believed she was haunting this place to help him; she wanted him to have what she had lost, and he must get it back. Then surely her ghost would rest. He needed Emma to take that message to his grandfather if he ever returned to London. He knew that this life was temporary until he could reclaim his title and birthright, so did not want to give Emma false hope or bind her to him, even if he did care for her.

The shadows shifted, dissolving into darkness, and the ravens – disturbed in their own slumber – started screeching in the night's sky.

The Turret

Three Months Later

Walking back to the alehouse in the summer sunshine, Will appreciated the change in atmosphere now that Peter de Bosiers and his prisoner, Hubert de Burgh, had left just over a month ago. The Stone Tower now stood empty, the building work had recommenced, and the inhabitants were once again allowed the freedom to leave the Tower's walls. The workers had returned to The Stone Kitchen, as had Jane Lund, significantly recovered from her illness. She certainly seemed brighter, there was a renewed vigour to her, and her mood had improved. Will had mixed emotions at her return, conscious that it put a new barrier between himself and Emma, and it had also curbed his own ideas to improve the alehouse. Jane after all, was the alewife, and therefore in charge.

Emma was sweeping the steps as he approached, and Will could not help but smile at her delight at seeing him.

'How were the pigs?' She laughed, knowing he liked feeding the ale mash to the Tower's pig litter.

'Growing well!' He stood next to her, lightly touching her hand. 'Who's that with Old Giffard?'

'I wonder if it's the new Constable? Didn't the men say he had arrived last night?'

'Let's hope he's better than Giffard. Are they coming this way?'

'Oh, Gawd, I'm going in. You can deal with them.' Emma dashed inside, leaving Will to deal with the two men advancing towards him.

'Ah, Lund, isn't it? This is the new Constable, Thomas de Blundeville, wanting to meet you.' The disdain was obvious in Giffard's voice. 'I'll leave you to it, Sir Thomas, and see you back at the Lodgings before I make my departure. I presume you have now seen everything I can show you of the Tower?'

'I guess I must have done, Sir Hugh; I can see you are eager to be gone, so I will trouble you no further.' Sir Thomas smiled as the man left. 'Will Lund, a pleasure to meet you. I hope you don't mind me dropping by like this, but I like to see where my men and workers will be spending their time. Could you show me the alehouse?'

'An honour, sir. You must forgive my surprise, but it is rare to have a visit from the Constable.' Once inside, Will was relieved to see both Jane and Emma, as he was nervous in the amiable man's company. 'My aunt, Jane Lund, is the alewife here; and myself and her daughter, Emma, assist her.'

'I hope you will find all to your satisfaction, my lord,' stuttered Jane.

'Well, the place certainly seems clean and tidy, which is a vast improvement on the alehouses I have seen in Rochester recently.' Thomas chuckled and the family relaxed.

'Would you like to taste the ale, sir?' Will asked tentatively.

'Yes, that would be most welcome.' Thomas was a pleasant surprise to Will. He seemed to take a real interest in the ale, and when he praised it and requested the alehouse supply the Constable's lodgings going forward, Will felt a certain pride.

As Will walked over to the Constable's lodgings two weeks later, he reflected on how different things were now that Thomas de Blundeville had arrived. At first his presence had concerned Will; he had noticed the older man appraise him and there had been a curiosity in Thomas' face as if he realised Will was out of place, but as the days had passed, an unlikely friendship between the two men had formed. Thomas, appreciating his ale, had encouraged Will to experiment with different herbs, which he was allowed to take from the Tower's kitchen garden.

Today, Will had a new flavour he was eager for Thomas to try. Will knocked on Thomas' study door and entered with his jug of ale, which he offered to Thomas. 'See what you think of this one, sir. I have added a new herb.'

'That does taste good! The best yet. Will, are you busy this morning? I want to inspect the Stone Tower and I could use your company rather than that tedious Steward.'

'Of course, I can accompany you, sir. The alehouse can spare me, I'm sure.' Will smiled.

'Good, good. Let's meet at the steps in an hour. I have some business to attend to first.'

Will left the house and walked slowly back across the Bailey. He could not believe his luck that the new Constable had taken an interest in him and he would finally get to see inside the Stone Tower. He had been waiting for an opportunity ever since Emma had told him about his mother and her imprisonment in the round turret. Returning to The Stone Kitchen, he told Jane and Emma of Thomas' request, being careful to avoid Emma's eyes in case they gave something away.

'The Constable seems to like you, Will, which can only be a good thing for us,' remarked Jane.

Emma, though she had been happy to have her mother back and in good health, was dismayed that she now had to be cautious around Will. He held back even though Emma was eager for him to show her more affection, and his kisses were fleeting and chaste. Emma ached for his touch and worried that his true station meant that she would never be good enough for him.

As Will finished his chores, he felt Emma watching him and turned to smile at her, seeing her face light up as he did so. It was not that he did not care for her, as he did feel strongly towards her. But he knew they could not carry on like this, and the more he saw her falling in love with him, the more he felt the guilt weighing heavier on him. When his grandfather returned to London, Will hoped there would be a chance to make contact with him and to leave his hiding place of the alehouse, but that would mean leaving Emma behind. He could hardly take an alewife's daughter into his grandfather's circle.

Will went to meet the Constable. He liked Thomas, perhaps because of the shared name of his old friend the Prior. He too was shrewd and clever, but in appearance the two men were so different. The Prior had been tall and angular like a sharpened sword, with hollow cheeks and the shaven tonsure of the monk, whereas the Constable was short and stout like a shield in shape, ruddy-cheeked with the rosy nose of a contented man, an abundance of copper curls, and a full beard peppered with grey. Will was glad to have quickly forged a relationship with him, despite his familial connections, and he hoped to learn from Thomas, to use his own brain, which was in dire need of some stimulation.

Thomas was waiting at the steps of the Stone Tower's forebuilding, a square structure which had been added by Henry II. It gave the Tower a stronger line of defence before entry could be gained to the actual keep.

'Ah, Will, here you are, good, good. Let's take a look at this place. See if anything needs attention. Never know if the King might want to visit, and it wouldn't do to have the place looking an absolute shambles.'

They walked up the steps to reach the guard room, where they were greeted by two soldiers who had been advised of their coming earlier when Thomas had sent word of his plans. 'I can tell the man is incompetent so I need to see it alone, and thought you would make good company,' Thomas explained to Will.

The soldiers had unbarred the great doors and ensured there was light coming from the wall sconces and, as they entered the entrance floor, Thomas noted that all the window shutters had been removed. There was no mistaking the slight draught coming through even though it was a summer's day. No fire glowed in the large fireplace to his left and no wall hangings covered the cold stone walls.

Will had never been in such a place before. If his mother had lived, and had his family survived, such places as this would have been common to him, but now he stood and took in the sheer vastness of the room into which he entered. If the Stone Tower had been intended to intimidate from the outside, then its interior certainly enhanced its reputation. Will and Thomas walked around the entrance floor noting the old rushes on the floor, the smell from the garderobes, and the general neglect of the place. Thomas muttering that there was much to be cleared up here and that his suspicions about the Steward had been right. They did not linger long in the two cavernous rooms where the Steward's official business would usually have taken place.

They walked over to the heavy oak door in the corner of the second room and Thomas explained to Will, 'So here we have the Great Stairs, and they are the only stairs to connect this floor to the top floor and the basement floor. A defensive feature. One access point is easier to guard and defend. We will go down to the basement first and inspect the storerooms.' They descended the spiral staircase slowly, feeling their way down the narrow stairs in the relative darkness, just the single light from the lantern Thomas had lit earlier and was now holding in front of him. They reached the huge door, which creaked loudly as Thomas heaved it open. Will thought they could have descended into the realms of Hell itself, as the oppressiveness of the room before them settled on their shoulders. Even with the lantern, the darkness stretched before them and the dampness seeped into their bones as they shivered in the cold.

'There's a well here somewhere. Always need a fresh water supply inside just in case of siege.' Thomas walked slowly forwards. 'This room, I believe, is used for the King's treasury when he is in residence, so I am pretty sure it's empty.' He swung the lantern gently around. The open door allowed some light to infiltrate from above, but he moved the lantern with care, not wishing the delicate flame to fail him in these murky rooms. There was a door to the right which Thomas opened, and they walked into another empty space. 'This, Will, is known as the Black Hall.' The room lived up to its name, as blackness encompassed them as soon as they walked in, the flickering candle shining a little amount of light on its interior. However, the echo of their feet exposed the size of the room, and the drip of water revealed the location of the well at its far end. But they could both make out the sacks of rotten flour and vegetables and smell the sourness of old discarded ale. There was also the sound of rats.

'No wonder the Steward didn't want me down here! Place is a disgrace!' cried Thomas. He jumped as a rat ran over his foot. 'Blast this! Let's get out before we are bitten to death.'

They scrambled up the stairs as fast as possible, ensuring the lower door was firmly closed behind them.

'That needs sorting out immediately. The man is mad leaving all that to rot,' Thomas grumbled. Will was glad to have escaped the darkness, and the sense of dread that had overcome him in the second room where he had seen the chains on the walls betrayed a sinister usage of that wretched place.

Thomas continued up the stairs to the upper floor, catching his breath as he went. 'Now, if the royal family were in residence there would be a screen right here, partitioning off the private room of the King,' he remarked, as they entered the Royal Apartments.

Will gazed up at the rafters, which gave the room a large, airy feel with the two giant posts that held up the roof above dominating the room.

'Yes, it's quite astonishing, isn't it? A clever trick. See how high the ceiling goes? So, from the outside the Tower looks a lot higher. You thought there were three floors? The pitched roof must be a later addition, as the roof in Rochester Castle is flat above the mural gallery. I am sure this roof must be blocking the gallery here. But doesn't it feel cold,

Will? It's a warm, sunny day out there but it might as well be winter in here right now!'

Will had noticed the air getting colder. At first, he had thought it was the chill of the basement still lingering within him but there was a warm breeze coming through the open windows and the sensation he felt was not only cold but that of being watched. Thomas seemed immune to that as he poked his head round corners, inspected the fireplace, and opened the door on the far side of the room.

'Ah, the Chapel. You must see this, Will. Could be the one chance you get!'

Will reluctantly followed Thomas into the Chapel. The room was remarkably tranquil and bright. Both men experienced the peace settling around them, and there was a desire to linger in its warmth and comfort away from the chill they had felt before. Reluctantly, they moved back through the ornate door and Thomas turned left through a doorway into the western chamber. It was yet another large room, devoid again of all furniture, with echoes of feasting past. It followed a similar design to its counterpart below. A large fireplace, recesses where the windows were, but also two large windows at the northern end which would flood the place with light when the shutters were removed. There was also one further staircase in this room. Thomas explained that this room was the Great Hall where banquets would be held, and that the staircase would probably provide access to the mural gallery above, now blocked off by the pitched roof, with further access to the turret level.

Thomas suggested they go back to the eastern chamber and use the Great Stairs to access both the gallery level and the turrets. Will shivered with anticipation. As much as he had found the tour fascinating, his aim had always been to see his mother's place of imprisonment. Now, as he climbed the stairs, the moment was almost upon him. Thomas led the way up the winding stairs and – looking back at Will in the gloom – remarked on how much colder he felt. Yet Will had started to feel a warm glow, which intensified as they reached the next level. Ever the stickler for detail, and probably because he was finding the climb quite exhausting, so many stairs in these large keeps, Thomas paused and looked at the now defunct mural gallery, the pitched roof obscuring the rooms below and taking away its exact purpose. He shook his head in wonder at such a deed, for now minstrels could no longer play above the Great Hall, but he supposed that the gallery could now be used for exercise or be a more convivial place for extra guests to spend the night. *Or as an extra prison space*; he shuddered at the thought.

And then they were outside the door of the round turret. A key was in the lock, and the door was stiff from lack of use as Thomas pushed against it and the two men entered. Without warning, Thomas felt intense hatred and anger directed towards him. His chest was gripped with pain, and he thought he would die there and then in the dusty, dirty room. And then a violent shove, so forceful he stumbled out of the room. 'Will,' he gasped, 'I need air…to sit down. Check the rest of the rooms and the roof, I must…' He hurried down the spiralling stairs, banging his hip against the jagged stone walls as the overpowering smell of what seemed to him to be decaying roses followed his descent away from that awful room.

    Will watched Thomas leave, concerned at what had come over him, but he continued to climb the internal stairs to the upper room as instructed. He pushed open the door, and as he entered, he felt an overwhelming outpouring of love which seemed to swathe his entire body. But he also felt the deeper sorrow of a life lost. The shadows danced as bursts of light seemed to spin around him, as he held up his gaze to bathe in a warmth he had never before encountered. Memories crowded his mind. A summer's day in the stillroom as roses burst into his senses and he heard whispers of love. He barely noticed the bleak, desolate room. The warm breeze that spun its way around the circle of arrow slits replaced the bitter biting winds of his mother's final days, but he could feel her pain and her desire for revenge so dark it gripped his own soul.

    He wanted to remain forever bathed in her love; to take away the grief he felt from her, but Thomas called him to tally no longer, to check the roof, and he knew he could not stay. However, as he turned to leave the bittersweet place, something glinted in the corner of the room, and he bent down to see what it was. The gold chain of a rosary with a ruby cross yielded itself from its hiding place. Immediately, Will smelt the sweet aroma of roses and, sensing it was his mother's, kissed it. Tears filled his eyes as he accepted the precious gift that Maude had left for him. Thomas was impatient now and he had to leave before the man got too suspicious. He hurried down the stairs, calling to Thomas that he was checking the roof as he opened the side door which led onto it.

As he stepped out into the bright sunshine, the view of London took his breath away. The city was laid out before him in all its jumbled glory. A sure testament that life continued. Will could see spire after spire competing with plumes of smoke rising from the myriads of chimneys. As he walked around the roof, he could see the glistening ribbon of the river dazzling in the sunlight. The small boats bobbing in and out of the larger ships, bringing in their cargo from unseen lands. People being ferried from bank to bank. Will was aware of how trivial and insignificant a life could be in this crowded city. Nothing emphasised this more than the bridge which spanned the river, with the crooked houses seeming to weigh down its very arches, and Will could see the rotten head of a traitor stuck on one of its poles high up on the bridge itself – a visual representation of, not just the King's power, but that of death over life. A large black raven landed on the wall beside him, startling him out of his morbid reflections, its darting eyes watching him as if it was curious as to his presence there. Will turned from its unsettling gaze.

Conscious now of Thomas somewhere below him, Will quickly checked the three pitched roofs for any damage and noted that they all seemed in order. The raven seemed to follow his progress, and he was glad to hurry down the stairs which led back to the first floor. In the Great Hall, he found Thomas resting in one of the window recesses, watching the works going on in the Inner Bailey.

'Are you feeling better, my lord?'

'Yes, yes. No idea what came over me earlier. Too many stairs, I think! Not getting any younger and I probably shouldn't talk when I climb stairs.'
Thomas mopped his brow with a kerchief, the cold of earlier chased away by the rising heat of the midday sun as he tried to pass off his hasty departure from the turret.

As they departed the Stone Tower, Will made for the alehouse, his hand curled around the golden chain, a warm glow within him and a spring to his step. Whereas Thomas slowly walked back to his own house mulling over his experience. He could not explain how he had felt as he had walked through the rooms of the old tower, and what had happened on those cold, curving stairs. He would have dismissed his feelings as fanciful, but the shove had been real, the malevolency he had encountered had also been genuine, and he could not shake off the fear he had felt.

When Thomas returned to his warm, comfortable rooms, he tried to push his thoughts aside and concentrate on the task at hand. He called for his servant, ready to start issuing orders to clean up the Stone Tower and to get things back to normal. His servant, however, handed him a letter, and his heart sank as he recognised the writing of his uncle, Hubert de Burgh, not long since a prisoner within these very walls.

Tower of Vengeance

The King, it seemed, had not appreciated the irony of the nephew of a recent prisoner being tasked with improving the security of de Burgh's old prison. Thomas had always admired his uncle; he had risen to power under King John and his son, the current King. Like all powerful men, de Burgh had his enemies; however, calling the King an imbecile, impotent, and effeminate perhaps hadn't been the best move! Thomas could imagine the chroniclers hurrying to record that one, especially the loathsome Matthew Paris scribbling away in his St Albans monastery. Thomas hadn't wanted the role of Constable but, after his success with the repairs to Rochester Castle, the King had been adamant that Thomas complete the works on the Inner Bailey here at the Tower.

Thomas hesitated for a moment, debating whether to read it later and get on with his business, but it weighed heavy in his hand. Reluctantly, he dismissed his man and settled down to read the letter with some foreboding.

Nephew,

I hear news that you are now Constable of the Tower of London, a position which was of course once mine and a place that was more recently my prison. I hope it brings you better fortune than it did to me. My exile is complete, and I wish I could hope for better days. But I wanted to warn you about a malevolence I encountered in the Stone Tower. I believe there is a vengeful spirit within its walls, and I am sure I know who it is.

Tower of Vengeance

Many years ago, when I was a young man serving under the old King John, I attended a great feast in Baynard's Castle, a small distance from the Tower. It was the home of Robert Fitzwalter. You will know of him and his family, and of the troubles they have had both with the old King and his son, King Henry. What you may not know is that Fitzwalter had a beautiful daughter, Maude, who was married to Geoffrey de Mandeville, himself a Constable of the Tower – what webs are weaved around that accursed place, now your responsibility!

King John, it would seem, had long desired the Lady Maude, and had been pursuing her for some time, but she had held firm in her love for her husband. Anyway, that night, John was fractious, angry with Fitzwalter and de Mandeville, who had been opposing him and daring to question his actions. John was not an easy man; he had a quick temper and an eye for desirable women. And what John wanted, John usually got. But Maude de Mandeville was no ordinary woman – she perhaps naively believed in her marriage vows and didn't understand the manner of the man she rejected. For that's what she did – she rejected the King.

I didn't see all that happened, because I was seated below the high table towards the back, as befitted my status then. But I heard the commotion, the shouting, as John called for his guards to take her away. I was told that in her rejection, she had shown such revulsion for him that it had angered him beyond belief. His fury was immense. This family of traitors plotting behind his back, and now this woman repulsing him in front of his own Court.

I heard little of her fate as I left soon after for Poitou, where I was seneschal for a number of years. I know she was imprisoned in the Tower and that both her father and her husband fled overseas only to return a year later apparently forgiven, and to play their parts at the signing of the Great Charter. Ironically, as you are aware, de Mandeville and I were both married at some point to John's first wife, Isabella – not that she brought either of us much favour or riches!

Maude and Geoffrey de Mandeville also had a son, who I have searched high and low for as not only has he been declared a traitor to the present King, but he murdered my dear cousin – if I had found the de Mandeville heir, I may still hold the royal favour. But he alludes us all.

I had forgotten the beautiful Maude, even when I arrived at the Tower a prisoner myself. However, one night as I lay in chains on the floor of my prison, I felt a presence and, in the gloom, I swear I saw Maude de Mandeville! Perhaps my mind played tricks on me. I was tired, in pain, and worried about my fate – death itself hung over me. But there she was. She hadn't aged. She still had that long, black hair that I remembered she wore loose down her back even after her marriage, and which swayed with the gentle rhythm of her walk. Those dark eyes that pierced your very soul, and the ruby red lips men longed to kiss.

Tower of Vengeance

I was transfixed as she appeared to glide towards me, and then she laughed. That sound struck terror into me as the room got colder, and I attempted to shrink away from her, but those awful chains prevented my escape. I closed my eyes, willing her to go away, but she whispered in my ear that she knew who I was, that I had been present at that unhappy feast, that I now searched for her son who I wished to kill to gain favour with the present King. Therefore, vengeance would be hers on one of the King's men. And then, infernal woman that she was, she cursed my daughter, Magota, and said she would be dead within the year. For why should I have the love of my child when she had been taken from her own son? And in my distress, I remembered King John had declared her a witch and I knew then that her curse would come true. And I wished to die in that actual moment, anything to be away from that beautiful, vicious face.

And nephew, you are now aware that my daughter sickens and her marriage to Richard de Clare is dissolved. All I can remember are those terrible words. Be careful – the Tower is cursed, and Maude's ghost haunts the place she was murdered, for surely John had her killed?

Forgive the ramblings of an old man, but I am afraid for my family and now for you, dear Thomas.

Hubert de Burgh

Kent 1233

Thomas didn't know what to make of Hubert's letter; he would have thought it far-fetched, and, as his uncle had admitted, probably the ramblings of an exhausted man in an extreme situation, if he too hadn't experienced something similar. Thomas had felt an unease as soon as he had arrived at the Tower, and his disturbed sleep testified to this. He remembered the fear he had felt just now within that turret, and now there was his uncle's letter with its mention of ghosts within the great Tower. Thomas had a nagging sensation regarding Will, who seemed so out of place here, whereas the spirit of Maude, if it had been her pushing him out earlier, hadn't affected him in the same way. It was as if the spirit had accepted him. *How curious*, thought Thomas, and he picked up his pen, thinking of the young man in the alehouse with dark hair and a charming smile.

Maude

I watch my son walk across the Outer Bailey to the alehouse from the rooftop where he stood just a moment ago. My heart breaks over being so close but unable to hold him, and even talking to him takes all my energy. I risked much that night in the alehouse, preventing him from running when I knew he was safe. It was a necessary action, but it drained me and for a long time afterwards I could barely manifest. I never knew that I would feel such pain after everything else I have endured.

I return to the room to regain my once-again depleted strength, but the room has changed since I left. It is no longer cold and empty. The Devil sits at a table which was not there before. He is playing with his deck of cards and motions me to sit before him. I am no longer a mere shadow. When the Devil is present, it is as if I have a physical body which can sit, can touch, and can talk as I used to before my death.

The Devil smiles, those benevolent eyes twinkling as he turns over another of his tarot cards. The Lovers. He smirks at the card, enjoying his joke once again, then discards it and turns over another. Death followed by Justice. He leans back in his chair and taps Justice with his long, elegant fingers.

'And how goes revenge, my beautiful witch?' He stokes the Death card. 'So easy, is it not, to kill in the name of Justice?'

Mark's kind face appears before my eyes. An apparition conjured by my companion.

'Such an innocent man yet you killed him.' The Devil smiles.

Tears prick my eyes. I cannot speak.

'And the de Burgh woman lies dying from your curse.' He enjoys my discomfort.

'I feel no pity for that man's sweet, pathetic daughter.' I spit out the words as I finally find my voice. 'He hunts my son even now in the hope of regaining power, and he watched my own downfall. De Burgh is no friend of mine. He deserves all he gets.'

'Your power impresses me – how it grows.' He speaks like a proud father. 'But what of de Burgh's nephew? The man you just sent out of here in fear – will you kill him, too, or perhaps use a curse?'

'He has been kind to my son, and he does not feel like a threat. In fact, I sense something in him which proves him useful.' When I had first approached Thomas, I had wanted to kill him, for he was the nephew of de Burgh, a man who sought to harm my son – and I had a great desire to protect Will. As my hatred built and I reached out to touch the man, I suddenly saw a flash of the future, where he had a message in his hands which held good news for Will. It was as if my own power of divination had stopped me from uttering the curse on my lips which would have sent him hurtling down the stairs to his death. My emotions then merely sought to expel him while I spent precious moments with my boy – there was no real malignant desire to hurt Thomas. I wonder at that.

'You have much to do to gain Justice, do you not?' The Devil breaks into my musings.

'I want my son to be safe. Then I will seek my own Justice.' I try to sound confident, but I falter.

'Are they not the same then?' The Devil is bemused and watches my inner turmoil. 'Revenge. Justice. So hard to achieve, but come now, you are starting to enjoy it, are you not? This Tower gives you such strength from its powerful walls. Draw from it – you have such potential, my dear.'

The Devil is right. I am starting to enjoy it, to see what these powers can do, but these emotions scare me, for it seems I cannot always control my anger and my hatred, and I am no nearer to Justice. And what happened to my old self? The girl who enjoyed her gardens, her stillroom, her quiet happy life…

The Devil is bored now and ready to leave me – he yawns and stands. Such a handsome man, all the better to tempt you.

'Be careful of what you are becoming and how this game plays out. And the gift you left the boy? This may yet betray you both. When you hid it from the guards, you must have already been channelling your dark powers without even realising it, as they really should have found it. How interesting. But I digress. Until next time.'

The room wavers, then he is gone; the room is drab and grey once again where it had been so warm and comforting. I am again a mere shadow, but on the old bare floor lie two cards.

The Empress and the Fool – I am left to wonder what they mean.

Comet

St Martin's Day – the day to begin the harvest, but the rain had not stopped for two months as summer had turned to autumn and as the river rose, ships tore free from their anchors in the battering winds. Westminster Palace flooded, and small boats bobbed through the apartments as others rode their horses through the corridors to avoid getting wet. Water forced its way through the cellars of all the houses, and in the Tower water seeped through its mighty walls, causing small lakes to appear in both Inner and Outer Bailey. Building work was halted as news from the country told of drowned people, destroyed crops, and lost livestock with the storms.

That evening, Will pulled his cloak around him as he left the alehouse, which thankfully being on the hill had managed to escape the flooding. He dashed through the heavy rain into the Inner Bailey to meet Thomas in the improved kitchen, where they had set up a separate alehouse for the inhabitants there. Thomas seemed agitated and at first Will thought it was the incessant bad weather that affected him.

'Are you well, sir?' Will enquired, worried as he did not seem himself.

'Sorry, Will. You are right, my mind is not focused. I have news which I can't share here as there are too many ears,' Thomas explained, and glanced around at the busy new alehouse. 'Let's go to my lodgings and have some warm ale.'

Thomas had grown fond of Will, who was undeniably handsome with those dark eyes, the brooding sensuous mouth, and the firm muscular body. But there was also that sense of displacement, as if the man didn't belong here, that Thomas had picked up since first making his acquaintance. His air of refinement had continued to puzzle Thomas. He had not believed the story about Jane's sister that he had been told – Will could never be related to such a coarse woman, although her daughter was pleasant enough to look at. Will's education was far beyond a measly village parson, nor was he a tanner's son. Thomas was not a man to give up easily on a mystery.

As they left the kitchen, the rain had finally ceased – a wonder in itself – and they stood awhile beside the Stone Tower, revelling in this moment of stillness now the rain no longer fell. As the city gave thanks to God for delivering them from the deluge, the sky lit up as a large star shot through the darkness like an emblazoned torch, leaving smoke and sparks in its wake. The ravens now rose like an almighty black cloud and, screaming upwards into the night, seemed to be chasing off the comet for fear it signalled the end of days.

Will wondered what the comet signified. The ravens' reaction intensified the belief that evil was coming and, within the Tower, some of the men sank to their knees in prayer. As quickly as it had appeared, the comet was gone, leaving no trace of its existence. The sky returned to darkness, but the rain clouds had dispersed and there was just the drip, drip,

Tower of Vengeance

drip of the gutters as the two men sloshed through the puddles towards Thomas' rooms. He had temporarily moved into the King's lodgings after the flooding to his own rooms, and people were already calling it the Blundeville Tower because, aside from lodging there, Thomas had finally got it finished and made it fit for the King himself, if he cared to come.

The fire had gone out in the grate, so Will set to building it up again, trying to remove the chill from the air, but at least Thomas had put up some wall hangings and the windows were shuttered tight against the cold night air. The wall sconces burned bright as the two men pulled up their chairs to the fire, tankards of ale in their hands. Will held a poker in the flames and then plunged it into each tankard, warming up the ale and releasing the pungent spices which he had added earlier. Thus, they had spent many an evening of late.

Thomas took a long sip of his ale, revelling in its warmth. 'I wonder what this all means for us. The rain, the comet, and those blasted rumours which I fear will mean further work for us. But more of that later. I have also been wondering for a long time who you are, Will. You can't hide breeding from those who look for it, and you are too educated and refined in your manners.'

Will stared at his friend, a feeling of dread rising in his stomach.

'And look for it I did,' continued Thomas. 'It unexpectedly came to me from a letter I had from my uncle about a ghost he thought he had seen here at the

Tower. Maude de Mandeville.' Thomas watched as the colour drained from Will's face, and saw the terror in those perfect eyes.

'Be easy, my boy. I wish you no harm. I am on your side,' he assured him, and Will felt less on edge. 'King John was an evil man. I knew what he did to women, not only your poor mother, and my uncle was ever the fool to trust in him and his son. Power corrupts the mind, and it certainly did Uncle Hubert – he pays for it now, but who pays for your mother's death and for the loss of your family?'

Will sat listening, unable to quite believe he might have found an influential ally after all this time.

'Therefore, on a hunch, I wrote to your grandfather a while ago now. He is overseas, so messengers take time, but I have heard back from him. He has been waiting to contact you since a woodman from Binham told him of your whereabouts six months ago.'

So, Harry had revealed his presence here but to his grandfather! Will thanked God for Harry of Binham, and a friendship which had obviously counted for something all those years previously.

'My grandfather knows I am here!' he exclaimed. 'Will he come and get me? I long to see him.' Will was overcome with joy. He caught the faint trace of roses in bloom, a happy smell, and he guessed his mother was pleased. He had sensed her more as the days had passed since he had found the chain; he had felt the warm glow of her love surrounding him and he could only rejoice in her presence, knowing she loved him.

'It is his greatest wish that you should be reunited with him, but he is alas a prisoner of King Henry. Another spate over land ownership. It would not be safe for you right now to go to him or to be revealed. The King is still no friend of your family, and your uncle – the current Earl of Essex, your title by birthright – is an ally of the King, and will not easily give up his earldom,' Thomas warned him. 'I am no friend of that man either. We must bide our time, for I will help you, Will, and we must be ready when the time comes.'

Will couldn't help but feel dejected that he would have to continue to wait, but his grandfather was aware of him and he had an ally in Thomas. His spirits were lifted and he had hope at last.

'However, we have a more pressing issue.' Thomas sighed reluctantly. 'It is said that we are to host a royal guest. That as we speak, the Princess Isabella, Henry's most beloved sister, is on her way to reside here at the Tower until her marriage can be arranged.'

This time Will felt a malignancy to his mother's presence, as the shadows flickered in the corner of the room. There was a coldness to her reaction as if she was displeased, and the smell of roses seemed to wilt as if a winter's frost had killed them.

'It is not good, Will. A royal visitor is never good news unless you are seeking an honour; and this, I fear, is not an honour for the Tower but a means to an end. For ask yourself this, but do so quietly as there are always spies – why would the Princess be brought here? There are plenty of other places she could go. Better places, drier places! Mark my words, no good will come of this,' Thomas said cautiously.

    Will wondered what Thomas could mean, but then for some reason he recalled the words that the old woman, Maria, had said to him on the London road: 'She is waiting.' He had not remembered these words since he had come to the Tower. But now they seemed to be forcing their way into his mind and his skin prickled. Maria had been dismissive of Emma so it could not be her, and it had been a warning which could not apply to his mother, who loved him.

    The comet seemed to sound a trumpet blast with a scream of ravens. The end of days? A Princess on her way. Both men pulled closer to the fire and wondered what this all meant.

The Princess

Isabella's eyes opened and struggled to adjust to the darkness inside the bed, where the curtains wrapped around shutting out the light and the early morning chill. She had slipped down from her customary sitting position until she was almost lying down. 'They say laying down is for the dead,' she whispered to herself, before she quickly pulled herself up. 'Perhaps then I am dead, gone to Hell for all my sins. For why else am I in this wretched place?' she muttered, feeling sorry for herself. Her brother may pretend it was a great honour, but the Tower was known as a prison able to hold her prior to marriage. She grew older; twenty-one was old to be a bride, even a beautiful royal one, and the time had now come for her to marry without further delay.

It seemed her brother could no longer trust himself in her presence; she had seen the coveted looks, the conflict in his eyes, and the struggle with his own desires – his father's son battling his father's vices. That wretched harvest feast where they had sat side by side on a pair of thrones in matching clothes as if she was his queen had only given rise to rumour that the King was too close to his sister. And when that meddling chronicler, Matthew Paris, described her as Henry's wife, the fool had panicked and cast her out. Was it but a genuine mistake by that idiot Paris or was he hinting at something more – it mattered not the damage to Henry's reputation was done. Marry she must, away she must go while Henry fell to his knees in prayer.

Isabella sighed at the dullness of it all and decided she needed to plan her way out of her boredom. For there was always a man fool enough to fall in love with her and she needed someone to pass the time with, to amuse her while Henry's advisors desperately found someone worthy of marriage to her. She had had enough of lecherous old men, with leathery skin, coarse whiskers that irritated, dry lips that slobbered, and rheumy eyes greedy with desire, and worried that was the kind of man her brother would see her married to. Men who were rough and cared little for the act of pleasuring her. She desired young flesh and a malleable mind. Surely she deserved some fun before her marriage, so Isabella determined that her next lover must be young and agile.

She heard her old nurse and confidante, Margaret Bisset, enter the royal chamber, already admonishing the young boy for dozing off by the fire, which he was supposed to have been tending throughout the night. The curtains were pulled apart, and Margaret's familiar tired face appeared to wake her mistress for the day ahead.

'How did you sleep, my lady?' she enquired.

'As well as could be expected in the circumstances. At least the furniture arrived ahead of us.' Isabella was stiff from the long, wet journey from Windsor and was now glad of the sumptuous fur dressing gown Margaret helped her into as she left the warmth of her bed.

Tower of Vengeance

'Well, William de Derneford, whom your brother, the King, appointed as your serjeant, has worked hard to ensure that the wall hangings are at least up and the fireplaces effective. It also seems that the Constable, Thomas de Blundeville, is competent enough considering he only had two days' notice of our arrival.' Margaret had been busy most of the night. She had been dismayed to see there was building work in progress and that the new Royal Apartments were not complete, so they had found themselves in this large draughty building. She had also asked de Derneford to check the garderobe. Unfortunately, the kitchen was situated in the Inner Bailey itself with no direct access to this building, but Jordan, the Princess' cook, had been impressed with the place, which they were told had recently been improved. Both Margaret and the serjeant had little to complain about in the circumstances, and it would hopefully only be for a short time.

'I just can't understand such haste! Why has my brother sent me to this awful place when my bridegroom hasn't even been decided yet?' Isabella interjected her servant's thoughts.

'You will feel better when you are dressed and have broken your fast,' Margaret cajoled her young mistress, knowing how quickly she could become angry.

'Once I am dressed, I want to see de Derneford.'

For Isabella, the chains of royal life, however invisible, were always there, and as much as she rebelled against her restricted life with her lovers and admirers, she was always a prisoner to the royal life she had been born into. And now she sat in her gilded chair as Margaret brushed her golden hair. She wondered what she would do to fill the tedious days ahead. William de Derneford stood before her.

'Princess, how do you fare today? I trust all is to your satisfaction?' He bowed to his mistress.

'My lord, I am already bored. When can we ride out and fly the falcons? Is there some place nearby that we can do this? And where are my dogs? I trust they are on the way, as we cannot hunt without them.'

'My lady, unfortunately the King's orders do not permit you to leave the Tower. He believes it is too dangerous for a princess such as you to be seen in London and the area. Your retinue is not big enough to protect you. The dogs are not permitted to join us. In fact, I am not sure what we can do with the falcons or all the horses.' De Derneford prepared himself for the storm about to come, but his hands were tied and he dare not disobey the King's command.

'Not allowed to leave? Has Henry completely lost his stupid mind? How dare he?!' Isabella screamed, picking up the goblet next to her and throwing it across the room; it smacked into the wall hanging, the contents dripping down the expensive tapestry. She rose from her chair, which toppled over in her fury, and those in the room collectively held their breath. But as quickly as her anger rose, this time at least, it faded almost at once, as she remembered who she was with and where she found herself.

'Leave me. All of you. I need to pray.'

Isabella gestured to dismiss her staff as she composed herself and walked into the Chapel, closing the door behind her. Her chaplain was absent, so she was finally alone. She felt the tears of anger and frustration prick her eyes – she never cried in front of her servants, or anyone else for that matter. Never show weakness, her brother Richard had always counselled her. She paced up and down, quelling the rage she felt against her fool of a brother, King Henry. She hated him for his weakness and could not stand to be treated like this.

The Chapel calmed her. She had scarce time for prayers; she played her role of course, as was required of her. Although mass was tedious and dull, she found chapels were useful to get away from prying eyes, unless of course she was at a public service, where she took care to look suitably pious. Marriage seemed almost preferable to this prison and how she longed to be free, to ride her magnificent grey horse, to fly her falcon, and to laugh at the hunt. That's what she needed – a hunt. If she couldn't ride to hunt, she would hunt a human prey, and her thoughts turned to her earlier desire for a young lover. She needed to find herself a distraction to amuse her and derive what little pleasure she could from being here. Suddenly, she noticed a slight movement above her and she quickly glanced up.

'Father Luke, is that you?'

But her words echoed back at her. Nothing. Her chaplain was nowhere to be seen. She shrugged and left the Chapel without a backward glance.

'Margaret, I would meet the Constable and the Steward of the Tower.' *Let us see what these two are made of*, she thought. Perhaps one of them could be her next prey.

Disappointment. The two men entered her chamber later that day and Isabella stifled a laugh. Thomas de Blundeville, the Constable, if he had been attractive or young, was not a man who found women desirable. She knew his type, but he seemed pleasant enough. He would be useful to her, she was sure, to make her stay as comfortable as possible, but not in the way she desired. The Steward was a nonentity, a stuttering, jabbering wreck of a man who wrung his hands as if they were in constant need of drying.

The Constable had at least offered her a stroll around the Inner Bailey to explain the ongoing building work and, although such things were a tedious bore, Isabella allowed him to accompany her, eager to agree to anything that would mean escaping this miserable room even if only for a while.

'As you can see, my lady, there are two twin towers separated by the Great Hall. The one on the right will be the King's and the one on the left will be for his Queen, when God grants his Majesty to marry,' Thomas explained to her, as they walked around the bustling Inner Bailey.

Isabella stifled her laughter at the thought of the poor woman who would marry Henry, as the

Tower of Vengeance

Constable pointed out the buildings which provided the services to both the new towers and the one in which she now resided. She noted the ale-stake swinging in the wind and fleetingly wondered what he would say if she asked to see inside! Of course, she would never wish to set foot in such a place, but it would have amused her to see his reaction. She watched as the door opened and she glimpsed a young, dark-haired man bidding farewell to one of her own staff. She paused for a moment to study him further, but the door closed and the man was gone.

She was too bored to make mischief today. The scene before her depressed her even more. The walls enclosed her further, and the sounds of laughter from the workmen seemed an insult to her presence – how could such low life seem happier than her? She pulled her fur cloak around herself and told the Constable she was cold; she had had enough exercise today, and she would let him know when she needed him further. Back to her gilded chair. Nothing for her today.

Thomas watched her return with her faithful Margaret to the Stone Tower. 'Such a beauty and such hard work.' He sighed, and hoped they found her a match soon, for he could see that the Princess was already bored and didn't the Devil make work for idle hands?

The Prophesy

Emma was full of excitement at the news that a real princess was here in the Tower. This was the first time a member of the royal family had stayed here for such a long time. She hoped she would see her even if it was merely for a moment. Will was busy in the new alehouse, The Golden Chain, ensuring everything was to standard for the royal household, so it was left to her to take Thomas his morning ale. He had quickly moved back to his old lodgings in case the Princess' serjeant complained about his use of the King's new apartments. As the building work had also been able to resume, it made sense for him to return to the Outer Bailey. The rooms continued to stink slightly, and his servants were trying to clear away the dirty water as she entered. Luckily, Thomas' study was upstairs, so at least he could work.

He looked up as she entered his study, and she registered his disappointment when he saw it was her and not Will who brought his ale.

'Ah, Emma, it's you. Thank you for the ale.' He liked the girl; she was always polite and always kind, but he knew she resented the time he stole from her with Will, even though neither of them had seen much of Will while he had been busy setting up the new premises. Today, though, she could barely contain herself as she placed his ale down.

'Have you seen the Princess, sir? Is she beautiful?' she asked eagerly.

Tower of Vengeance

The currency of beauty is always the thing we value most, he thought, as Thomas answered her, 'Yes, I have indeed seen her, and she is a beauty.'

'Oh, I wish I could see her.'

'She will be here awhile and is allowed to exercise in the Inner Bailey, so I'm sure you will see her at some point.' He could see this delighted her, but before the giddy girl could leave, he remembered something that had been niggling him. 'Oh, Emma, before you go, do you know why Will called the new alehouse The Golden Chain? It seems an odd choice and he changed the subject when I asked him.'

'No, I don't. He was vague with me too. But does it really matter? It's making money after all, and with the Princess here with all her retinue, it can only make more.' And then she was gone, practically skipping out of the room in anticipation of seeing Isabella.

I'm getting old, he thought. *I no longer crave this life in the King's service. I need to be gone, back to my own house in the country where Martha, my dear sister, will have a warm fire and good food. Simple pleasures away from all this.* He knew Will would soon be gone, too, when Fitzwalter made inevitable peace with the King, and he did not like the thought of being in the Tower without his friend.

Will had already returned to The Stone Kitchen when Emma got back. He had seemed preoccupied since the night of the comet, as if something was weighing on his mind. Emma had become accustomed to his moods but still felt hurt as he distanced himself from her. She was now nineteen and an age when she should have been long married. Luckily, her mother wasn't pushing her into getting married, though she had mentioned one of Aunt Joan's sons as a potential match. Emma had seen her spotty-faced cousin when she had visited Joan, but he was a poor comparison to Will. While Will was in her life, no other man stood a chance. Although he had never made her the promise of marriage as such, she knew he cared for her, as otherwise why would he be so respectful of her when they could easily find the opportunity to lie together?

'How was Thomas?' Will asked. 'I haven't seen him for a few days, but hopefully the Chain won't need so much of my time soon.'

'Missing you!' she teased, and he laughed with her. 'And he's seen the Princess. He says she is a beauty, and I might get to see her!' She squealed in excitement.

'I am sure she is not as beautiful as my girl,' he whispered, and stole a kiss after checking that Jane was not in sight. Emma blushed, reassured in his affection, but she longed for more, and her hand moved downwards and stroked the hardness she felt under his tunic. The kiss got deeper, and his hands gripped her buttocks as their passions rose. A sound from the kitchen brought them to their senses and they reluctantly pulled apart before they were caught.

'Later,' Will promised, squeezing her hand, and the dull day now seemed brighter for Emma with promises of more passion to come.

Tower of Vengeance

* * *

The Tower settled into its new routine as the royal household made their presence felt. The days dragged on for Isabella, and Emma had yet to see the royal guest. One cold morning, Will set to clearing the space around The Stone Kitchen where the storm's debris had collected and, at the same moment, Isabella wandered from her bedchamber into the Great Hall, where Margaret and her girls were sewing by the fire. Isabella hated to sew, even though all young ladies should, so she thought to read awhile in one of the window recesses. She had one of the servants remove the shutter so she could at least see outside and get some light. The man placed her gilded chair in the alcove and made sure she was wrapped in furs with a goblet of wine at her side.

    The book soon bored her with its religious homilies, and she glanced out of the window, looking out at the city. A sound made her look down and she saw Thomas shout over to a dark-haired man outside yet another alehouse. He turned from his task and a smile formed on her lips as she watched him return Thomas' greeting. It was the same man she had glimpsed before – young, strong, and pleasurable to the eye. From where she sat, she could see the fine face and the strength in his arms as he heaved an old barrel away from the wall of the house. He stopped to talk to Thomas, and she knew she had found her prey. But how to quarry him? This one would require a clever plan to get such a peasant into her chambers.

Tower of Vengeance

'Margaret,' she called over to her trusty servant, keeper of all her secrets and procurer of her desires. 'Find out who that is,' she whispered, pointing to the young man. Margaret nodded, discreetly leaving the chamber to seek out her mistress' latest whim. As Margaret shut the door, one of the large wall hangings abruptly crashed to the floor, making the girls scream and Isabella shout out to one of her ushers.

'Alfred! For goodness sake, get that properly fastened before it kills someone.' With that, she retreated to her own chamber unaffected, it would seem, by the violent act.

'Yes, my lady!' Alfred looked at the tapestry in astonishment. The straps were not damaged, the brackets sturdy; it was as if the whole thing had flown off the wall. He called for help to re-hang it and checked the other wall hangings in the room, all tightly fastened as that one had been. The girls watched wide-eyed and whispered of ghosts and other such like, and Alfred could not disagree with them.

'The name is William Lund. Runs the alehouses with his aunt, and there's a female cousin too,' Margaret revealed on her return. 'A plain girl not worth worrying about.' Isabella had raised a questioning eyebrow. 'By all accounts he's quite intelligent for an ale man, and he's also a friend of the Constable, which is interesting.'

'I can imagine he is. Thomas obviously has taste.' Isabella smirked.

'He's popular with the men and brews the best ale in the Tower.'

'Does he indeed? Well maybe we need to sample his wares.' The two women laughed as they planned their next move. Margaret saw the colour return to her mistress' cheeks and saw no harm in her soliciting a flirtation before her marriage.

Isabella, walking with Thomas the next day, could see he was surprised when she mentioned her dissatisfaction with the ale her own household had been providing for her. He believed they were brewing it in the Stone Tower's Black Hall in the basement.

'Perhaps it is the damp down there,' he suggested, still bemused, as he would have thought she would prefer to drink wine.

'You may be right, but I simply cannot drink it much longer. I like a cup of ale each evening in place of wine, you see.' She glanced over to the alehouse. 'My usher, Alfred, tells me there is much better ale from there. Who's the brewer? I would have him bring me a sample.' She smiled innocently, waiting for Thomas to take the bait.

'Oh, well that would be Will Lund. Are you sure you wish to meet him? I could arrange for your usher to bring you some,' Thomas suggested, thinking that would be more fitting for a lady in her position.

'No, I prefer to meet those who supply me, so I can ask questions directly. My father, King John, always said the details were important.' She doubted that very much, but she found it was always useful to remind people who her father was – that she was a king's daughter who was used to her orders being met, and that normally meant she got her way.

'Quite so, my lady. I will fetch him to you this afternoon.'

Isabella could hardly receive the brewer in her bedchamber, so she waited in the Great Hall in her gilded chair by the fire, glancing for a moment at the wall hangings. Alfred, noting her gaze, hoped no further mishap would occur, and felt a slight shiver run down him.

The door opened and Thomas entered with the young man carrying an ale jug – she almost laughed at the absurdity of the jug as her ruse to get him here, but instead she studied the man who bowed low before her. Her eyes met dark eyes, and she was pleased with what she saw. *Yes, he will do nicely.* She nodded to him to pour her some ale and raised her goblet to her lips, all the while keeping her eyes locked on him, noting the effect she was having on him. Margaret smirked, resigning herself to more secret assignations while her mistress sought her pleasure, noting the chemistry between them.

Will had been prepared to hate her – for she was a reminder of everything he should have had, and after all, her father had killed his mother, which was where all his family's problems had begun. But as she had turned towards him, he had noticed the languidness of her body, the curve of her breast against the blue silken cloth. Her sensuality had struck him like an arrow. Her perfect beautiful face with dark black eyes set within alabaster skin, ripe red lips curving into an expectant smile framed by the lustrous long hair spun like gold that bewitched him. He wanted her in that moment – nothing else mattered – not revenge, not his mother, and certainly not the girl he had left in the alehouse who could never really have his heart. And as his eyes met hers, he saw the matched desire as her pink tongue teasingly brushed her lips.

'Your ale is good, Master Lund. We will have it served to us each evening after we dine, but I must insist that you alone brew mine, and you are also to serve it to me so that I can be sure no one else has brewed it,' she ordered him.

'My lady, it will be an honour.' He bowed in polite deference.

A pleasant voice too, she noted. 'You may go,' she dismissed him. *Never let the hunt be too quick, for the anticipation was as good as the actual kill* – that her father had taught her, even one as young as she had been, and it had stayed with her.

'Is that normal, my lord, for the local alehouse to supply the royal household?' Will turned to Thomas.

'Well, your ale is good, Will!' Thomas laughed and slapped Will on the back in jest. 'Come, it's a huge honour and will enhance your reputation.' When they left the Stone Tower, he asked what Will had thought of the Princess.

'She is beautiful, but I was so nervous I was focusing on trying not to drop the ale all over her. I promised Emma a detailed description of her, but I couldn't even tell you the colour of her dress.' He laughed.

'It was blue if that helps, and you will have plenty of opportunity to study her if you are to take her ale each day.'

'Yes, I suppose I will. Emma won't like that. She will want to take it herself. Instead, she will be constantly asking me questions.' Will sighed, deliberately playing down the effect the Princess had on him.

However, in the Royal Apartments a gust of angry wind flew through the vents and extinguished all the fires. But Isabella and Margaret whispered in the Chapel, as the raven, perched on the Tower's roof, watched as all the foolish people practised their deceits and spun their harmful lies.

Maude

I can no longer rest. Why, when we are so close to Will getting away from here, does this have to happen?! Thomas has proven a useful friend, too, and all seemed to finally be going well. But now the arrival of John's daughter consumes me with a dread that will not leave me. My son thinks to hide his emotions from me and the girl, but he underestimates both of us. The alehouse girl will realise eventually that she has been usurped in his affections; she will notice his distraction and the smell of another female on him.

And I, I saw the look that passed between them. The mutual lust. That promise of what is to come. The Lovers card taunts me once again.

Oh, Will, you fool. You may think she feels the same, but you are merely a plaything, a diversion before she leaves for her grand marriage. I see her and her servant, that wheedling Margaret, whisper in corners plotting Will's ensnarement, and I curse that I cannot save him from his desires, but he blocks me from his thoughts. I try to push my way in, but he has inherited some of my own power and he is able to resist me. He knows all too well that I would disapprove, and like any child he will not want to hear my warnings; the lust is already upon him and there is no reasoning to be had.

I watch the Princess sleeping, I watch her eating, I watch her constantly. She has her mother's golden hair, but she has her father's dark eyes which are pools of pitiless black. Her face is delicate, and she feigns being in need of protection, so that foolish men declare they will die for her. Her lips, light as a pink rose, curve in disdain or are artful in temptation.

She thinks she has power, that as a princess she will have a better life than those around her, and her success with men gives her confidence regarding her unknown marriage. That she will mould her husband, that she will get riches and power and all that she thinks she deserves.

She forgets her mother's fate. Her namesake – Isabella of Angoulême, who was married to the King as a child. I saw her once at court. A haughty bitch of a woman who thought she was so clever as she looked down on us all and cared not for John's affairs. It was said she got her own pleasure outside of the marital chamber. But John never crowned her, never allowed her power or financial independence. He disdained her more than any other woman in his life – I think he even admired me for rejecting him – he only wanted the heirs he could beget on her.

After his death, she was quick to leave England, abandoning her own children for the man one of her own daughters had been betrothed to. The son of a man she had herself once been promised to! What webs this family weaves. They care not. And what a brood mare she has become – a further nine children to add to those she bore John.

There is no power in marriage for a woman, simply a need for heirs – it was ever thus. I pause to remember my sweet Geoffrey. How fortunate I was

Tower of Vengeance

in my husband, but I knew my role and in that I let him down – only the one son to show for our union. And even Will is unable to be his father's heir…

And now that son wants the she-wolf herself. And I feel helpless as I watch it play out as no good can come of this. And the Devil whispers in my ear – 'Choose your revenge carefully for she must live out her lifespan already decided; you can influence her future happiness but be careful what you wish for her. There are always consequences.'

I want to argue with him – this was not what I envisaged on the crossroads with Death. I thought by now I would at least have some revenge, some compensation for my life lost, but instead I am faced with this debacle where I seem to be losing even more.

He hands me a card – Temperance once again – and I watch as the winged angel pours the present into the future. The card wants me to be patient, to show some self-control.

But I cannot wait. I have a curse to make.

The Hunt

Following his first meeting with Isabella, Will returned to The Stone Kitchen with the image of her secret smile imprinted on his mind. It was quiet and he thought back to the day he arrived, marvelling at how much his life had changed. Unbidden, the words of the old woman on the road came back to him as a kind of warning. He shook his head as if to shake the memory away, trying to convince himself that the woman who had been waiting for him was his mother and not the woman he had just met.

'How was it? What is she like?' Emma asked eagerly, as she pulled him down to sit beside her at one of the tables by the glowing fire.

'She liked the ale,' he said calmly, deciding it was better to say little than to betray his feelings for the Princess and hurt Emma, who had only been loyal and loving towards him.

'She liked the ale? Is that all you can say?' She laughed, looking at him in disbelief. 'You and your ale! That's all you and Thomas think about. I want to know what she looks like. Come on, Will – tell me!' she encouraged him.

'Well, I was a bit nervous, so I kept my head down like Thomas told me to, but I think she had blonde hair. Oh yes, oddly she has the darkest eyes,' he added.

'That's it? Dark eyes and blonde hair?' Emma sighed, frustrated that Will didn't appear to be the most observant of men.

'I think her gown was blue and she had a gold circlet on her head.'

'And what did she say?' she pressed him.

'Only that she liked the ale, and I am to provide it to her each evening after she dines.'

'How exciting! Can I take it to her, do you think?' she wondered.

'Er, no, she was adamant that it had to be me, for some reason, as the brewer.' Will looked sheepish.

'Oh, that's a bit odd, isn't it?' Emma was puzzled. 'But then I have heard that only a few people are allowed to serve royalty, and isn't there a taster in the kitchen who has to try everything before it's served to the Princess? Perhaps you will have to taste it in front of her. Make sure you don't drop dead!' She laughed.

'I guess so. But, Emma…' he said hesitantly.

'What, Will? What's wrong?' She spoke softly, leaning towards him and taking his hand.

He stopped. She hadn't realised who Isabella was. To Emma, she was a princess, and she had never been close to such a person before.

'Nothing's wrong, I'm fine. It's a lot of extra work though. What with the new premises we might need to get some more help,' he suggested.

'That's true.'

'What's that about extra help?' Jane bustled into the room carrying jugs of ale ready for the next set of customers and Will, relieved at her intervention, explained the extra duties required from their royal guest.

'What good news.' Jane smiled, pleased at this turn of events, and blessing the day Will had come into their lives, as The Stone Kitchen now thrived. They now had a second alehouse in the Inner Bailey and the royal family wanted their ale.

Emma and Jane were both delighted over the success of Will's ale and had no reservations as Will left that evening to deliver his ale to King John's daughter, believing it was a huge honour to their alehouse. Will climbed the stairs to the royal chambers, the light and warmth contrasting to that summer's day when he and Thomas had first been inside the dilapidated Stone Tower. Now, the apartments felt alive with people, and he could hear the chatter of Isabella's ladies, the faint hum of music as he was led by one of the royal ushers into the Great Hall.

And there she was. In her gilded chair by the fire, looking as beautiful as one of the paintings on the church walls in the Priory. To him, she was an enchanting vision as she sat tapping her long, beautiful fingers as she waited for him to relieve her boredom. The older woman, Margaret, quickly jostled the ladies into the bedchamber next door on some errand with the royal wardrobe, leaving him alone with the Princess. There was a sense of anticipation as Will and Isabella surveyed each other fully for the first time with no other eyes on them except each other's.

Isabella smiled. Her prey had arrived. Time to hunt. But not too swift. She enjoyed the thrill of the chase.

'So, you bring my ale, Master Lund? I hope it tastes as good as I desire.' She smiled coquettishly.

'My ale is very desirable, my lady.' He moved across the room and poured the ale into her goblet, watching her intently as he did so.

'Yes, it still pleases me,' she announced, after taking a sip and licking her lips.

It made such a change to hunt a young, unaffected man, but she needed to be sure of him. As she looked at him, she wondered how it would feel to touch such smooth, unwrinkled skin. She had an urge to kiss the full mouth, to hold onto the strong arms, and to have that moment of complete control. For here was a relationship in which she would have the power, and how it progressed would be hers to decide – unlike her marriage, which would not be of her own making.

But he was still a man, and she needed to make him feel virile. She would need to play the innocent Princess to keep him in her thrall for

Tower of Vengeance

however long she was forced to stay here. She might have to play the long game. No need to rush. Anticipation was part of the sport.

'You may go,' she dismissed him, taking pleasure in the dismay in his eyes. He had clearly hoped for more, which she took great satisfaction in, now clear on his longing for her.

Will left the warm chamber unable to shake the sense of disappointment. He was so wrapped up in his own thoughts that he didn't notice the sudden chill in the air or even the smell of roses which followed him as he left the Tower. He had wanted to stay, for surely he hadn't imagined the way she looked at him. To seduce her would be such revenge on her family – to spoil her for her bridegroom – and he would derive great enjoyment from doing so. It would be no hardship to be with such a beautiful woman when the desire was mutual. Perhaps her dismissal of him today was nerves. After all, she was a delicate, cultured creature who, being so closely guarded, would surely have no knowledge of carnal pleasures. He blushed thinking of her and was glad of the hot, noisy alehouse, where he immersed himself in the rowdiness of the men, pushing all thoughts of Isabella from his mind.

Later, when it was quiet and Jane had gone to bed, he had greedily kissed Emma, rough and frantic, trying to slew his frustration, making her gasp with his intensity. Emma as always had been willing, begging him for more as she loved him with an innocence he did not deserve. He had wanted to take her, knowing it would make her happy and satisfy his lust, but the guilt would be too much. He had desire for Emma but not the love she desperately craved. Will also knew that he would be finally ensnared if he took her maidenhead, as he would feel the pressure to marry her after such an act. And marriage was the furthest from his mind as he thought of the Princess in the Tower even now as his mouth sought Emma's.

* * *

In the evenings that followed, Will climbed the Stone Tower's stairs with his ale and each time his longing for Isabella grew. She smiled, she moved gracefully around the room, and occasionally she touched his arm as he poured the ale before quickly lifting it away and speaking in that soft, lilting voice of mundane things. But he always felt her dark eyes on him. She took an interest in The Stone Kitchen, how he brewed the ale, the different herbs he used, and his plans for the future. She asked him about his family in The Stone Kitchen and he told the story he had given to Jane when he first arrived. She had expressed sympathy as his heart had beaten that little bit faster as he told her the well-practised lie.

Isabella watched him from her window as he walked across the Inner Bailey, after dismissing him for the evening. She had got him to open up to her, but she needed to make sure she meant something to him, so he would never betray her. He had to love her. For it was always a risk to lay with a man who might boast about bedding the King's sister. He didn't seem the type to talk of his conquests, but he was after all a man – she needed to make him feel special, desired, loved. She saw a young brown-haired girl greet him warmly, noticing an obvious familiarity, an affection about them. The girl laughed at Will and playfully pushed his arm as they strolled back to the alehouse. *This must be his cousin*, she thought, her eyes narrowing as she acknowledged a rival. She smiled as she felt herself aroused. It only strengthened her determination to have her prey. The girl was nothing compared to her, and she would delight in taking her prize.

When Will returned the next evening with more of his wretched ale, she was ready for him.

'I believe you mentioned your cousin? What was her name? Tell me more about her. I am interested in those that live here.' She smiled encouragingly.

'Oh, her name is Emma. She's a nice girl, bit younger than me. Her father, my uncle, was killed just before I arrived here,' he replied, not knowing what else to say.

'Is she not married? I thought such girls were married by now?'

'It's hard to meet men here in the Tower who aren't soldiers or workmen.'

'Does her mother not know of any suitable boys in the city?'

'I'm not sure.' He shook his head, waiting for the conversation to end.

'And you? What do you think of her?' She raised her goblet to her mouth, studying him closely as he replied.

'She's my cousin, so I don't think of her as anyone other than a friend.'

A lie, she thought. Yet if he lied about Emma, he would lie about her and not reveal any dalliance between them, so she was satisfied she could trust him and was ready to swoop in for the kill. She rose from her gilded chair and stood close to him, touching his face softly with her fingertips.

'I would hate to think you had a sweetheart, especially as I grow fond of you,' she murmured, watching the effect she was having on him.

'There is no one,' he hesitated, 'but you.' The words surprised him, but he could not take them back and he knew them to be true.

She blushed and moved away slightly, dropping her hand from his face. The door opened suddenly and her serjeant entered in a panic.

Isabella turned, sharply, and asked, 'Do you not knock?'

'Apologies, my lady, but the King's messenger is on his way.'

'Then we will receive him and discover what news he brings,' she said, recovering herself.

The moment gone, she dismissed Will with no further ado, calling for Margaret as the serjeant went to meet the messenger, trying to hide her frustration that her moment of longed-for seduction had been thwarted.

The Thief

Emma walked into the Inner Bailey the next morning on her way to The Golden Chain to check on the brewing there. The cold December air made her walk quickly, pulling her rough, coarse cloak around her and ducking her head against the tiny flakes of snow beginning to fall. When she looked up, she noticed someone in front of her dressed in furs, attended by guards, and realised it was the Princess. She paused as the woman turned and noticed Emma on the path.

'You are the alehouse girl, are you not?' Isabella asked, a mixture of curiosity and disdain on the delicate face.

'Yes, my lady.' Emma meekly bowed her head in deference, unable to believe she was face to face with the Princess at last.

Will had been right about the Princess' eyes – they were so dark against the pale skin – and the hint of blonde hair that crept out of the fur hood. But to Emma, they seemed like the eyes of a thief she had once seen in the city – black, pitiless, cunning, and callous. She shivered, this time not from the cold, but from what she recognised in that face. Then she thought of Will's mother and what she must have seen on Isabella's father's face all those years before. Her childish delight at meeting a princess had gone as quickly as the snowflakes dissolved on the ground before her. But then Isabella smiled, and the darkness of the eyes lessened, the moment passed, and there was radiance as if the sun had burst through the dark of night.

'I have heard about you from your cousin, Will. Perhaps you can bring me some ale sometimes. I grow bored of the company of my ladies, so you can enlighten me on alehouse life!' She laughed, and Emma wasn't sure if it was at her or with her. She bobbed her head in acknowledgement as Isabella dismissed her, and she carried on her way to The Golden Chain.

Isabella watched the girl as she went. *Pretty enough*, she mused. She would need to move faster with Will, for the messenger had brought news of an offer of marriage from the Holy Roman Emperor himself, Frederick of Sicily. She liked the idea of being an empress. It was a title that sounded worthy of her. She knew hardly anything about Frederick. All Constable Thomas had informed her was that he was twice widowed with two sons, and would be a useful ally for her brother, the King. She cared not, as she was desperate to leave this dreary place and take up her new prestigious role. However, there was time yet to have some fun with the alehouse boy, and she smiled at the thought.

That evening, Isabella dressed herself with care for her meeting with Will. She was fed up with the blue delicate colour her brother Henry liked her to wear, and he always ordered her gowns made of the same blue colour as his own weak eyes. So today, with Margaret's help, she perused her wardrobe for a different colour. Her eyes stopped on a rose-coloured gown which gave an impression of delicacy, of innocence, and youth. Instead of wearing her usual circlet of gold on her head she had white ribbon threaded through her hair. There were no flowers to be found during winter in the Tower or in the city itself, but she wanted Will to see a young maid rather than the princess the gold circlet represented so a ribbon would have to suffice. She needed to take away the fear the crown could represent to such a man as Will. She knew she could trust him now and he longed for her, so she determined to make herself obtainable, within his reach and she smiled with the artifice of it all. A part to be played before she left for a bigger stage.

When Will entered the room, she immediately saw that her ruse had worked. Although he tried his best to mask it, she could see desire burning in his eyes. He walked across the room where she stood alone by the fire, her pale skin slightly flushed by the heat. He set the jug down on the table and took her hand in his, lifting it up to his lips.

'If you permit me to be so bold, my lady, you are beautiful tonight.' She was impressed by his courage, his conviction in her own desire igniting hers. She made herself quiver slightly; her eyes met his in feigned astonishment as she parted her lips in anticipation. His eyes never wavered from hers as he drew her closer to him. This time there was to be no repeat of the interruption of that first attempt some days earlier. She had given strict instructions to Margaret to ensure they were not disturbed. The far door was bolted, guarded by one of her most loyal ushers and Margaret herself now stood outside the door Will had entered through keeping watch.

She gently pressed herself against his chest and could feel his heart pounding. She had to wait to let him take the lead playing the sweet virgin he believed her to be. Experience had taught her that no man liked a brazen whore unless he was paying for it and certainly not if the whore was a princess who was supposed to be pure and unattainable. He stroked her golden hair, looking at her in wonder, as if she were a rare jewel. She placed her hand onto his coarse tunic, feeling him stir as he pulled her closer to him, and she suppressed a smile so as not to look too eager. And then his lips were crushing hers in intense desire and she moaned as she felt herself triumphant. And yes, his lips were soft, his arms strong, and he was hers at last, this prey feeling more satisfying for the wait.

Hearing her moan, Will worried that he had gone too far and forgot himself. He moved to pull away.

'Don't stop. I want you so much. From that first day. Did you not feel it too?' she whispered, drawing him back.

'Yes, of course I did. But you are a princess, and I could be killed merely for kissing you!'

'Who would know?' Isabella stroked his face, soothing his fears. 'My servants are loyal, and you would not tell anyone would you? I will be leaving soon to marry, so would you deny us the time we have left together?'

Tower of Vengeance

'I would never betray you,' he murmured in assurance.

'Be my first, Will, don't let some withered old man take my maidenhead. Let it be an act of love, not duty.'

She stepped away and let Will gently unfasten her dress so that it fell to the ground. Her pale, naked body glowed in the firelight as Will quickly undressed. The strong, muscular body of youth was everything Isabella had hoped for in her final affair before she wed and became Empress. Her gift to herself worth more than the gold and silver her brother gave her to buy her love. She shivered in anticipation as she held out her hand to Will, careful to look nervous and let herself be led for this first time at least.

Will paused as he left the Stone Tower, pressing himself against its cold walls as he realised that he had not felt his mother's presence that night. Usually when he was in the Tower, he would feel her nearby whether by the dancing shadows, the familiar scent of roses or just the warm glow of her love encasing his body. Ironic that Isabella's father had wanted his mother to submit when her own son had now taken his precious daughter's virginity. He and his mother should be happy as his revenge had been easy. If circumstances had not conspired against him, then as William de Mandeville, Earl of Essex, he could have married Isabella in a strategic match which would have aligned the King with an old powerful enemy. But Henry saw him as a traitor, a murderer, a son of a witch, with his grandfather still a prisoner and the title that was his by birthright could not be claimed. His anger rose at the injustice of it. It all came back to King John and his mother's rejection that had marked his life.

  He suddenly realised that in his haste to leave, after Margaret had called out that it was time for Isabella to go to prayer, he had left behind the ale jug. It gave him an excuse to go to The Golden Chain to pick up an empty one, and if Emma asked where he had been all this time, he could say he was there checking on the new premises. He did not feel like he could face her yet, his guilt at what he had done gnawing away at him despite his feeling for Isabella. Situated in the Inner Bailey, the Chain was proving popular with the inhabitants there whereas The Stone Kitchen mostly catered for the soldiers of the Outer Bailey. He had a brief word with the new man, Simeon Sutcliffe, who had been hired to run the place for the Lunds, and checked on the ale to ensure it was of good quality.

  When he returned to The Stone Kitchen a short while later, it was also busy, and Emma was occupied with serving the men. Will slipped behind the bar and began pouring the ale into jugs setting to work as normal.

  'Oh, you are back!' Emma smiled happily.

  'Yes, I popped into The Golden Chain to see if everything was alright there.' The lie came easily to his lips. Emma discreetly squeezed his hand under the bar completely unaware that Will's heart had been stolen from her by the woman with the thief's eyes.

Tower of Vengeance

Maude

'She's the woman Maria warned us of, isn't she?' I demand of the Devil, who stands unmoved by the fire. I am pointing at my murderer's daughter asleep in her bed, restless in her dreams after her antics with my son. The Devil smiles, and as I look down, I find I am now holding the two cards: The Empress and The Fool. My fool of a son has fallen for this Jezebel that is Isabel. He believes he has had some sort of revenge on her by taking her virginity, when that had long gone and she had tricked him. Her mock cry of pain reverberated in these very walls where I shrank from their encounter. I watched her later drink down that herbal concoction that her accomplice, Margaret, in her dark deceit, had prepared for her, one that would purge her of his seed.

    I tried to communicate with Maria today. To ask her about her prophesy. But found only emptiness.

    'Your friend is dead,' the Devil tells me, reading my thoughts. 'Passed into my realm. There was no further need for her here. You are strong enough without her now.'

    I feel yet another loss. This one is so hard to bear. Maria has been a constant all of my earthly life and all of my spiritual life. Without her I could not be what I have become, and my son would not be here. I think back to those early days of death and how she found me in this spirit land, helping me shape my power and guiding me through the initial pain. I have felt untethered these past days and now it all makes sense. I sob for my dear friend – am I destined to watch everyone I love die? The thought makes me shudder and I feel the familiar unease over this Devil's pact.

'Her prophesy has come to pass. You alone must now decide what to do. Your son has given her his heart, for the Empress is enchanting, is she not? And so clever. I quite admire her you know.' The Devil strokes her pale face, and she stirs in her sleep. He knows his words anger me, deliberately trying to bait me, and I toss my long black hair, gathering my strength, pulling it in from the stones that surround us as I feel my hatred swirl towards the bed, its tendrils wrapping themselves around her sleeping form.

'I curse you, Isabella of England, daughter of a murderer,' I whisper. 'Through your marriage you will achieve the title you most desire, but you will not know happiness in your husband's bed. He will love another more than you and all your beauty, all your cleverness will be locked away and you will wither away as I have. Your marriage will be a prison of sorrow. And you will finally know what love is but too late, and with that love I wish you great loss. I want your heart to break like mine so all that you hold dear crumbles into dust. I cannot kill you, but I can give you a living hell. Your dreams will be of these walls, of my son, of the raven who even now calls out your destiny. These are your last days of happiness. Enjoy them while you can,' I warn.

My power wanes as my curse takes root.

'Is that the best you can do?' The Devil sneers beside me. 'There are others such as her. Plantagenet heirs who beget sons while your son lives in an alehouse. The Earl of Essex may even marry the alewife's daughter.' He laughs as he contemplates such a match, knowing he vexes me further as I am rendered powerless.

He is right. She is not the only child of that man, my murderer. I will regain my power and curse them all and their marriages – why should any of them know wedded bliss? They will not have the joy that I had so briefly.

'Be careful what you wish for,' he whispers, and he is gone.

I look down at the cards in my hands.

They have changed.

The Wheel of Fortune spins frantically. The Tower's walls are falling. I toss them away, not wanting to see what they foretell.

But there is another card: The Emperor. Dominant, arrogant. He seems to wink at me from his Imperial throne. My heart lifts.

My curse lingers as I disappear into the stones. It will give me some justice for my son's broken heart.

It will not be enough for my death though. The King's spawn must all pay.

The Earl

Christmas came to the Tower a few weeks later, but Henry did not come to London that year, not even to see his own sister. For Isabella, it was the final confirmation that her brother could not trust his feelings enough to be near her even at Westminster, the favourite of all his palaces. Instead, he stayed in France with the stretch of water keeping them further apart, and she realised that the brother she was once so close to would not see her again before she was sent abroad to be married.

Isabella continued to distract and amuse herself with her latest fancy. Will's devotion flattered her, his body sated her, and she enjoyed his company. She had taken an interest in the girl Emma too, and to dispel any rumours she allowed her to bring her ale every other night. It kept Will at arm's length, too, as there were days when his presence bored her, suffocated her, and became tedious. The girl was an easy piece of prey. Emma was dazzled by this miniature royal court and was in awe of the Princess, unaware she had stolen her love from right under her nose.

Isabella also spent time with Thomas, and she found she enjoyed his company. He was amusing, clever, and discreet. She wondered if he had his suspicions about her and Will, as he was a clever man and observant, but if he did, he chose to turn a blind eye to it.

And then for Isabella, there was joyous disruption as word came that her favourite brother, Richard, Earl of Cornwall, would be arriving within the week. Her beloved brother, so like her in sexual appetite, would not however forgive his sister for having sex with a mere peasant, so it was imperative he remain oblivious to her dalliance with Will.

That evening, as Will and Isabella were getting dressed after laying together, she told him of her brother's impending visit.

'He must not see you in my company. You will give yourself away and then we are both in trouble. He will only be here a few days, but he has the eyes of a hawk,' she warned him.

'Shall we get Emma to serve you both?' Will suggested.

'No, I don't think that would be a good idea. Richard is a man who likes new conquests, so it will be safer to get one of my ushers to collect the ale.' She dismissed Will, eager to purge his seed from her spent body.

Will hated the idea of her brother visiting, which would keep him from Isabella. Despite initially taking her maidenhead for revenge, he now found that he was under her spell and had fallen in love with her, even though she was the daughter of the man who murdered his mother. He found he would do anything for her, and when she smiled and he looked into those dark glittering eyes, he forgot his own revenge; taking her virginity now seemed like it had been an act of love just as she had said. He wanted only to be with her, and each day his rage at his own fate ate away at him. Thomas had sent further messengers for news, but no word had come from his grandfather. Fitzwalter remained a shadowy figure, frustratingly out of reach of his grandson, keeping him at the Tower, which was beginning to feel even more like a prison. If Will could be declared Earl of Essex and reconciled with the King, he naively thought he could then pursue Isabella for his wife. He had claim to her body after all, he reasoned to himself, so why not her marriage hand? Isabella loved him and he knew they would be happy. But without the earldom, he was just the alehouse boy and his dreams were fanciful.

Within the week, the Earl and his men clattered into the Outer Bailey, horses whinnying and restless in the cold air, and tired after the long ride. The Earl was to lodge in the new Royal Apartments, which Thomas had ensured were ready for their first royal guest. Thomas himself was there to greet the visitor and take him directly to his sister, both impatient to see each other, as other men sprang into action, helping the Earl's guard dismount and unloading the baggage carts.

Richard shuddered at the bleakness of the place as he took in his surroundings, and wondered what on earth had possessed his fool of a brother to incarcerate their beautiful sister in such wretchedness? He worried what life this had been for Isabella, and only wished he had been able to come sooner. The Stone Tower had changed in the time since he had last been here, although he rarely visited.

There was more structure to the Inner Bailey, new royal lodgings, an improved Great Hall, and a new alehouse. Thomas de Blundeville, the resident Constable, had done a good job, and he could report back to his brother that London's premier stronghold was definitely improving. The short, stout man at his side also seemed affable and his men efficient.

Richard was once again struck by the size of the place as he entered his sister's quarters. She stood at the top of the Great Stairs, waiting to greet him as radiant and as beautiful as ever. The most beautiful of all John's children – and also, he believed, the most cunning, which was why he felt such a kinship with her. He smiled as they embraced, for it was far too long not to have seen her, but royal life had kept him busy.

Isabella breathed in the smell of him – the mix of earthy sweat, leather, and horse which she loved so much. It felt so good to have him here, for he knew her the best and loved her for who she truly was.

'You look well even in this awful place!' Richard drew back to look at his sister's face.

'And you look dusty and dirty!' She laughed back at him.

'I wanted to see you straight away. It's been so long. I have so much news and the latest on your marriage.'

'How much time do we have?' she wanted to know.

'Barely a few days while the men rest. We have come straight from France at Henry's orders to see you, then we return to Padua to complete the marriage negotiations.'

'On Henry's orders?'

'Yes, he wants me to talk over the match with you to see what you think,' he explained.

'As if I have a choice!' She snorted.

Realising Thomas and her ladies were in the room, Richard hugged her again. 'Later, my dearest, we will discuss it once we are alone,' he promised her, before taking his leave.

Will watched from The Golden Chain as Thomas showed Richard to the Blundeville Tower, where he was to lodge during his stay. He could only make out dark hair and the broad build of a fighting man. The Earl of Cornwall was not a man to cross, according to the men who drank at The Stone Kitchen. Will needed to keep a low profile during his visit. He glanced at the round turret and wondered about his mother and whether she would make her presence felt. Isabella had told him of unsettling things that had frightened her ladies, of a sensation of being watched, especially when she prayed in the Chapel of St John with its upper gallery where shadows lurked, and of a foreboding which crept into her dreams. He worried what Maude was up to. He had tried to engage with her, to get her to leave Isabella alone, but she ignored him, and there was a feeling of intense disappointment, the smell of roses no longer sweet and vibrant but rotten and decaying.

The Falcon

Later that afternoon, Richard and Isabella had walked to the stables to admire Isabella's falcons. The birds were restless now with the limited hunting they had, although her men were allowed to take them out to the fields and forests beyond the city.

'I hear Frederick is a lover of falcons,' Isabella had remarked, as she stroked her favourite bird's soft breast, its dark, darting eyes mirroring hers as she watched her brother.

'He is a great hunter,' he agreed, as they left the stables.

They watched as a raven swept past them to land on the walls of the Stone Tower. Isabella shuddered as the large black birds cried as if in lament at their presence.

'It's as if those grotesque birds are holding the Tower together there are so many of them!'

'So, if they all fly away the Tower falls?' Richard jested.

'Imagine what the soothsayers would say if that happened!'

'Henry would need all the prayers he could get.' He sneered.

And laughing they had returned to her rooms to dine with Thomas, her ladies, some of his men, and other senior servants at the large table dominating one side of the room. Now Richard and Isabella sat alone before the cavernous fireplace, their ale poured, their dinner finished.

'Why do you insist on sitting in this vast room rather than your bedchamber? Surely it is more comfortable in there?' Richard looked around the room as he stretched out his legs towards the fire.

'I prefer to keep my chamber private. All these people coming to stare at a princess and her bed! Besides, this room has better light during the day and my ladies have more room to dance and amuse themselves,' Isabella reasoned, omitting to mention the views this room gave over the alehouse and both Inner and Outer Bailey so she could catch glimpses of Will. Her bedchamber was boxed in by the Chapel and had limited views on one side which looked down at the neglected gardens of the Tower and towards the tedious grey walls which protected the fortress. She had quickly grown bored of it within a few days. At least the Great Hall allowed her some glimpses into an outside world from her gilded prison.

'I'm glad to see you at least have a decent-sized household and your table is certainly plentiful.' Richard sipped his wine appreciatively, his stomach satisfied from the meal not long finished.

'So, tell me, brother, am I to marry the Emperor?' Isabella asked.

'I am to meet Frederick's men at Westminster in the next few days and if all goes well, I will return with them to Padua to finalise the marriage contract

Tower of Vengeance

with the Emperor himself. Once it is agreed, Henry will then announce your nuptials.'

Isabella let out a sigh of relief. *Finally, to be free of this place and to have a marriage befitting my status.*

'Have you met Frederick yet?' Isabella enquired.

'Not yet, but the match is a good one for both England and Sicily,' he assured her.

'What knowledge of the man? I hear he is twice married already with heirs?'

'Yes, he has sons already, so at least there will be no pressure on you to produce one. He's a learned man and he does like to hunt. I'm told his palaces are luxurious and he likes to move around his kingdom. You will be happy and have everything you could desire, dear sister,' he promised.

She wondered what her brother wasn't telling her. She had known him long enough to know he was selecting his words carefully, and she felt a tiny prick of doubt as the candles danced as if in agreement.

'It's a grand marriage you will have. Better than Joan or Eleanor's.' They drank as they reflected on their sisters' marriages.

'Yes, I do not envy either of them,' Isabella agreed. 'Poor Joan, ten years old when she was sent to Scotland to marry King Alexander. I was told she cried for days before she left. I wonder how she does now with no heir to show these fifteen years later.'

'And Eleanor married to the Marshal's son at nine and widowed at sixteen,' Richard added.

'I wonder how she is coping in the nunnery. Will her vow of chastity last?' Isabella arched an eyebrow at her brother.

'I hear she grows restless.' He smirked, and they laughed at their sister's misfortune.

'And what of our dear brother Henry? Who is he looking to marry now?' she asked, wanting to hear more on the rumours that had reached the Tower.

'An Eleanor, I believe. But then they all seem to be called Eleanor,' answered Richard sardonically.

'Or in our family's case, Isabella.' She arched an eyebrow.

'Ha, yes!' Her brother smirked. 'Our father of course, married two Isabellas – including our dear mother – as well as giving you that name. I guess it was easy for him to remember.'

'And you too have a wife called Isabella,' she reminded him, laughing at his oversight.

'How could I forget my dear wife – the Marshal's beloved daughter. A finer man than me or our Kingly father.' The bitterness was palpable. 'And two dead sons are all we have to show for it so far. Thankfully, her father is not alive to mock me for such failure.'

'Did you see our mother when you were in France?' Isabella changed the subject quickly, realising how his marriage angered him.

'Of course not. She wants no reminder of her other family now she has remarried and has even more children. Gosh, Bella, what parents we have – no sooner does our father die than our beloved mother runs back to France and marries her old suitor's own son.' Richard reverted to his childhood name for his sister as he remembered those turbulent years when they were all so young. The bewilderment and shame they had felt when their own mother deserted them.

The talk of all the unhappy royal marriages cast a dark shadow over the evening as Isabella wondered what lay in store for her, but she was under no illusion of romantic love. She hoped that hers would be a marriage of equals. She was certainly a match for any man. Frederick may be older but he too had experience and power, which she admired. She was also artful, deceitful, cunning, and above all she was beautiful and knew the ways of men. She felt prepared for her marriage.

For his part, Richard hoped she would be happy as Empress. He thought that of all his siblings, she was probably the most like him. Richard knew of her lovers, but he feared Frederick was not a man who would be easy to conquer. From what he heard, the Emperor had strong views on the role of women in his court, which might restrict his sister's freedom. There was talk of harems, secluded wives, and a dazzling mistress who ruled his heart, along with their son who was treated like a crown prince.

Suddenly, Richard wanted to be away from this place, to be in the bed of a willing whore, and to no longer feel the eyes of his sister upon him searching for answers he couldn't give her. He couldn't help but wonder if they were cursed in their marriages and if Isabella and Henry would follow this pattern.

'Is it true that one of Father's mistresses was murdered here?' The words were out before he could stop himself.

'You joke, surely?' Isabella pulled her fur cloak around her, chilled by his words as her face drained of colour and she recalled the fears she had shared with Will over the strange feelings and incidents that had happened during her stay.

'Ha, ha. Your face!' He laughed as he tried to make jest of it. He hadn't meant to scare her and wasn't sure why that old rumour had unexpectedly surfaced in his mind.

Later, when he left Isabella, he paused on the Great Stairs and looked up toward the circular turret where he believed the woman had been held. He was grateful to be sleeping that night in the new Royal Apartments rather than in the Stone Tower with all its cruel secrets.

Richard's arrival had been the talk amongst the soldiers drinking in The Stone Kitchen that evening, and his men had proved to be amiable, pleasant company. Their master, it seemed, even with his ruthless reputation, treated them well and instilled a discipline in them that had taught them to respect the places they went to.

'You have a pretty lass there,' one soldier remarked to Will after observing how he looked at Emma. 'Be careful not to lose her or let our master see her! He has a wandering eye.' Both Emma and Will had taken it in good spirit and now as they were clearing up at the night's end, she felt happier than she had in a long time. Since Richard's arrival, Will had not been required to take ale, so had been around much more and they'd quickly fallen back into their familiar routine and regained their closeness.

Will too was enjoying the easy company of Emma. She was the person that knew him best, as well as knowing his true identity. Even though he had a passion for Isabella, he cared for Emma because she was constant and never-changing. Isabella appealed to him because she was worthy of his status, and she intrigued him with her beauty and the power she had over him. He did not know how he had found himself in this position. He did not want to break Emma's heart for she meant too much to him, but right now he wanted to feel her arms around him and have the comfort of her unwavering love. Emma placed the last of the empty jugs on the bar and in this moment, working alongside her, it was as if no one else existed, and they were back to a simpler time. They both laughed as Jane shouted at them from the kitchen that she was off to bed, leaving them to finish clearing up.

Will bolted the door, banked down the fire, and joined Emma into the kitchen to help wash up the remaining pots and jugs ready for the next day. They worked in companionable silence. The fire in the kitchen flickered for a moment and the shadows shimmered as a faint smell of roses drifted into the room. It was gone before it was noticed, as Will took Emma's hand and pulled her in for a kiss.

    Silently, they moved into Will's bedroom. Jane slept deeply in the room above, the long working days taking their toll, so they would not be disturbed. Will slowly undressed Emma, being gentle and taking care. Emma kissed him again, showing her desire for him and that it was time, they did not have to wait any longer. She tugged at his tunic and his desire intensified. It was just them, caught in a rare moment of belonging together, of wanting each other.

    Later, as Will slept, Emma slipped from his bed, gently placing his arm, that had held her to him, back by his side. She dressed quickly, and quietly crept up the stairs to her own bedchamber to ensure she was in her own bed when her mother awoke. She could hear Jane's gentle snores in the next room as she got into bed. Her body ached and tingled from Will's touch. She could feel where his hands had caressed her skin, where his fingers had pinched her nipples and probed the very core of her, making her wet with desire so that when he penetrated her, she had been ready, the pain sharp but swift and the climax quick. He had whispered that it would get easier with time, but she hadn't minded. He was hers now and as she lay in the dark, she smiled with joy and happiness, for surely, he loved her as much as she loved him. He would not leave her now. As she finally drifted into a deep satisfying sleep, her thoughts were of their future and the children they

Tower of Vengeance

would have.

Maude

The Devil places the Hanged Man in my palm…I want to toss it away. My family has already sacrificed enough, our lives changed beyond all recognition. The card signifies further suffering, and I worry about what Will has done. He plays a foolish game when he should have been focused on regaining his inheritance. I can only hope it is not too late.

'But you know the card does not lie,' whispers the Devil.

I watch the three of them slumber from my shadowland with their different dreams, their different lives.

If only the jezebel could be gone now before it is too late. Before the girl finds out Isabella is indeed a thief and Will's heart is already lost. For it is. Soon it will be tossed aside, and his life once again will be shattered all because of that wicked family. These golden people whose lives revolve around a golden crown of power with no thought for us mere mortals. Destruction, hate, and death go in their wake, and we can but hope we survive their whims, their desires.

I did not.

The girl and my son are playthings, and they too will be discarded. Time is running short for them, and I fear how it will play out.

The Wheel continues to spin.

Tower of Vengeance

I look to France, where my grandfather is imprisoned. He is Will's one hope to regain what is ours and to get him away from his unwise entanglements.

The Devil laughs. He teases me with another card. The Star denotes hope, but he flicks it between his fingers so that it is gone too quickly, and it fades to dust.

The Marriage

Four Months Later

The day had finally come. Richard had impressed upon his sister the importance of this moment – it was time to take centre stage and shine. At last, Isabella would escape this cold castle, the endless dreary days, and the intense eyes of a man who had once been a welcome distraction but who she was quickly tiring of. It was now time to move on.

Isabella rose from her gilded chair and made her way over to the great chests which dominated the room, watching the household controller check each item as it was carefully stowed away. Nothing must be missed, nothing forgotten, and nothing squirrelled away by deceitful hands. Each item the servants packed represented her status, her importance, and her family's power. She watched as Margaret folded the robes of gold silk, the cloaks of scarlet and cendal, the burnet tunics and the green cloth of Ghent lined with miniver with great care. Isabella smiled when she saw the two dressing gowns lined with fur bringing back memories of other nights gone by in other beds where men had caressed her beautiful soft skin, and the pleasure she had taken in those encounters. She would have to pack away those memories with her old bed, which was being replaced with two new ones made from cloth of gold and furnished with soft silk mattresses. She was to become an empress and a dutiful wife.

Tower of Vengeance

As the strands of sunlight pushed their way through the small windows, the silver and gold goblets and plate glinted from her private Chapel as they were stowed in the chests under the watchful eye of her tedious chaplain, and she could see the covertness in his eyes. The King had supplied such riches here – perhaps there was guilt here after all, she pondered, for not seeing her, for not saying a final farewell. Cloths of gold, amices, new copes, and altar towels all in the finest materials from across the realms he ruled. There were even new robes and cloaks provided for her new knights, for her squires, clerks, chambermaids, her chaplain, and her physician. Henry was also sending a large household for her of fourteen kitchen maids, a washer woman, and several grooms and messengers. All to be packed away in the coaches and carts that would transport them.

She walked over to the smaller, stronger chests which held her precious jewels and picked through the riches there. The necklaces, rings, and amulets sparkling at her touch. And then the centrepiece a crown on which was carved the four martyr saints of England unto whose protection Henry had committed her, and for a second, she felt a frisson of fear. What was he protecting her from? The crown was now malevolent in its splendour, and the packing chests foreboding in their size. The sturdy locks represented a new prison as surely as the one she now stood in. She pushed away her dread – she would soon be an empress. It had taken four more months since Richard's visit for her marriage to be announced and tomorrow she would proceed to

Westminster for the solemnisation of the union between her and Frederick of Sicily. Then in five days' time she would sail to meet her husband, begin married life, and dazzle on her new stage.

    Later that evening, as the chests were moved downstairs into the lower floors of the Stone Tower, the jewels and gold locked in the treasure room next to the Black Hall, Isabella dined with Thomas. She felt Will's eyes upon her as he served the ale. She had grown weary of him as she knew she would, but she still lusted for his touch, and why not a few moments of satisfaction before she left? When Thomas went to use the garderobe, she whispered to Will to meet her after evening prayers on the staircase between the crypt and the Chapel. It would be too late to receive him in the Great Hall, and so close to the wedding she had to be careful no one outside her inner circle discovered them.

    Will returned later under the cover of darkness, with the few soldiers in the Stone Tower guard room letting him pass as they knew him by sight and always appreciated the extra ale he brought them. He quietly slipped through the doorway at the near end of the entrance chamber and into the Chapel crypt. In anticipation, he climbed the winding stairs, and there on the tiny recess – lit by one flickering sconce – stood Isabella, radiant in the candlelight. She pulled him to her, kissing him urgently, tugging at his tunic as he lifted up her pale blue gown. Their coupling was frantic, as if the sands of time were ticking faster and faster towards the moment they would finally part. They both felt the sudden burst of

Tower of Vengeance

satisfaction. Pleasure quick and spent. Their foreheads rested on each other for a moment as their hearts slowed again.

'You must be gone,' Isabella whispered, as she straightened her gown. Eager to be alone, her use for him sated, and ever mindful of his seed trickling down her leg, needing to be quickly purged from her.

'How can you bear it?' he asked, holding her wrist as she went to turn away.

'I bear it because it is my duty,' she snapped, tired of his cloying ways. She withdrew her hand, reminding him with a disdainful glance of the trespass he made on her royal person, and was gone. Will slumped against the stone wall, deflated by her callousness, knowing he had lost her. He could hear the curfew bell ringing and knew he would be late returning to The Stone Kitchen. The Tower was quiet now as the inhabitants began to find their beds for the night, but he managed to use the garderobe, to wipe away the traces of his encounter before he returned home.

Will left the Tower as quietly as possible; the night was cloaked in an inky darkness and little stirred within the walls, just the sounds of the river beyond with the boats ferrying their last few passengers punctuating the silence. He kept to the shadows in case a soldier should see him on patrol but made it back to The Stone Kitchen without being seen. His heart lurched as a figure rose from beside the glow of the dying fire, and he breathed a sigh of relief when he saw it was Emma.

'Will, at last. I was worried about you.' She went to hug him, but he gently pushed her away and poured himself a pot of ale.

'I was just helping out in the Chain. It is busy there with all the marriage preparations,' he explained.

'Are we alright? It's just that you have rarely touched me these past few months since that night. I just feel so confused.' A tear started to run down her face.

'I told you that we can't risk you getting pregnant. Your mother would never forgive us,' he reminded her, as he took her in his arms and began to softly stroke her hair.

'Do you still want to leave? I want to know what our future holds. I keep thinking of that night and what it meant to you and to us. But I know how much finding your own family means to you,' she admitted, tired of the unknown that haunted their relationship.

Will had not told Emma about Thomas' knowledge of his identity and the messages crisscrossing the sea to his grandfather. His departure may be sooner than they thought, and he had felt guilt over that night when they had finally slept together. He had been careful not to make any promises of marriage that he might not be able to keep when his birthright was restored, but now looking into her tearful eyes he found himself wanting her again.

Tower of Vengeance

'I love you, Emma,' he said, kissing her hard, knowing her weakness and owning his lie. His eyes would have betrayed him, but his lips and his body could tell a different tale as he quickly lifted her tunic and gave into his own lust. Desire washed over Emma; the words she had most wanted to hear scurried away her questions, fears, and doubts.

After they had parted to their own bedrooms, Will was in turmoil. He had wanted to reassure Emma of his affection. At times he had such tender feelings towards her which he did not experience with anyone else, and he could not control his need for her. He felt disgust at himself for having had both women in such quick succession, but most of all he wished he could love Emma as she deserved to be loved. As he climbed into bed, he hated himself for what he had done that night. She of all people did not deserve this.

* * *

The next morning brought a bright May day as Richard, Earl of Cornwall, entered the Outer Bailey accompanied by the royal heralds with the royal standard held before them. Richard's retinue of knights, squires, and pages followed, banners streaming in the spring breeze, horses dancing as if in rapturous delight, and then the royal coach regaled in silk with its honour guard ready to transport Isabella to Westminster Abbey.

Tower of Vengeance

The Tower inhabitants, not used to seeing such pageantry, crammed on every step, wall, and nook for the best vantage point, waiting for the Princess to descend from her Royal Apartments and make her journey to the Abbey. Isabella was glorious in her splendour when she emerged. Her blue silk gown shimmered in the sunshine; her golden girdle catching the light sent glittering sparks out to the transfixed crowd. She wore a light purple cloak trimmed with royal ermine around her shoulders, and on her head the crown which Henry had gifted her with the four martyr saints of England. Since the Princess had arrived six months ago in the flurry of winter snow, the Tower inhabitants had thought of her as their own, her presence enhancing the Tower's status – providing an aura it didn't previously have – but now they were reminded of the royalty they'd had amongst them and how she was destined for greater things.

Isabella paused on the steps and savoured her moment. Today she would become an empress, married by proxy in Westminster Abbey, that most sacred of places, and then she would be gone. Nothing would diminish her blaze of glory; she would continue to glow. She had been born for this day. Isabella of England.

As the royal party left for the Abbey, the Tower returned to its daily duties, awaiting the Princess' return before she left for good.

'Well, that was wonderful, wasn't it, Jane? She looked so beautiful!' Joan declared, turning to her sister-in-law as the procession came to an end.

Tower of Vengeance

'Aye, she certainly did.' And the two women returned to the alehouse and settled on one of the benches.

'Where's Emma and Will? I thought they would be watching?'

'Supposedly, they are too busy brewing ale.' Jane looked at Joan, who raised an eyebrow, not believing her daughter and nephew were really preparing The Stone Kitchen for morning service.

'I know you've had your concerns about them, but has something happened?'

'Oh, Joan, why couldn't the foolish girl fall in love with the likes of Simeon?! No, she has to fall for Will.'

'You said you now doubt that he is your nephew, so why are you so concerned? He seems a good lad.'

'I'm not sure who he is anymore, but you are right – he's done a lot for us. He's worked hard, opened a second alehouse, we serve royalty now, and his friendship with the Constable has been advantageous. Life has been much easier for us with him, I don't deny it. When we lost Mark, I thought we would lose everything. Will gave us a new start.'

'And Emma? You think she loves him?'

'I know she does, but I worry he might not love her in the same way. He's constantly restless, never truly at ease, as if he is waiting for something better.'

Joan placed a hand on Jane's arm to soothe her.

'I am sure it will work out.'

'I hope so, Joan. Why did I ever think running an alehouse in a place like this was a good idea?!'

Tower of Vengeance

The Golden Chain

The day had been a triumph. The crowds in the city had cheered and thrown flowers at the royal possession as it made its way to Westminster. Richard had breathed a sigh of relief for London was not always fond of its royal masters, but today the sun had shone, and Isabella with her charm had enchanted the sullenest of peasants. She had smiled and waved throughout, cunningly letting her veil shift slightly so that they could see her face for brief moments. There had been some jostling, a faint jeer here and there, but his men had managed to quell any glimmer of unrest, unobtrusively ensuring it had not grown into something larger. And he had made sure to distribute the flowers in advance.

And now Isabella was back inside the Tower for her final few nights. She sat alone in her gilded chair marvelling at the day. The cries from Frederick's ambassadors of 'Vivat Imperatrix! Vivat' echoing in her ears. Closing her eyes against the Stone Tower's walls, contemplating her Imperial life in the splendour of the Sicilian court, she smiled. She finally had the life she deserved. She wanted this time alone, to savour the day that she had long waited for.

'Your ale, my lady,' Will offered her.

'You startled me! I asked to be alone.' She was brusque and annoyed to see him. He was already in her past now that she was married and ready to begin her new life.

'Please, my lady. Let me at least give you this one thing to remember me by. I love you; I know there is no future for us but at least if I know you have some part of me, I will feel some happiness.' In earnest, Will held out the golden chain with the ruby cross that he'd found a year ago in the Stone Tower. It had been his mother's rosary and now he handed it to the woman he loved.

'Why, it's beautiful,' she lied, as she accepted the gift that seemed to burn at her touch, while the room seemed to darken slightly. Isabella felt repulsed by the love she could see in his eyes, and knew he expected a declaration of love in return, but none would be forthcoming from her. She shivered as once again the room chilled, and she looked to see if the fire had somehow gone out. The fire hissed as she gazed at it; she jumped slightly and wanted him gone, her ladies around her, anything to get away from the malignancy of the moment. She would be glad to be away from this place where she had never felt comfortable, the sensation of being watched always present.

'Thank you for your service, Lund.' Isabella's serjeant broke the spell as he strode into the room, followed by dear, loyal Margaret. 'You will no longer be required by the Empress. The Emperor has ordered that only her household may now have access to the Imperial apartments, and his men will now stand guard to ensure this is adhered to.' Even Isabella was surprised at this command, before she remembered the new knights who had been added to her retinue, realising now that they must have come from

Tower of Vengeance

Frederick to oversee his bride's journey. She curled the chain in her fist so nobody would see what she concealed as Will was finally dismissed. Her lover was gone, and she was now a wife.

Will returned to the alehouse in a daze, as it was far from the parting he had envisaged for them. Isabella had been frosty towards him, and he was surprised she was taking her marriage vows so seriously when he was the one she loved. The Stone Kitchen was busy with everyone celebrating the royal wedding in a convivial mood, and he had no time to think about the fact that he had lost Isabella for good.

'Emma, I left an ale jug in the Princess' apartments, could you fetch it?' he asked her when there was a brief moment of calm, realising he had been jostled out in such a hurry he had forgotten it. She wondered why he didn't go himself, but there was no time to ask as the men demanded more ale from him, and it was better that he remained here in case the merriment of the patrons quickly soured. She made her way to Isabella's rooms but noted the soldiers were more stringent, checking anyone who entered. She had to be approved by the officer in charge before she was allowed up the Great Stairs, but they deemed the alehouse girl no threat to the new Empress. An usher went to find the missing jug while she was instructed to wait outside the Great Hall. There was only the screen that divided the royal bedchamber from the place where she stood. It allowed a makeshift corridor from the stairs to the Great Hall, and gave some privacy to the bedchamber, but she could hear voices within.

Realising it was Isabella and Margaret, she pressed herself against the screen to listen to their hushed conversation.

'Oh, look, Margaret, he gave me this awful gold chain as a keepsake! It seems he did indeed love me, so I must have played my part better than I thought.'

The two women laughed. Emma's heart seemed to stop, and she felt light-headed all of a sudden.

'Well, he can marry the alehouse girl now. He'll soon get over it when she gives him children, although I bet she does not please him as you did,' Margaret said with a laugh.

'I asked him once if he slept with her and he said it had happened once – a mistake – as if I cared. He said it was like bedding a piece of wood. He forgets she was actually a virgin. I can't believe he thinks he took my maidenhead. How does he think I learnt all those positions and how to tease his cock so well! He served a purpose, I suppose, and I will miss laying with him,' she said with a giggle.

A door slammed somewhere and the two women quickly stopped talking, but Emma had already heard enough. Will had lied to her and played her for a fool when all this time he had been with Isabella, even falling in love with her so deeply he had given Isabella his mother's chain, which was his most precious belonging. She remembered when he had shown it to her – how it was a beloved gift that he always kept so close, the single possession he had from his mother. She noticed the room had changed – a sense of despair swirled around her, the wall sconces flickered, and there was a coldness that was unusual for the May evening. The usher, finally returning with the jug, noticed her pale face and asked her if she was alright. She grabbed the jug and somehow made it down the stairs, through the entrance room, and out into the darkness of the night. Once outside in the cool evening air, she felt her breath come in gasps as her grief overcame her, wanting to howl at the night sky and to run as far away as possible. She did not know how she would be able to face the man who had betrayed her.

 She returned to The Stone Kitchen and made herself busy to avoid Will, not bearing to look at him. When the alehouse was emptied, Jane quickly retired to her room, leaving Emma alone with Will.

 'So how does it feel to bed the King's sister?' Emma spat the words at him, picking up the nearest ale pot and hurling it at him with all her strength. 'And don't deny it. I heard her talking about you and her. Does it make you feel powerful? Special? Because I can tell you this – you mean nothing to her.'

 Will felt the anger pulsating from her and realised his deceit had been uncovered. He moved closer to her and grabbed her arms, desperate to silence her so as not to wake Jane. 'Emma, please stop this. You know not what you say.'

 'Don't you dare deny it, Will!' She withdrew from his grip. 'Do I mean so little to you? I was never good enough, was I?' Will paused, not knowing whether to try to touch her again, to comfort her as the tears fell down her cheeks, or to finally own the truth.

'You even told her about us – that it was like bedding a piece of wood. Did you think of her when you bedded your piece of wood?' she sobbed, before slapping him as hard as she could. 'You think she loves you? You fool. Go ask your royal whore what she really thinks of you. You were simply a conquest to her. A good one but nothing more. I hope it was worth it.' Tears streamed down her face, and she wept uncontrollably.

'I'm sorry, Emma. I should have told you the truth. I don't know what I can say to you. I didn't mean for it to happen.' His heart was racing; he had never meant to hurt Emma in this way.

'You have no idea of love and neither does she. I hope one day you do realise what love is because this is not it. I can't even look at you. You disgust me.'

'I do love you, Emma, you have to believe me. We could be happy, couldn't we? It's you I want a future with.' In that moment, Will realised that Emma had always been his fallback. If all else failed he had her; he could marry her, try and make something of his life. Without her, all that remained was the glimmer of hope that was his grandfather.

'Are you deluded? You can't expect me to just go on as before! There is nothing left for us now.

She has destroyed us like her father destroyed your mother.'

At the mention of his mother, he could smell the decaying scent of roses, feeling his mother's sorrow and anger at his actions.

'You gave her your mother's chain! You break not just my heart but your mother's too.' She held up her arms as he went to reach for her again. 'Enough. We are done.'

'Don't walk away,' he whispered into the silence, as she left him alone surrounded by the debris of the night's drinking, and the realisation that his life had tumbled down around him, leaving only the ashes that smouldered in the fireplace.

* * *

In the Stone Tower, the atmosphere had seemed to shift; the men felt uneasy listening to the cries of the ravens outside, the ladies in their beds moved closer together to gain comfort from the night's shadows, and the household warily finished off their tasks as the Empress would be leaving in a few days. Margaret felt the change and wondered at such alchemy, for she had long sensed the magic of another. It had eluded her, it troubled her, and even now she feared it – for though they would soon leave, who knew what damage it had already done. Who was there in the shadows causing such unrest? She glanced at Isabella sleeping, seemingly oblivious to anything but her new life and relieved she had now broken things off with the boy from the alehouse to make a fresh start and avoid any scandal. Ysend, Isabella's maid, was helping Margaret tidy up, and they quietly continued as Margaret tried to shake off her fears.

  Ysend was a young girl from one of the better peasant families, whom Margaret had acquired during their days in Winchester to serve the Princess. She was strong, quick to learn, and placid in temperament. She was also a plain girl, useful when there were men around, as none took much notice of the sturdy, short maid with the slight squint. She was loyal to her mistress, worshipping the beauty she could never have. Margaret knew she had chosen well, as such devotion was hard to find, and she had proved a useful addition to the household.

  'Ysend, can you go down to the serjeant and tell him we are set for the night. He can secure the Stone Tower, and then off to bed with you. I will stay with the mistress.' She wanted no harm to come to Isabella tonight, and would ward off the dark magic she felt whispering within the walls.

  The girl finished folding the blue gown Isabella had worn earlier and placed it carefully in the chest. She took one of the candles from the wall recesses to guide her down the Great Stairs, saying goodnight to Margaret as she left the warmth of the bedchamber. She felt the cold immediately. Being a country girl, she was not one for fanciful thoughts, but tonight she felt a strange presence near her. She shrugged it off.

    'Silly fool. Naught here but shadows and cold stone,' she told herself, as she hurried on her way.

    She shone her candle down the winding stairs, checking that nothing was lurking in the shadows, and chiding herself for her fanciful imagination.

    'All clear?' she shouted, so that anyone coming up would know she was coming down. Silence. No answer came. She swung the candle round up towards the blackness when she thought she heard a noise. Again nothing. Up ahead, her bed lay waiting in one of the nooks of the blocked-off minstrels' gallery, but further up lay the circular turret where no one dared to go. The thought of her bed seemed to rouse her. She simply needed to complete her errand as she had done on numerous evenings, and then she could sleep for it had been a tiring few days with the preparations for the marriage ceremony and departure. She took a step down, then another; *soon be there*, she thought, laughing at her fears. Then she felt a shove in her back, her foot slipping. Desperate to steady herself, she dropped the candle, plunging her into darkness, and then the tumbling descent down the stone stairs, her body twisting and turning until her head cracked on the final step. Her journey completed. Her life ended before she could understand where the faint scent of sickly roses was coming from.

The Farewell

Early a few mornings later, after dawn had broken and another restless night, Emma went to see the serjeant, who raised an eyebrow when she requested an audience with the Empress. The household was already in turmoil following the death of the maid a couple of nights ago and he had more than enough to do, including finding a replacement.

'She won't see you,' he said dismissively, eager to move on to one of his numerous more pressing tasks.

'Please can you ask her? Tell her I have found her golden chain,' Emma said firmly.

'You can hand it to me.'

'No, I want my reward. At least tell her.'

'Very well, but she will not see you.' The girl was persistent, he would give her that. He decided to humour her.

A few minutes later, Emma was shown into the royal bedchamber to the astonishment of the serjeant, who had been sure she would be refused access. Isabella sat alone on her gilded chair, bemused by the girl standing there.

'I hear you have a golden chain belonging to me,' she said calmly.

'No, my lady, I fear it is you who has a golden chain which belongs to another. And now you owe me for the theft.' Emma looked at Isabella in defiance.

'I owe you? I hardly think I owe you for what you never had.' Isabella realised the girl had more guile than she had originally thought.

'You may laugh, but I know Frederick's guards stand just beyond that screen,' she hissed, 'and I would be more than happy to tell them all about you and the alehouse boy. What I saw with my own eyes. Oh yes, I can lie as much as you, and they will know I had access to your chambers serving you ale,' she warned her, and Isabella's smirk faded. 'Perhaps a search of this room could find the actual chain in question. I'm sure that's not a risk you're prepared to take, because you want out of this accursed place. Well, so do I. So, here's what we are going to do. I am leaving with you as your new maid. A fair trade, don't you think? I want a new life away from here as much as you do. Let's both get what we want,' Emma bartered.

Isabella contemplated the girl with fresh eyes. She had underestimated her, which could be Isabella's downfall if she did not tread carefully now and appease her. She was not so meek and submissive as Isabella thought, and not willing to settle for a man who didn't love her it seemed. She had courage, she would give her that, and perhaps she could prove useful. The girl was right – she couldn't take the risk of losing what she held most dear, which was a marriage that would make her more powerful than her sisters and even her own brother, a mere king. They might not believe the girl, but rumours would start, and she wanted nothing to tarnish her reputation.

'If it is what you want, so be it. Go collect your belongings and say your goodbyes, for now you will enter the royal household and Margaret will need to give you some training. There will be no going back, you realise?' she warned the alehouse girl.

'I understand, and I promise to serve you well,' Emma replied.

'Good. One last thing – how did you know about the chain?' Isabella was curious to know.

'Walls have ears, my lady, and you have been careless with your talk.' Isabella blushed scarlet at how indiscreet she had been and was only grateful that the person who had overheard wouldn't bring everything she had wanted crashing down. She dismissed Emma and tried to recover herself, recognising that she had become too arrogant as she had revelled in how well she had manipulated Lund and his cousin.

Emma turned and left. It was done. She would leave this place with her love rival but at least she would get away and could forge a better future for herself without the need of a man. When she had heard of the maid's death, she had seen her chance and grasped it, for she could not stay with a man who did not love her whatever he promised her.

She had told no one of her plan, so her mother was distraught when she returned and broke the news.

Tower of Vengeance

'I will never see you again!' Jane wailed.

'It's an honour to serve the royal household. Father would be so proud,' Emma said brightly, keeping a brittle smile in place as she pretended it had been her ambition all this time. 'Imagine the places I will see,' she feigned enthusiasm.

'You won't see places, only piss pots and dirty sheets, you silly girl. You won't have the freedom you have now,' Jane chided her, as if serving coarse men each day was a better life.

'No, I will have a different kind of freedom. Please be happy for me. It's for the best, Ma.' The two women embraced as Emma said her final goodbye.

Emma slipped out of The Stone Kitchen while Will had been at The Golden Chain, not wanting to see him before she departed. When he returned, he found Jane crying and, feeling the absence of Emma, he knew something had happened.

'I don't want you here any longer. My daughter has left because of you. She didn't say as much, but I know,' Jane sobbed. 'You can take Simeon's place and run The Golden Chain while he comes here. I know you broke her heart, and you swore an oath that you wouldn't hurt her. Now I have lost her. Get your things and go, I won't share my alehouse with you any longer.'

Tower of Vengeance

Fitzwalter

Five days after the wedding solemnisation at Westminster, Isabella of England left the Tower of London for the last time escorted by Richard, Earl of Cornwall, and the Bishop of Exeter on behalf of the King, with the Archbishop of Cologne and the Duke of Brabant representing Frederick. There had been letters of congratulations, encouragement, and endearment from the King to his beloved sister, but still no visit, no final goodbye to the new Empress. If Isabella felt his absence, she didn't show it, and the Tower inhabitants were not so reticent as once again they gathered to say goodbye to her. Their Princess of the Tower. They cheered and waved as the procession finally left, but this time there would be no return and the place already felt empty and quiet. Now lacking that royal sparkle that Isabella had given them.

Will had not gone to see the Empress and her retinue leave. He had heard the cheers from The Golden Chain, where he readied the alehouse for the day ahead. He looked up in surprise as Thomas entered, out of breath, his face flushed with excitement.

'Thomas, I did not expect to see you so soon after the Empress' departure. Are you quite well?' He quickly poured the panting man a pot of ale as Thomas sank onto a bench.

'Are we alone, Will?' he managed, as he gulped his ale, recovering his breath.

Tower of Vengeance

'Yes, there's just me, as the serving girls have gone to the market for me, after of course watching the Empress leave. What's happened?'

'A letter, Will, I had to bring it to you as soon as I could. Read it.' Thomas was smiling as Will cautiously unfolded the letter and began to read.

Dear Sir Thomas,

Forgive me for the long delay in writing to you. I am now a free man and have finally made my peace with the King.

I cannot tell you how glad your news made me all those months ago in my imprisonment. When Will, my grandson, left the Priory I had no idea where he had gone. Of course, I secretly put out feelers for news of his whereabouts, but the King and others looked for him too and it was a dangerous time as I feared for Will's safety. The woodman from Binham brought the surprising news that Will was at the Tower of London, but until you contacted me, I had no way of getting news to him without alerting those others to his presence there. It was a shock that he was there, a place which saddens my heart as it is where my dearest daughter, Maude, lost her life. I can never forgive myself for her death. I blame myself for not doing more to save her; having to leave her to that man's mercy whilst I and her husband escaped abroad broke my heart. I knew I had to keep her son safe for her sake as much as my family's.

My joy at his survival knows no bounds and it is my one wish before I die to ensure he receives his birthright and that I can see him once again. Will was but a child when I last saw him and it touches my heart that you say he has grown into a strong, resourceful young man. There is further good news. Will's uncle, the current Earl of Essex, has fallen out with the King, and I believe Henry will look favourably on a new young earl. Unfortunately for you, Thomas, your Uncle Hubert has lost any chance of reconciliation with Henry, so there is no longer any need to appease him for the death of his cousin. Thomas, my good man, I appreciate how hard this must have been for you to protect my grandson at a time when your uncle could have used Will as a bargaining tool to regain favour. You will always have my eternal gratitude.

In the light of all this news, you need to instruct Will to be ready to leave as soon as I am sure it is completely safe to send one of my men to bring him home. I have told no one else as yet about Will's existence. I still need to tread carefully – my heir, my other grandson, is but two years old and a ward of one of my enemies. How I wish my son, Walter, were still alive to help, but as you may know, he died not long after his son's birth. My life is full of sadness, and the loss of both of my children grieves me so very much, which is why I long to see Will and entrust in him my family's future. Together we can return the Fitzwalters back to their former glory.

Tell Will it will not be long now. Our wait will soon be over.

Richard Fitzwalter

Tower of Vengeance

Will's hands had started to shake as he read the letter, and his heart felt as if it would burst with joy.

'Oh, Thomas! It's the best of news today of all days. I can hardly believe it after all this time.' He grabbed his friend's hands.

'I could scarce believe it myself after all this time, all our hopes,' Thomas beamed.

'What he says is true, my friend. You could so easily have given me up to help your uncle. I can never repay you for that.'

'I do not believe in innocent people dying for the sake of one man's fortune. My uncle knew the dangers that come with being close to the Crown, as your own family can readily testify. I have tried to stay on the outskirts of such politics and to judge each person as I see fit. You are a good man, Will,' Thomas was adamant.

'Well, I don't really feel that at the moment.' Will sighed, remembering Emma's shattered face when she had discovered his betrayal.

'I did mean to ask you about your change of circumstance, and of course Emma's sudden departure with the Empress, but was waiting for the right time. Do you want to tell me what has happened?' Thomas asked gently.

Will briefly told Thomas what had happened between him, Isabella, and Emma, knowing he could trust his friend not to betray his confidence regarding the newly crowned Empress. 'So, you see, I have truly mucked up my life here, and broke poor Emma's heart, which she did not deserve. I've been such a fool, Thomas,' Will finished his sorry tale.

'Good grief, Will, that was a very dangerous path to tread. You realise you could have been killed for just touching the King's sister. However, it seems she well and truly used you, and you got your comeuppance by losing Emma too. No wonder the poor girl left.' Thomas shook his head. 'She loved you. I could see it in her face every time she looked at you. Did you ever love her?'

'I don't know, to be honest,' Will admitted. 'I like her; she's kind, funny, and generous, but I think at the back of my mind I always believed she was not good enough for me. Conceited, I know, but my aim has always been to leave here, and how could I arrive at my grandfather's court married to an alewife's daughter? I would have been laughed at and not taken seriously as his grandson, let alone the Earl of Essex. Isabella was more befitting to my status, which heightened my desire, and of course there was an element of revenge when I thought I was taking her virginity. Then I got swept away by her and I found myself falling in love with her.'

'And men are ever fools for a beautiful face. Answer me this, Will, if Emma had been a worthy match, say the daughter of an earl, would you have loved her then?' Thomas challenged him.

Will had never thought of Emma in these terms before as his equal, and he realised how shallow he must seem when he answered truthfully.

Tower of Vengeance

'Probably, because she would be everything you could want in a wife. I look back now and I see her kindness, her loyalty, her beauty, and how she made me feel safe. I really have been stupid, haven't I?' Will groaned.

'She's gone now. You have learnt too late. Such is youth,' mused Thomas. 'You could have fought for her, you know, in your grandfather's court. Yes, it may not have been the match your family would have wanted for you, but you could have argued how much she had saved you these past few years. Your grandfather would have recognised loyalty and love.'

'I didn't even think of that. I was just blind to status, to my birthright, and I only wanted to leave here.' Will was dejected at the thought of what he had lost.

'But now you must move forward. You cannot gain what is lost but you can regain your birthright. Come, we have much to prepare for, but we still need to tread cautiously.'

Sunlight streamed through the alehouse's small windows and there was a glorious scent of summer roses as the two men embraced at their joyous news.

Maude

The Devil and I stand in the empty rooms of the Royal Apartments, stripped bare now of all its glittering finery, leaving only the old, cold grey stone behind.

'Was that part of your revenge?' asks the Devil, shuffling his pack. 'Killing that innocent servant girl?'

'I did it for my son,' I spit out the words. 'The alehouse girl would have trapped him here, and there must be no more temptations for him. He must leave and claim his birthright. This will be revenge on all those who have denied it to him for so long.'

There are no ties to bind him now apart from me, but I will be happy for him to leave, to get what is rightfully his. It is everything I have ever wanted for him. Killing doesn't get any easier, but it is a price I am willing to pay for the one that I love the most.

'Innocent lives come at a cost, you see. There is a tally to be paid for Mark, Magota, and Ysend, and your actions will eventually cost you.'

'I do not care. I am already dead, trapped here, watching my murderer's family prosper. Why should my son suffer? Their lives were expendable,' I say defiantly, but I feel a creeping sense of unease. The Devil is right – why should innocent lives be taken? My emotions drive me too much, I know – I

Tower of Vengeance

cannot harness them as I should. Have I become a monster?

The Devil smiles as he reads my mind. 'To play the cards, you must learn to control your heart. Otherwise, the game cannot be won.'

'Yet this feels like a game I can never win,' I protest, trying to recall when the pact we made included winning at the Tarot. I wanted revenge, but it seems the cards have a part to play in this and I am playing whether I like it or not.

'Time, of which we have so much, will tell,' the Devil says cryptically, as he deals two more cards.

The first is Strength followed by Death.

Of course, I must remain strong – there is much to do, and I must prepare to lose my son. I do not fear the Death card, as it also means great change, the death of an old life, so I am confident that this signifies the start of a new life for Will.

These are good cards, and they renew my faith in my actions, which after all have been for the right reasons, haven't they?

The Devil smiles. He has such a beautiful smile – seductive, teasing, and promising. I shudder at my sudden desire. He laughs as he senses my discomfort, walking across to me and running one of his long, elegant fingers over my lips. I tremble and my eyes close at the thrill of being touched again.

'Remember, you must pay,' he whispers, his warm breath caressing my cheek. I feel his lips touch my cheek. I hunger for him. I arch my body towards his.

He has gone. I am left alone with my thoughts on what I have started.

The Return

Eighteen Months Later

In the pale light of the September morning, Jane stood on The Stone Kitchen's steps, enjoying the breeze while she could. The summer had been unusually hot, and the drought felt across the country affected the crops which they needed to brew the ale, leading to shortages, so it had been tough for business. As prices of this precious commodity had increased, Jane was struggling once more to make ends meet. She could hear Simeon attending to the brewing below, trying to eke out their meagre supplies. She was hoping today would bring a much-delayed delivery from the monks of All Hallows, as the soldiers and the increasing number of workmen demanded more and more ale in the relentless heat to quench their first. This had been the second summer the crops had failed to deliver in abundance, a second summer since Emma had left and, as Jane looked at the cold, forbidding Stone Tower, it was as if it too had lost its lustre since that May day last year when the Princess and her vastly extended household had left, taking Jane's only child with her.

Jane noticed more prisoners arriving each day from across Henry's kingdom, and the Stone Tower, once a royal residence, was now a grim prison where the soldiers said men and women were dragged into its lower floor and chained to its unforgiving cold walls – the Black Hall finally living up to its name.

Tower of Vengeance

Where once the walls were adorned with colourful tapestries, the Royal Apartments, Jane had been told, were now divided into small cells to confine rebels, traitors, and more recently the Jews of London who failed to pay the King's taxes. *No wonder*, she thought, *the city's residents hate the place so much.* And with the increase of prisoners came more soldiers to guard them and a Constable to keep them in line. Bernard Crioyl was much more ruthless and not as amiable as Thomas, who had retired to his home in Kent not long after Emma had left. But Thomas had become an ill man, and Jane had just heard that he had passed a few weeks ago. Henry continued to fortify his premier fortress, with the building work continuing apace as the King sought to ensure he had a refuge from the troubles that seemed to consume him like a curse. At least now he was married, and the wedding had brought some light relief to an otherwise restless city. The Tower was a hive of activity and dust and noise, with the workmen busy on the renovations.

Jane watched as the first of the autumn leaves fell from the trees, fluttering across the Outer Bailey as if signalling a change to come. The morning bells started to ring out as the city's gates once again opened and the day began.

The morning passed into afternoon as more carts rumbled through the Tower's gates, bringing the much-desired supplies of grain, materials for the continuing construction work, and more unfortunate prisoners. Amidst the carts came a modest escort of six horses bearing the colours and banner of Baldwin de Vere, one of Henry's most trusted messengers to the Imperial Court of Frederick. The riders paused in the Outer Bailey and a woman carrying a small baby was helped to dismount.

'We bring you home, Mistress Lund, as per the Empress' instructions,' said de Vere's young squire who had been tasked to complete Emma's journey to the Tower, whilst de Vere himself had left them at Westminster to take messages to the King from Italy. Emma thanked him, taking her modest bundle from one of the other squires. They were eager now to re-join their comrades at Westminster, where they would get food and rest after days on the road. They certainly did not want to linger in the Tower, as its reputation brought chills to even the bravest of men. They turned the horses around and were gone before the Constable himself had noted their arrival.

Emma shifted her son's body as he awoke, squirming in her grip. Together they took in their surroundings, blinking in the hazy sunshine and careful to avoid the carts that continued to arrive. In Emma's eyes barely anything had changed, with workmen still continuing with the never-ending building work, but so much had. It seemed a lifetime since she left, dressed in a rabbit fur cloak meant for another girl, serving the woman she had detested, leaving behind everything she had ever known after her heart had broken. Now she had returned in her own fine clothes denoting her service to the Empress. The ale-stake continued to hang over the door of The Stone Kitchen, and she hoped her mother was still living there. She had left Italy in a hurry and had been unable to send a message to her mother about her arrival. She entered the alehouse and time stood still as the familiar scent of the ale assailed her senses, the room no different; the faces of the soldiers could have been any from her past time there. She was surprised to see Simeon busy pouring the ale, and a young girl passing through the tables of men – a ghost it seemed for a moment of her former self, but the girl was real enough as she served the ale and joked with the men.

'Am I a stranger in my old home now?' Emma whispered into her son's soft curls as he wriggled, tired from the journey.

But then out of the kitchen bustled her mother, who with the discernment of the alewife instantly knew when someone unexpected had entered. She stopped, wondering who the striking, well-dressed woman with the baby was who stood in the doorway. Emma smiled hesitantly as Jane looked quizzically at her. Emma saw the realisation on the older woman's face, the sudden delight as she quickly rushed towards her.

'Is it you? Is it really my girl?' Jane gasped.

'Yes, Ma, it's me!' she answered, smiling broadly at her mother's incredulous face. 'And this is your grandson,' she said, and she held the boy out towards her. He stretched out his arms as Jane hugged him to her in disbelief.

'Well look at you, my handsome boy!' She looked at Emma for explanation.

Tower of Vengeance

'He is Will's son, Ma, that's why I have come home,' Emma explained, anticipating her mother's question.

The baby, now hungry after the journey, started to cry and fuss at his strange new surroundings. Simeon looked up at the noise and realised who had returned. Jane told Emma to go through to the kitchen and as her daughter went ahead, Jane pulled Simeon aside.

'Don't go sending word to The Golden Chain about this, do you hear? She will see Will when she is ready,' Jane ordered him, and Simeon, an unassuming man, shrugged in acceptance before carrying on with his work.

The two women went upstairs to the bedchambers they used to share. Jane's room still belonged to her, but Emma's now housed Ruth, the young girl she had seen downstairs.

'You will have to share with me for now while you decide what needs to be done,' her mother said.

'Is he here?' asked Emma tentatively. During the long journey home, she had worried that Will would be gone before she had a chance to introduce him to his son. After all, she had known his desire to be with his real family, and without her or the Empress to tie him to the Tower he may also have left of his own accord. There had been no way to hear any news about the Fitzwalters or even the Earl of Essex at the Imperial Court. The only choice left to her had been to come back to the Tower and trust that either

her mother or Will still remained and that she had a home to return to.

'Yes, he lives and works at The Golden Chain. I couldn't have him here after what he did to you – I know he was the reason you left, so don't deny it, although I had no idea that this would be the consequence,' she said, pointing at the child who now greedily guzzled at Emma's breast.

'His name is John,' she told her.

Jane flinched at the name – memories of the old King and his monstrous ways still lingered even now. It was a strange choice, and she was surprised Emma hadn't named the babe after her beloved father Mark as a way of remembering him.

'It was the Empress' wish. She was after all my mistress, and she supplied the means for me to return here after his birth in February. I had no idea when I left that I was pregnant. And then of course I had to wait to recover from the birth before we could even attempt the journey,' she explained.

'We heard all her household had been sent back after she arrived at the Emperor's court. I waited to see if you would return. I was worried sick as I had no idea what had happened to you.'

'I was lucky that the Empress argued I couldn't return so soon when she learned of my condition. So, arrangements were made that I could stay until after the birth, and I lived in a quiet house with two other ladies of her retinue who have remained there, and then as soon as I was able, I planned my return home.'

'It would appear that the Empress was good to you.' Jane smiled, glad at her daughter's fortune when things could have easily turned out differently.

'The Empress is much changed; I am ever grateful to her for my son, for he lives because of her kindness and her courage.'

'And Will? I never did know what went on with you two that made you leave as you did, but I knew that something had come to pass, and after that I couldn't very well let him stay.' She shook her head.

'It was a stupid quarrel. I thought he was sleeping with the Empress' laundress, which he denied. On the journey to Sicily, I finally spoke to the girl and she told me it wasn't true, and I felt such a fool! So, I had to return to put things right. Unless he has already found someone else?' Emma lied calmly, eager to make things right now that they had a son who deserved the happiest life they could give him.

'No, there is no one as far as I am aware – he's been quiet of late. Constable Thomas retired and died quite recently, which upset him as they were close. I rarely see him myself though. I guess that will have to change now if you marry him.'

'I am sad to hear about Thomas – he was a kind man to us all. And as for Will, he is a good man and I know he will provide for us,' Emma declared confidently.

Tower of Vengeance

'Well, my girl, I think you had better let him know he has a son before rumour flies before you!'

As the soft rays of the sun started to fade with the advancing evening, Emma carried John over to The Golden Chain. Memories flooded back as she passed under the shadow of the Stone Tower, through the gate of the Inner Bailey towards Will's home. This was the moment she had anticipated the most on the journey back to England, wondering how she would feel seeing the man she once loved. She had hated him for so long. There had been such emptiness until she had held John in her arms and felt so much love for her son. John gave her peace, and she hoped Will too would now feel the same.

In The Golden Chain, Will was overseeing the Chain's staff, ready for another busy evening. It had grown to accommodate the extra inhabitants – soldiers, workmen, and prisoners who all needed ale as long as they, or in the case of the prisoners their families, could pay.

Will missed Thomas. The man who had shared so much with him. The joy at his grandfather's freedom and then the tragic news of Robert Fitzwalter's death had come just as Will had been ready to leave. Old age had finally caught up with his grandfather and now no one in his family knew of his existence. Not long afterwards Thomas had left, and it was with great sorrow that the two friends had parted. The news of Thomas' death had been the final blow and Will was glad to be alone now, busy with The Golden Chain, the days merging into countless others. Now there was nothing left except endless days of brewing ale. His mother's grief was palpable in the stone walls, disturbing the already wretched dreams of the prisoners, twisting her anger into tormenting these poor souls. The cloying scent of roses was too much for Will, who pushed her spirit away from him, rejecting her sorrow, wishing now he had never heard her name.

Will walked out of the alehouse to get some air and he almost walked into the woman standing there. Their eyes met and he smiled, as if all the joy had come back into his life. The sounds of the Tower and the alehouse behind him receded, and the air hung in breathless balance.

'Emma,' he whispered.

Tentatively, she smiled back, and John reached out a determined fist and grabbed at Will's tunic.

'Hello, Will. This is John, our son,' she came straight out with it, and waited nervously for his reaction.

'Mine? My son?' His voice cracked as he put out a hesitant finger towards John's small hand. John grasped it firmly as Will and Emma started to cry.

As they stood there, finally reunited, even as the smell of roses encircled them reminding them of another force in their lives, Will hoped that what had once been lost between them could now be regained, and perhaps after all there could be a new beginning, another kind of loving forged by their son.

Tower of Vengeance

But the raven's cry above foretold a different story.

Maude

The Death card mocks me and my hope of a reversal of fortunes is snatched away after my father's demise and with him all my son's hopes. The Wheel of Fortune spins again. My rage was great, and I tormented the unfortunate prisoners who hung from their chains in the Black Hall. I fed off their wretchedness, draining their energy until the weak died of fright – their bodies are still suspended in their gruesome dance. I no longer care who I kill.

'I warned you of a price to pay,' whispers the Devil in my ear.

I turn toward him and push him, screaming. 'Go back to your hellish kingdom; you give me nothing! Look at my son. What does he have left? Where is my revenge? You promised me revenge!' I argue, but I feel so helpless.

'Wait.' He gives me a card – the Sun.

My raven screeches at the window. Desperate for my attention. The Devil has vanished once again. I go to see what has disturbed Erin.

The girl has returned with a son.

I laugh at the Devil's card, which signals marriage, children, happiness. Something has been left for Will, and the girl will get what she most desired. The alehouse girl will wed the Earl of Essex. But for my murder she would never have been so fortunate.

Tower of Vengeance

And what news she brings with her! Finally, I can rejoice. My curse on her marriage worked and the jezebel got what she deserved. I can read Emma's mind as her thoughts briefly flicker with memories of the precious Empress. I sense emotions of seclusion, powerlessness, and of being unloved. Such joy I feel at this.

But that woman helped the girl return. I pause and wonder at such kindness in one such as her. But she has had one last laugh on us – bestowing her father's name on my grandson in a cruel irony which haunts me.

I sense my son's happiness. He needed this, something to lift his spirits after the bad fortune he has endured of late. Our family line will continue, which is good news at last.

But the boy intrigues me. For I glimpse something in his dark eyes that troubles me, and there is no webbing between his tiny toes which both Will and I have. He seems such a happy, contented child though with none of the malevolence of his namesake, so perhaps all will be well.

I return to my turret with some hope restored, but the Devil is not done with me today. He has left four cards on the dirty, dusty floor.

Two cards have landed upside down and I turn them over cautiously.

The Magician reversed – the trickster laughing at me.

Tower of Vengeance

I shudder at the next card. The Sun is now reversed, burning away the happiness of marriage and giving me such a foreboding over Will and Emma.

And then of course The Moon with all its deception, sinister in my eyes.

And finally, The Tower again with its falling walls…always falling…

My raven flies up into the sky, screaming at these portends of doom. Once again, I despair.

The Falling Walls

Six Years Later

Will watched his wife sleeping, revelling in the quiet time just before dawn while their two young sons continued to sleep. He gazed tenderly at Emma's familiar, lovely face, which looked so peaceful in the faint morning light. Her eyes opened and she slowly stretched.

'Are the boys awake yet?' she whispered.

'No, all quiet at the moment.' He smiled and went to reach for her, feeling a sudden desire to hold her.

'No, Will,' she flinched, and shifted away from him. 'I don't have the energy right now. Matthew woke me in the night again and you of course, slept through his screaming.'

'Is he still having nightmares? I was hoping he would grow out of that by now.' Will's desire now dampened as he felt her rejection; the flinches that had happened so often since her return surprised him still, but he guessed his old betrayal still rankled her.

'He's three, Will, just a young boy.' She was exasperated with him now.

'Do you ever wonder if my mother has anything to do with it?' Will ventured, expressing something that had been worrying him since their son had started having the dreams.

'I told you, I don't want her mentioned in this house. The past is gone, and I want no more to do with ghosts. Matthew is just Matthew. He's different to John, who has always been an easy child, but that's normal with children. Now, I need to get up and get on with my day. I need to go to market later.'

'Emma, do you love me anymore?' Will felt compelled to ask. So much had changed these past six years – not just the second addition to their family, but adapting to life together in The Stone Kitchen. Jane remained with them, now occupying Will's old bedroom downstairs, but she was getting slower and could only help so much. The Tower was ever busy, and running both alehouses took up so much of their time that there was little left over for themselves.

'Of course I love you. I have always loved you – probably too much.' She laughed bitterly. 'I should be the one asking you that question.'

'You know I do. I'm here, aren't I? We are married with children.' He had never told her how close he had been to leaving the Tower; he had simply told her that his grandfather had died and that his future lay with her and their family now. 'But you don't seem to love me anymore.'

'It's always about you, isn't it, Will? You never change. I have given you two sons, and you whine about not getting enough sex, because let's be truthful, that's what this is about, isn't it?' With that, she angrily left the room to wake the two boys next door. Will sighed and wondered how he always seemed to say the wrong thing. He loved his family but there was still part of him that craved the life that had been so tantalisingly within his grasp. He felt the strands of resentment from both him and Emma lingering in the walls of their bedroom.

* * *

Emma returned from the market later that day and was still bedazzled by the whiteness of the Stone Tower, which the King had ordered to be whitened just last year, such was his fashion with his royal buildings. It was brilliant against the greyness of the day, the raindrops making it sparkle as if it were a cloak adorned with precious stones. She was startled out of her reverie to see a large number of soldiers dispersing and luggage trains disappearing through the Coldharbour Gate into the Inner Bailey.

    She guessed from the size of the escort that someone important had arrived, and remembered that just last night in the alehouse there had been talk amongst the men that more prisoners were on their way and that this time it was royalty itself. They had heard that coming to the Tower were the Welsh Prince Gruffudd and his sons Rhodri, Davydd, Maddock, and Owain. More captives from the Prince's army would follow on foot bound by chains, to be sent down to the Black Hall, where darkness and rats and who cared what else awaited them. Their Prince and his family, it was believed, would be taken to a more comfortable prison fashioned out of

Isabella's old apartments, but with less of the luxury than the King's sister had been afforded. It had at least steered talk away from the rumours being spread in the city by a hysterical priest who had claimed to have had a vision from St Thomas Becket, who he said struck at the Tower's walls bewailing 'why do you rebuild them?' as the walls tumbled at Becket's command. The same walls which had indeed partially collapsed the year before. Such talk had made Emma and her mother shudder.

Emma now hurried into The Stone Kitchen to find Jane, whom she had left tending the children. John was an amiable boy with a sweet nature which belied his dark looks, but Matthew, being a more difficult child, was prone to flashes of anger and impatience.

'Here's your mother now, boys!' Jane sighed with relief, and Emma could tell that there had been some trouble between her sons.

'What's happened?' She already felt weary, ready to pacify the continuous arguments between them.

By the time Will returned from sorting out the ale delivery at The Golden Chain, the boys were quiet once more, as Emma readied the counter for service and Jane prepared the pottage for the meals.

'We're going to be extremely busy for a few days at least,' Will warned, as he helped pour the ale into the jugs as the first customers started to arrive.

'Yes, I saw. Whose men are they?' she asked, to see if he had heard more than her.

'Richard, Earl of Cornwall escorted the new prisoners,' he replied, taking the jugs to serve the men.

'You look as white as the Stone Tower! What's wrong?' Jane gasped, when she came back into the bar.

'Nothing,' Emma said with a shrug, but disappeared into the kitchen to compose herself before the rush began, and to check the children weren't making a nuisance of themselves.

Early next morning, after a restless night, Emma took the boys out to play on the Tower's green within the Inner Bailey. It was safer from the comings and goings of the carts, the horses, and the men. The weather was dry and mild as the boys chased the last of the falling autumn leaves. Christmas would soon be upon them. John was chasing one of the ravens across the lawn, chuckling with delight as the bird swooped around his dark head as if it was playing too. Matthew was restless and needy by her side, no longer wanting to play, a look of disgust on his face at the raven.

She froze as two figures approached her from the direction of the Blundeville Tower. It was foolish of her to have come into the Inner Bailey. Perhaps she would go unnoticed if she kept her hard down. She clutched Matthew's hand tighter and tried to get John's attention, but he was chasing after that wretched bird, and she watched in horror as he ran straight into Richard, Earl of Cornwall. Richard and his Steward laughed at the young boy and looked around to see who he belonged to.

'My lord, I beg your pardon for my son,' she said, bowing her head and reaching for John's hand. Her hood slipped down, giving Richard a glimpse of her face, and she saw the smirk of recognition appear as he realised where he had seen her before.

'Well, if it isn't my sister's maid!' He laughed at the absurdity of meeting her here of all places, and then he looked once more at John.

'Your son, I take it?'

'My name is John,' the little boy said shyly, looking up at the strange man.

'Yes, my lord, and this is my other son Matthew. I am married to William Lund, from the alehouse,' Emma said calmly, trying to keep her voice even to hide the nerves she felt rising inside her. Imbert de Pugeys, the most recent Constable, strode over to meet Richard, and she felt relief for a moment that he had business to attend to.

Richard signalled for Imbert to wait and for his Steward to go ahead, leaving them alone.

'We need to talk, Mistress Lund. To renew our acquaintance and remember old times,' he said, sneering at her. 'Unless you would rather I talked to your husband instead?'

Clenching her fists, she felt the familiar revulsion his presence had had on her all those years ago, and wished she could get as far away as possible from him. However, she knew she could not trust him not to follow through with his threat, and so just nodded meekly to acquiesce to his demands.

'Meet me after the noon day repast on the walls of the second entrance tower – the one they now call the Beauchamp Tower. It's sectioned off at the moment as it needs repairing, so we will not be seen there. Do you know where I mean?' she hurriedly whispered, while the boys were distracted by a black feather which had fallen from a raven.

'Yes, I saw it as I entered yesterday. Come alone so it can be just like old times,' he mocked, brushing her arm before walking away to attend to his affairs.

She hurried away, not wishing to spend a moment longer in his presence, for she had the misfortune to know what he was really like. He had finally cornered her on the ship to Italy when she had been fetching ale late one night for Isabella, who had not been able to sleep. She remembered the smell of the salt air, the screaming gulls, and the ship pitching and creaking as she had crept into the darkness of the galley as the rest of the passengers slept. He had grabbed her from behind, his hand over her mouth so no one would hear her call out, and his signet ring digging into her lips, his other hand wrapped around her waist already tugging up her tunic.

'My sister's pretty maid, at last we are alone and it's time to have some fun. Do not bother to cry out. I'm a prince of England and I can do what I please with the likes of you. No one will come to your aid, so your cries will not help you.' He removed his hand from her mouth and pushed her over the barrel as he yanked up her tunic. She couldn't move for fear, and her voice felt caught in her throat so that if she were to scream, no noise would come out. Her legs were trembling, and she knew not how she would keep upright. And then he pushed her legs wider and suddenly he was thrusting inside her, as her face dug into the barrel, tears spilling down her cheeks. He was done quickly but she remained where she was, unable to move as he adjusted his clothing, and then he slapped her across her exposed buttocks.

'Not your first, am I? My little whore,' he taunted her, before lowering his face next to hers and whispering, 'If you tell my sister, I will slash this pretty face, do you understand?' She had nodded, the overwhelming sense of shame meaning she never wanted to speak of this ever again. He had left her then and she had been careful not to be alone again on that long, arduous journey to Padua and the Emperor's court, to remain safe from his advances.

It was her worst fears come true to see him again like this. Isabella may be manipulative, but she was loyal to those who were good to her, whereas her brother was just callous and dangerous. Emma had to protect her marriage and her family, the life that they had built here in the Tower. She had no choice but to meet with him to find out what he wanted, for she would do anything to protect those she loved.

Tower of Vengeance

When she returned to The Stone Kitchen, the boys were good for once, and she sat and watched them play by the fire. She loved her children – they were the best of her, they had healed her through the heartbreak and united her with Will. She wished her marriage was better and that Isabella and her brother had never come between them, for then they could have been truly happy rather than bearing the burdens they both did.

'Are you alright, love?' Will asked, as he came up from the cellar.

'I'm tired, so just wanted to rest awhile. Two children are a handful, aren't they?' She forced a chuckle, which sounded brittle to her ears.

'That is true!' he agreed, and bent down and kissed the top of her head, putting his arm around her. She tried not to recoil as tears pricked at her eyes, but Will, feeling the flinch once again, quickly moved away to pick up John and Matthew, swinging them around much to their delight. Emma, unable to watch, left the room abruptly and busied herself at the counter, desperate for the day to be done and Richard to be gone from their lives for good.

The day which had started so brightly had now taken on a grey hue. The drizzle of rain pattered down on the walls as Emma quietly left the alehouse and made for the Beauchamp Tower at the arranged time. The area around it was busy with workmen and the traffic of the various trades and suppliers, so she passed unnoticed to the side stairs which would take her up to the walls. She had come here not so long

Tower of Vengeance

ago with Will, who had been told of the view across the river, of London's bridge and the spires of the city. It now stung to be reminded of that when she came for a rendezvous that threatened to tear her family apart.

    Emma hid herself in one of the corners of the wall as she waited for Richard. She heard a horse gallop across the causeway at great speed, its rider shouting an urgency that would clear the way for him. She sighed, her heart racing at the thought of this meeting, of the man's demands, and the overwhelming desire to get back to her family. She would have to persuade him to leave her family alone; he must not know the truth, he must not believe John was his. What could he possibly gain from another bastard son anyway? Best to leave it be as the truth would surely destroy them all.

    A raven landed on the wall opposite her, and seemed to be looking straight at her, its dark eyes darting about. Its feathers were the colours of John's hair, she thought – that black, blue sheen he had was so like the bird's and as dark as the night sky. The bird ruffled its feathers, shaking off the drops of rains, watching her as she shivered and waited. Another ruffle of its feathers and a tiny rose petal, dislodged from the raven's wing, drifted to the ground to Emma's amazement. It cocked its head quizzically. Then, with one last look at her, it took flight along the river, disappearing into the gloom of the day.

Tower of Vengeance

* * *

Richard was making his way to the steps to meet the girl when a messenger detained him.

'I am the Earl of Cornwall, man. Hand me your message.' He recognised the badge of Frederick's Imperial Court and wondered what news he brought so urgently.

The man reached into his satchel, removed the sealed letter, and handed it to Richard.

'I was told to come to you, my lord, and that you would tell the King.'

'No! This cannot be true!' Richard howled as he read the letter.

'I'm sorry, my lord, to bring you news that the Empress Isabella died a month ago in Padua.'

There was a mighty crack. Time stopped. The rain seemed to pause as it fell, and the ground felt as if it was shifting beneath them. At the sound of rumbling stone, the messenger's horse bolted with its rider towards the Inner Bailey, as the ravens took to the skies in a multitude of blackness and foreboding.

'The wall! The wall is falling again!' screamed one of the workmen, looking up at the Beauchamp Tower as a piece of stone came crashing down. Richard, sensing the catastrophe, ran towards the Inner Bailey. People began to panic and scatter in all directions as more and more pieces of stone fell

Tower of Vengeance

from the wall, and there was a rumbling deep within the vast depths of the walls as if the whole Tower would fall with it. Men were already trapped under the rubble, crying out for help as the wall continued to crumble. It seemed to be falling forever but within moments it was a pile of stone, for in a heartbeat there was a stillness as dust settled around the ruins, and then the air was rent with the cries of the wounded as people ran to help, already beginning to pull at the stones.

In The Stone Kitchen, Will had heard the ominous sound of the wall cracking as he had been clearing the bar. Jane came running out of the kitchen alarmed.

'What is that?' she asked, and then the sounds of the wall falling filled the room, and from the commotion they knew the worst had happened. 'You go and help, Will. I will stay with the boys,' she ordered him.

Will rushed to help. Richard prepared to leave, having his men make a way through and, taking only his bodyguard, rode past the rubble, blocking out the cries, much to Will's bemusement, who thought it was typical of the family to always protect themselves and wondering what was so urgent that he would abandon the Tower in its hour of need.

By dusk, the men were almost done; there were no more pleas for help, and the bodies were laid out under makeshift shrouds in the Tower's Chapel. The injured were taken to St Katherine's Hospital to be looked after by the holy orders, and Will and

Tower of Vengeance

Simeon handed out ale to those who needed it.

'There's a girl under here!' came the cry, and men urgently pulled stones away in the hurry to get to her. And Will looked around for Emma. He had not seen her return, had he? Perhaps she had slipped past, but no, she would have come over to him, to reassure him and to give help. He went cold and his heart seemed to stop. And he scrambled over the stones, desperate now to disprove the thoughts in his head; she could not have been on the wall, of course not, she had gone out somewhere and was delayed in the city, it would not be Emma, not his Emma lying there amongst the rubble. But when one of the men glanced at him with such sorrow, Will collapsed to his knees in despair.

Maude

The Devil is by my side as we watch my poor son collapse amongst the ruins as he finds his wife's body.

'Why did you kill her?' he asks incredulously. 'She loved your son and was a good wife and mother to their children.'

'Because she brings a lion cub to our door.'

'You know this for certain, do you? That John is Richard's son?'

I was so sure, but his question makes me pause for a moment and I begin to doubt myself. John is sweet and kind and does not share his father's temperament – if it is indeed the Earl of Cornwall. Matthew is the worst of my son and the girl, born in resentment and unhappiness, with a webbed foot to show for it, which John does not have. But then I am not sure that my own brother had it. I wish I could ask Maria what it signifies, but she of course is gone, and I feel her loss once more.

'Richard believes John is his and the girl hid a dark secret, I am sure,' I insist, as the Devil watches me. 'I could not let her destroy my son. It would break him, and I could not risk it.'

'But how does this help you? You lose sight of your revenge,' he warns me.

He is right. There is no revenge in the girl's death, for Richard lives. However, I had cursed his marriage like I had cursed his sister's, and I had rejoiced when his wife had died last year, with three children dead too and one son destined to die young. He will never be happy in his marriage beds, of that at least I am sure. But I wish I could do more to that man – to make him genuinely suffer. For men can always get more wives, more children.

'My son's happiness must count. And Isabella, that bitch, is finally dead and that makes me rejoice. Will is free at last from both women,' I say triumphantly, hoping that it is yet not too late for him to regain his title.

'Can you not see what you have become, my beloved? A true servant of mine after all,' he goads me.

I realise I am beyond caring. My soul is ever darker in the Devil's vice-like grip which tightens around me. I find I enjoy killing these miserable people, gaining my strength from them, and soon I will send the Welsh Prince tumbling off these walls to give me even greater power, and maybe I will take one of his sons too – they are not of King John's blood, so their lives are mine for the taking. I smile at the thought of Death embracing them.

'Richard will return for the son he believes is his, and what will you do then, my creature?' the Devil asks, and places a card in my hand. I turn it over to see The Chariot – it pulls us in different directions, denoting a war to come and a battle to be fought for all our souls.

'Your turn to deal. You have shown you are mine and worth a place in the game.' The Devil hands me the pack.

The cards tingle in my hands; a small flame ignites the pack and the cards crumble to dust, leaving me with four cards.

The High Priestess.

The Hermit.

The Hierophant.

The Star.

None are Justice, which I crave with all my heart, but my wishes count for nothing in this game.

The Devil is gone, leaving me to wonder what these cards mean.

The High Priestess holds much sacred knowledge and can divine the spirits. I feel her power and I smile, for I sense an ally.

The Hermit sits inside his cell with soul-searching eyes, and I sense a role to be played, but not yet awhile.

The Hierophant sneers beneath his priestly robes. I shudder at his Godliness, for his God forsook me years ago.

Tower of Vengeance

The Star twinkles and lifts my heart. Perhaps there is hope after all.

I look for Erin, my raven, but she has not yet returned to my side. She has no love for the Devil and his games, and I too grow weary of them.

PART TWO

The Chaplain

Thirteen years later

As autumn declined and winter approached with its shortened days, it brought with it such unendurable cold with a frost that seemed as permanent as the Tower's walls. The north wind pushed Matthew across the Outer Bailey and into the Chapel's meagre shelter, although there was hardly respite from the cold here, just flickering candles illuminating the anguished faces of the saints looking down on him from the Chapel's walls, as if reproaching him. Matthew brushed off the snowflakes and shivered for a moment, stamping his feet to regain some warmth as he hurried to relight the charcoal braziers, before going to check on Brother Geoffrey, the Hermit, who lived in an enclosed cell. Matthew brought him food each day yet as it got colder, the man seemed to diminish further, his feverish devotions emanating from blue lips. Matthew admired such fervour, to be close to God, but even he could not imagine life within the tiny, enclosed space that the King had incorporated into the improved Chapel some years ago. Matthew came here to escape earthly concerns and his tiresome family; it was also the place he felt closest to his mother who had died when he was three.

    The Chapel had been his solace from an early age in a childhood tarnished by grief when the chaplain, Brother Anthony, had taken pity on the

Tower of Vengeance

troubled child and turned Matthew's eyes to God. Let his brother, John, have the dirty, rowdy alehouse with all its sinners. Matthew had the glory and love of God, who would surely punish all those who did not fall on their knees and repent their sins. Each day, he chanted several masses for his own mother's soul, so she too would ascend to Heaven, to God's grace. For he hated to think of her death, which had been so sudden and brutal without time to confess, repent, and be shriven, so he must do what he could to save her soul for all eternity.

He had so few memories of her, being so young when she died, but he knew she had loved him, more so than his father and his great-aunt Joan. He was not close to his family. He detested them all, yet it was John he hated most. He hated his dark looks, his happy disposition, the way people liked him – even the soldiers would ask for him and pet him like one of the King's exotic creatures in the royal menagerie, with him lapping it up as if it was his right to be loved. Matthew would sulk in the background, his blaze of red hair a source of jests, his pale skin luminous even as he hid in the shadows. He was even teased over his fear and hatred of those hideous black birds who would swoop down on him whenever they spied him, sensing his distrust and disgust. They were surely not God's creatures.

Matthew moved around the Chapel, checking the candles, adding more charcoal to the braziers, and muttering prayers as he did so. Brother Geoffrey was also in prayer, his blue lips forming the words. Matthew felt God's love wash over him as he performed his duties before the evening service. The Chapel door swung open, caught by the north wind, as Brother Anthony hastened in, chilled from his walk from Candlewick Street.

'Heavens, Matthew, it's bitter tonight! I appreciate the King's kindness with my lodgings, but sometimes I wish they had been closer to here, if not within the Tower itself. I am almost frozen.' He sighed, hurrying over to one of the braziers to warm his hands.

'Shall I fetch you warm ale, Brother?'

'No need, Matthew. It is God's will that we suffer this cold to make us stronger. His love will make us warm. Let us pray together while it is quiet and then you can tell me the news.'

They knelt in front of the altar and gave thanks to God for their day. Matthew gave his own thanks for the man beside him who had saved him in so many ways and showed him the way to salvation. He had been six years old when he had first met Brother Anthony. The chaplain had not long arrived at the Tower, come to help Brother Peter, who was getting older, somewhat forgetful, and spending more time in The Stone Kitchen than the Chapel. Brother Anthony was the youngest son of a knight, his lot in life to enter the Church, so he had been young and enthusiastic. He had soon grown bored of his duties as the Tower chaplain, with its itinerant flock of differing soldiers, constables, and visitors.

Coming to extract Brother Peter one evening from the alehouse, he had noticed the two young boys who scurried around the place. John was full of it even at ten years old, yet Matthew was shy and withdrawn. They had reminded him of his own relationship with his older brother, who as heir had been so sure of himself and his position in life. Anthony could also see that Will, their father, was struggling to control the two boys, who seemed bright; their minds were sharp and their arithmetic good, as they knew how much each customer owed. Anthony had returned to The Stone Kitchen while it was quiet the morning after. Anthony proposed to teach the boys simple reading and writing and Will had quickly agreed, perhaps keen to get his boisterous boys off his hands for a few hours.

Matthew slowly had begun to enjoy the lessons; the peace of the room set off the east side of the aisle, where Anthony had set up his makeshift school and the Chapel itself revealed its wonders to him under the Brother's guidance. And now some thirteen years later, Matthew was preparing to make his own vows to God and become a chaplain with Brother Anthony's grace and support. Matthew had been a great help to the chaplain, especially since the death of Brother Peter five years past, and the Church in turn was now Matthew's family, his comfort, and his vocation. Matthew had felt he had not been good enough, not as handsome nor as charming as John, but now he felt a sense of pride that he had bettered himself and was not destined to life in the alehouse.

His mind briefly wandered from the prayers Brother Anthony was saying with his sense of superiority, and he felt a sense of shame which he would later attempt to atone for with his horse whip, hidden under his narrow bed in the room he shared with John. Each strike on his bare back would drive away his impureness. He looked forward to the day when he, as the King's chaplain, could move to his own rooms in the city, away from his family, and able to scour his body without fear of being disturbed and ridiculed by his brother.

'Come, Matthew, let us light the fire in our room and warm up before evening prayer begins. I'm eager for news of our new prisoners. The people have been wild with speculation since they arrived!'

The prison carts had trundled over the causeway just before sundown as the Tower garrison assembled to meet the armed escort. Matthew had watched from the Chapel's porch, hidden from view as he spat out his curses, for the prisoners were Jews, Christ murderers. Just under a hundred men were to be imprisoned in the Tower to await their fate. They had been tried and convicted in Lincoln of the murder of an eight-year-old boy.

'They crucified him with a crown of thorns and threw his body in a well,' whispered Matthew to the astonished chaplain, who had also heard rumours of such an act. 'I heard the charges read out by the officer as he handed them over to the Constable,' Matthew confirmed, remembering the audible gasp from those who had gathered in the Outer Bailey to take the prisoners into their prison within the White Tower. The infamous Black Hall was ready to chain them to its cold damp walls.

Tower of Vengeance

'I am told that they do this every year to insult our Lord Jesus! And the King protects them for their money!' Anthony sighed.

'The soldiers say we should follow the Earl of Leicester's lead and expel them from our towns, our cities, this country,' Matthew repeated what he'd heard in The Stone Kitchen.

'Simon de Montfort is indeed a wise man, but the King forbids them to leave, and this is what happens! None of us are safe from them. It was bad enough when we had that Jew, Abraham of Berkhamsted, imprisoned here. He defecated on an image of our Lady and the baby Jesus by placing the icon in his privy. His wife took it out and cleaned it, so he murdered her!' Both men crossed themselves and muttered prayers to cleanse their thoughts of such an act.

'Don't forget the King pardoned him because he paid seven hundred marks. And now there are even more here in the Tower who taint the very air that we breathe!' snarled Matthew.

'Will they be executed soon?' Anthony asked him.

'The soldiers say that they will be hung any day. But each day we seem to have more brought here, because the godly people of London are reporting more crimes.'

'Let us pray, Matthew, for us to be rid of them. God wills that they rot in Hell.'

Tower of Vengeance

* * *

As the two men fell to their knees, talk in the alehouse turned from the prisoners to the famine which gripped the country. The year had again been barren, and land lay uncultivated, as it seemed a great plague swept amongst the crops, the cattle, and the sheep. The summer had seen bodies piled up in streets across the land, as food shortages had meant the poor starved, and now winter was bringing little respite.

'I saw two thousand dead bodies placed in a graveyard in St Edmunds,' stated one man, who had travelled far to get work in the Tower. Being a blacksmith, the Tower had been in need of his trade, as the King ordered more weapons to be made with the unrest stirring in his kingdom.

'Bloody noblemen are alright though – they got corn from France, so no starvation for them,' another man berated, as he gulped his ale.

'What do you expect from the likes of them?' grumbled the blacksmith.

'If this weather continues, more will die, and then what will they do?'

Another man, a soldier this time, leaned closer to his fellow drinkers and whispered, 'I hear de Montfort is unhappy and could be on the move against the King.'

Tower of Vengeance

'And what will the Earl of Leicester do? Make the north wind stop blowing? Stop the snow from falling and make the crops grow?'

The men all laughed at the blacksmith's words and ordered more ale. Ale that was subsidised by the King because it was served as part of his men's wages. Will thought of the irony of these men criticising the man who paid for their own ale, as he served the men. Will had become weary of it all – the cold, the famine, the soldiers and the workmen, and living in a place that was marked with grief for him. First his mother had died here, and then his wife. Both deaths had left Will with questions as to what had truly happened to the women he loved, and he felt burdened most by Emma's death, cursing himself for ever showing her that view. He knew she had been tired that day, that the boys were always a handful, and she must have escaped for a moment of peace. He should have noticed Emma was struggling. He had let her down once again and he could no longer make it up to her. He would have given all the earldoms in the country to have her back.

He had tried to bring up his sons the way Emma would have wanted. The chaplain had helped, giving them an education. But Jane had died not long after her daughter. The grief of losing Emma had been too much for her. Will had relied on the ever-resourceful Joan, who had found him Bess Smith, wife to one of the Tower blacksmiths, Abe; and along with her two daughters, she had helped look after the boys as well as The Stone Kitchen. He had needed all their help as he expanded the alehouses to provide basic food and better ale, adding fine wines to The Golden Chain because it supported the inhabitants of the Inner Bailey. The Stone Kitchen had expanded in size, as the Tower had filled with blacksmiths, tanners, butchers, bakers, etc. to ensure it could withstand a siege, with an ever-resentful London looking to their King in Westminster.

  Will watched John joke with the soldiers at one of the tables as he brought the ale. He was a natural in The Stone Kitchen – he loved joking with the customers, his good humour dispatched many a fight, and he always took any teasing in good spirits, especially when it came to his success with the women. For John had a charm and a handsomeness that broke many a female heart, although he was careful enough not to upset any girls within the Tower walls. Will had learnt to turn a blind eye to the times John crept back home having bribed a friendly guard to let him back in the Tower after the curfew bell had tolled.

  Emma would have been so proud of Matthew, he was certain. His place in the Chapel a worthy step up for an alehouse boy, although his son didn't know about the money Will had used to ease his path to acceptance within the Church. After his wife's death, Will had found a significant sum of money hidden in Emma's dower chest, along with a tiny scrap of brown hair, which he knew couldn't have been John's as he had always had striking raven-black hair, and Matthew's fiery red had never been as light as this. He assumed she must have got the money from Isabella in lieu of service, yet even though Will was resentful that she still touched their lives, the money had been useful. He had briefly wondered about the hair before throwing it on the fire – he had no need for it.

As well as using the money to secretly pay for Matthew's chaplaincy in the Royal Chapel, Will had also made the alehouse improvements, which kept him occupied and busy while securing a good future for his first-born son. But Will was tired, exhausted from the long days at the alehouse, which got harder in his advancing years and with the weight of his grief. He had tried to give up any hope of recovering his own title after the death of Fitzwalter, and with his own family to provide for, he could not risk the lives of his sons for his own ambition – he owed that at least to Emma. Although it didn't stop his resentment for a place which now felt like a prison for him, haunted by the memories of what he had done, and by the ghost of his mother who lingered at the edge of his life as much as he pushed her away, scared at the power he could feel around her.

Tower of Vengeance

𝒯he Elephant's Cage

John sat eating his supper as his brother glared at him, Matthew's pale face showing the disgust he felt for him. John could never understand why his brother disliked him, especially when John had tried all his life to be a friend to his younger brother. Matthew had returned from evening service in one of his dark moods; *prayer obviously hasn't beatified his heart*, thought John. For a man of God, his brother seemed an unhappy soul, and God's love certainly hadn't made him easier to live with! Hopefully when Matthew became a fully ordained chaplain he would move out and leave them in peace.

    John finished his pottage and grabbed his thick cloak, ready to brace the cold and head over to The Golden Chain to see how they fared. He nodded to his father as he left The Stone Kitchen, which was indeed quiet tonight, and ignored his brother, who had not spoken a word to him. The cold air clung to him as he trudged across the Bailey to Coldharbour Gate. He loved the Tower on nights like this, when nothing much stirred and it was still. There was just the odd light from the bakehouses as the bakers watched their ovens; the sounds of the animals sometimes disturbed the air, and the soldiers ever watchful at their posts were quiet under night's mantle. Even the ravens were hushed now, but he could feel their dark eyes following him, the true sentinels of the Tower, always keeping watch.

Tower of Vengeance

    As he made his way through the snow, thick now on the ground, he looked for signs of the ghost lady. She was no secret to him or his brother. As young boys they had been aware of a presence as they explored the Tower. Both boys were known to the Tower inhabitants and had free rein to wander as they played, as long as they didn't go into the guarded areas or prisons. They knew their boundaries and how far they could push the tolerant soldiers.

    One glorious summer's day, John and Matthew had managed to sneak into the White Tower after they had finished their lessons with Brother Anthony. The White Tower was a place they had never been into – it was a glittering temptation, forever in front of them but always out of bounds. But that day it was surprisingly easy as the rest of the Welsh prisoners were gone; the prison rooms lay empty and the guards were relaxed, revelling in a rare sunny day. The boys had slipped past them and crept up the grand stairs hoping to glimpse the Royal Apartments, which they knew from alehouse gossip were on the second floor. They heard voices from the rooms they wanted to explore and were startled, not expecting anyone to be inside.

    They had darted upwards until they saw a smaller staircase leading to an open door, gladly seeking sanctuary within it to avoid being caught in their mischief. For a moment they were united in an adventure, and John had felt pure happiness at the accord between him and his brother. They found themselves in the circular turret, where they could see through the window slits the city beyond the Tower walls. There was another staircase leading to another level, and the boys were eager to see the view from there and had willingly gone up into the room above. The dust which had gathered on the wooden floor seemed to sparkle as if the sun's rays had penetrated the gloom. The room below had been cool, even in the summer's heat, but this one seemed to emanate warmth, and there was a beautiful, sweet unknown smell. Matthew's face had changed from the giggling boy he had been to one of fear and distrust.

'There is devilry in this room,' Matthew gasped, overwhelmed by a sense of dread.

'No, there isn't!' John scoffed. 'It's so peaceful, and look at the lady in the corner, she is smiling at us.'

Matthew had screamed and genuflected at the ghost, before running headlong down the stairs and out of the turret. John, left alone, smiled at the spectre. 'Who are you?' he whispered, but she placed a finger to her lips and disappeared, as if she was melting into the walls.

In Matthew's hurry, he had been heard by the guards inside the Tower as he had rushed terrified down the stairs; and not long after, John and his brother were being marched home, where Will was admonished by one of the officers for letting his sons roam so freely. Will had been forced to offer his apologies and a mug of ale before the man hurried back to explain to the Constable how two boys had managed to breach their premier prison! Matthew

Tower of Vengeance

was shaking with fear and rage, muttering of evil spirits and the Devil's work.

When John breathlessly explained to his father what he'd seen, Will told them it was probably the shadows in the turret playing tricks on them. It didn't matter if his father continued to deny it, because John had continued to sense her, knowing when she was near because of the lovely fragrance. There was a warmth to her presence, and he instinctively knew she wouldn't harm him. Now, as he entered the Inner Bailey, there was no sign of her in the darkness of the night. The White Tower loomed above him, filled with its new prisoners, the Jews of Lincoln, awaiting their deaths. The guards acknowledged him curtly as he hurried past towards the warmth and clamour of The Golden Chain.

It was busier here than The Stone Kitchen. The residents of the Inner Bailey had braced the cold and were merrily supping in the alehouse. Simeon's wife, Ruth, had a good reputation for her food. She came through from the kitchen complaining of backache, large with child, and John asked if she needed to get a message to Great-Aunt Joan, who had offered to send help when the baby was coming.

'I don't think the babe is ready as yet, but I have such a hankering for garlic, and we have none in the kitchen,' Ruth replied.

'There's some in the King's garden – I saw some earlier today, growing along the back wall of the Chain,' said one of the serving girls, eager to get John's attention; like many, they thought him handsome.

'I'll go,' offered John, always happy to help. 'I know what it looks like, as Bess uses it all the time, and my cloak will keep me dry and warm.'

'Oh, thank you! But don't worry if you don't find it in this snow,' Ruth assured him.

John laughed, ready to take on the challenge of finding a frozen garlic bulb and impressing the girls – he had seen the lust in their eyes and had basked in their attention.

He tramped back through the snow to the kitchen garden, past the huge storerooms and workshops where the bakers' fires glowed, and past the stables where the horses snickered in their stalls. At the end of the stables loomed the old elephant's cage, which always made John smile. A few years ago, the King had been gifted yet another animal that had ended up at the Tower. Previously he had been given three leopards by the Emperor Frederick on the occasion of his marriage to the King's sister, who it was said had stayed here in the Tower before she was wed. The leopards had languished in one of the old towers along the Tower's walls, until they had fought each other to death, bored and hungry from neglect.

The elephant had been another wonder for a short period, and the King had ordered wine, such a precious commodity, to keep this one alive. John was sure its keeper had drunk most of it, and soon enough both keeper and creature were dead, and its empty cage rotted in the corner. As John passed it, he heard something rustle inside and realised the heavy iron

Tower of Vengeance

door of the cage was bolted across, and that there appeared to be fresh straw heaped up inside.

'What creature have we got now?' he murmured. In the darkness he could see nothing, so he returned to his task. His feet crunched under the snow, which he scooped away from the wall, and sure enough there nestled the hardy bulb of the garlic. He captured his prize and hurried back to the warmth of The Golden Chain.

The next morning, as John ate his breakfast with only his father for company, he remembered the animal in the elephant's cage.

'I'm sure I saw fresh straw in that old cage last night. Has the King had another gift arrive?' he asked his father.

'No, lad. I heard talk last night that some soldiers threw one of the Jewish prisoners in there,' Will replied, stoking the fire in the kitchen.

'But why would they do that? The prisoner will freeze to death.'

'I forgot all about it until you mentioned it,' Will admitted. 'It's quiet now, so grab your cloak and let's go and check on the poor wretch.'

The morning was brighter with the winter's sun. The smiths were busy hammering away; the smell of freshly cooked bread wafted in the air from the bakehouse as the other workers were steadily appearing to start their day. The cage itself was set back slightly from the stables, left neglected against the Tower's outer wall, but John noticed once again the chain and freshly piled straw.

He gripped his father's arm and nodded towards the cage. 'Look! I can see a piece of cloth under the pile of straw,' he said, and they rushed closer. They peered through the bars and called softly into the depths. The straw slowly moved, and from under the now-visible cloth appeared a small dark head, large green eyes blinking at them struggling to keep open.

'Help me, please,' a faint voice croaked.

'Good heavens! It looks like a child,' exclaimed Will.

'It can't stay in this cage, Father. It will die!'

'I'm not sure the Constable will care less about a dead Jewish child, John,' Will conceded. 'Despenser is Leicester's man, and he hates all Jews.'

'But we can't just let the child die,' pleaded John. The child had sunk back into the straw, desperate to keep warm.

'We have to do something,' John urged Will, tugging his father's arm.

'Aye, John, we must. But there are too many people around now. We'll bribe a guard to turn a blind eye to give it some warm ale and food, and then try to think of a plan.'

Tower of Vengeance

They quickly returned with the ale and a piece of fresh bread, along with an old cloak for warmth, which John slipped through as Will kept watch.

'Drink the ale quickly to warm you up. We'll come back as soon as we are able, I promise,' John whispered.

'Strange one that,' a voice called as they hurried away. Luckily it was Ralph, a soldier that frequented The Stone Kitchen and was known to them. 'She came in with her father Elias le Evesque, both on the charge of plotting to poison the King. However, I think this is Leicester's way of trying to cut off the King's money, because the Evesques are a wealthy family. That's all I better say.' He glanced around him, ensuring no one else had heard.

'The prisoner is a girl? We thought she was a child,' Will persisted.

'No, that's no child – I would say she is the same age as your son there. For some reason the Constable had her thrown in the cage. Just be careful that Despenser doesn't catch you.' And with that, Ralph turned away.

'John, no word to your brother about this,' Will warned, and John nodded understandingly.

* * *

After the morning rush, Will left the Tower telling his sons he had business to attend to in the city. He made his way to Eastcheap, not far from the Tower and close enough to the great warehouses on the river's wharf, where Joan lived. She was sewing in her solar when he arrived, and she cheerfully welcomed Will into the warm room with its cosy fire and plentiful candles. The years had been kind to Joan – plump cheeks and a sturdy figure attesting to good living and a happy home. Her hair was greyer, and she was slower of movement, but she was sharp of mind, and most of all a keeper of secrets and a lover of excitement in her otherwise mundane life as an alderman's wife. Since Jane's death, Will had relied on her counsel and her support regarding his sons.

'So, what brings you here? Is it Ruth? It must be near her time?'

'Ruth is fine, although I'm told it won't be long now, and last night she was happily eating garlic John managed to find for her in the snow!' They both chuckled.

'Which son is causing trouble this time then?'

'Well, neither really,' he said, and told her John's discovery of the young Jewish girl in the elephant's cage.

Joan sighed as Will finished his story. 'It was the talk of the Guild last night. Elias is a good man and a friend to the King and Queen. This does not bode well. Listen, if you can get the poor girl out then bring her here to our stables. Our stableman can hide her until we can find a way to get her out of harm's way.'

Tower of Vengeance

'It will need to be done at night before the curfew, and I should be able to get Ralph, one of the Tower soldiers, to help,' Will reasoned, thinking of how he could manage this.

'If you can get her out, tell the gatehouse guards that she is one of the Chain girls going to fetch the midwife for Ruth. You or John say you are accompanying her as it's dark and the streets aren't safe for a young girl.'

'I don't want Simeon and his family caught up in this.' Will was protective of his friends.

'Don't worry, we will get round it somehow. The guards are easily fooled.' Joan smirked.

'But Despenser is bound to find out the girl is gone!'

'Not if your friendly guard says she died and was thrown in the burial pit?' suggested the ever-resourceful Joan.

'We are asking a lot of Ralph,' Will fretted.

'It will be fine, and Despenser won't care if she's dead – saves him the trouble. Just get her out before she freezes to death.'

With that Will took his leave, eager to not see someone else die in the Tower if he could help it.

Maude

Even now I remember what it's like to be a prisoner here. The fear as you enter through the gates and see the Tower in all its terrifying splendour. The roughness of the guards as they fling you into your cold, filthy prison, and that awful realisation that your life may never be the same. Gone is happiness, family, and joy to be replaced with despair, loneliness, and sorrow, knowing you are unlikely to leave here alive. One minute you have all you desire, the next a living hell. Imagine it for one minute. Place yourself in my turret or in that elephant's cage. Right now, she is closing her eyes, waiting for death, delirious in the cold, grateful for my son and my grandson's kindness in giving her some respite against the thirst and hunger, the extra cloak reminding her of a warmer bed where previously she had slept without care.

  Of all the prisoners who have come here these long years, she is the one who has resonated with me. Usually I care not; I take what power I can from their dying souls, laughing at their pitiful cries for mercy, for forgiveness, and for God's love. Where was God when I needed Him? But I digress. I have the Devil after all.

  Time is a blink of an eye for the spirits that remain on this earth. Your own death seems merely a day ago, but when you look around your mortal family have grown. My son gets older, his hair turns grey, and he grows wearier as he struggles with his

Tower of Vengeance

sons. He does not realise how fortunate he is to see them grow, to be able to help them become men. I watch them all, connect with them in different ways. John is my joy, my hope, my Star of the Tarot, and although he does not know who I am, we have such a bond – he has to be a de Mandeville, but for those eyes. I try to talk to Matthew in his dreams; after all he has the webbed foot, so he should share my gift, but he is God's servant with his protestations of godliness, his hairshirt, and his self-flagellation. He is fanatical in his beliefs, which does not bode well. He denies his heritage. The Hierophant who repulses me.

And now comes this prisoner, this girl in the cage. I recognise the power within her and I know she is the High Priestess of the cards I dealt. She senses me too and has no fear of me. She needs to be saved as she has a part to play in my revenge tale – for are we not all characters in search of a minstrel to tell our story? She is clever this one. Just what we need. The Devil agrees, although she is not his servant. Her beliefs are too strong for him it seems.

But what of the Hermit? What part is he yet to play?

And where is the Magician who haunts my dreams?

The Burning Cross

John walked quickly across the Bailey hoping that he had not been seen. He had taken a risk leaving the alehouse during the afternoon rush, but he worried that the poor girl would not live until the night when they hoped to free her, so he slipped her some food. He did not see Matthew leave the Chapel where he had been taking confession.

Matthew, surprised to see his brother out of The Stone Kitchen in the middle of the day, retraced John's footsteps marked in the fresh snow, which had fallen once again. He followed them to the old elephant's cage, where he saw the fresh straw.

'You there! What's your business?' shouted a patrolling guard who had spotted Matthew hovering by the cage.

'I was wondering what new beast we have here,' Matthew replied, turning towards the guard, allowing his cloak to fall slightly to display his holy robes, so that there would be no trouble.

'Sorry, Father,' the guard stuttered. 'But there's a Jew in that cage and the Constable would not be happy seeing such a Christian man as yourself administering to it.'

'How dare you. Administer to a Jew?' spat Matthew, his anger rising at the accusation.

Once again, the guard apologised and meekly hurried away.

Tower of Vengeance

'Do penance for your filthy words!' shouted an enraged Matthew, as he too hurried away, keen now to be away from the cage and its wretched prisoner. He returned to the Chapel, which was empty apart from the Hermit, and Matthew fell to his knees in front of the altar, praying for cleanliness after his close encounter. And then it came to him as he muttered his rosary amid the dirty straw, he had seen an ale mug. His brother was helping a Jew.

As Matthew returned to The Stone Kitchen, the afternoon rush had subsided and only Bess was serving, slowly going around collecting pots and checking the men were content. Matthew stopped by the half-open door, where he could hear Will and John in the kitchen whispering. He strained to hear but from what he could make out it would seem they were planning to help the prisoner escape!

'Are you mad?' Matthew burst into the room, his anger rising in his throat. 'That is a Christ killer you plan to free!'

Will and John leapt up in shock at Matthew's unexpected entrance.

'I will not let you do this unholy act. I will tell the Constable if you do this. It goes beyond what we believe,' he spat out his words.

'Matthew, you are overwrought,' soothed Will, gesturing his son to sit down and calm himself.

'So, you would let an innocent girl die?' John challenged him. 'That is your Christian kindness?'

Tower of Vengeance

'How do you know she is innocent? And I will not sit down! Take your hand off me, Father! Too often you ignore me, push me aside, but this time I am serious! You will listen to me as a man of the true God. As the soon-to-be King's chaplain, I cannot allow my family to do this. You will bring shame and punishment upon us,' he warned them.

Will removed his placating hand from Matthew. 'I agree, we should not interfere with the King's orders, and this has always been my way. Keeping away from the Tower's prisoners as much as we can, allowing justice to be served by the King and his men, but this is not right,' Will protested. 'She is a young girl with no recourse to justice, no voice to be heard in that filthy cage. Would your God and His son want her to die in such a way?' Will tried to reason with his son – who was now pacing the kitchen – looking sternly at John to keep quiet, so as not to provoke Matthew further.

'My God does not recognise Jews,' Matthew was adamant. 'There is no forgiveness, no justice, no love for those that killed His son, who left Him on the cross to die. You think He cares about this girl? He would want her dead and in Hell!'

'You are the one who is mad. You are the evil one here,' John spoke up, unable to be quiet anymore as his brother spewed such poisonous hatred.

'You dare to say I am mad?' Matthew turned towards his brother, eyes glaring in open hostility. 'When you are the one who connives with witches,

Tower of Vengeance

with ghosts, and no doubt the Devil himself. Oh yes, I hear you talking to that wretched spirit!'

'Enough!' Will stood between his sons. There had always been an uneasiness between the boys, but now they were older, the chasm between them had only widened.

However, Matthew would not listen any longer and swept out of the room. As he left the alehouse, eighteen of the prisoners walked past him, shackled at their hands and feet, no escaping their fate, already different to when they had arrived a few days ago. Now there was no hope, simply a sad acceptance of what lay before them. Heads bowed, a slow shuffle, no sound except the clanging of the heavy chains slowing their progress as the guards ordered them to keep moving. The exertion caused them to breathe heavily and the whiteness of it streamed forth into the cold air from trembling mouths mocking them, seeming to emphasise how few breaths they had left, one last cruelty.

Matthew heard one of the guards whisper, 'Why only this lot? Why not all of them?'

'I heard it was because they refused to be tried by a Christian jury back in Lincoln.'

'Hardly going to be allowed one of their own kind on a jury!' scoffed the other man.

The sight of the Jews leaving to be executed lifted Matthew's spirits as it was all they deserved. Now he must pray; God would give him strength and resolution to go to talk to Despenser about his father's plans to release the girl.

Inside the Chapel, the candles welcomed him in, and the wooden cross suspended over the altar seemed to be spreading arms in an embrace of love. Matthew prostrated himself on the cold stone floor, expressing his adoration for his Lord. He prayed for God's forgiveness, His compassion, and His guidance, but there was no answer. The Chapel was strangely quiet.

'Have you deserted me?' Matthew whispered. A chill seeped through his bones and a weariness washed over him. He resolved to wait for Brother Anthony. He would know what to do, for God would surely confer to him. He would be here soon enough to take evening prayer; there would be time to speak with him then. Matthew scrambled to his feet and went into the warmer side room, closing the door, and heaping up the brazier before he settled into one of the chairs, falling into an exhausted, deep sleep.

The Hermit opened his eyes. He sensed something was different somehow. He looked around for his meal. 'Forgotten again by that useless boy,' he muttered to himself, as he felt hunger and cold. His cell door was unlocked and open. He knew he should not leave but one small transgression would not hurt, and his stomach grumbled with lack of food. He wrapped his threadbare blanket tighter around his thin shoulders and stumbled into the chancel. On the altar was a lump of stale bread and the dregs of sour wine left over from the communion that the lazy boy had not cleared away. He nibbled at the bread, savouring the rigid crumbs, and washed it down with the heady wine. Some relief from the hunger at least. He was startled by a sound behind him and spun round in haste. Not wanting to be caught out of his cell swigging from the communion cup like a desperate peasant, he dropped the cup, which clanked loudly as it hit the stone floor and rolled down the aisle. His eyes rounded in terror as he made out an indistinct figure coming towards him, almost floating in the air. What devilry was this? He stumbled backwards, fear gripping him as the figure advanced towards him. He tripped on his own blanket in his attempt to retreat, crashing into the altar, pulling down the altar cloth as he tried desperately to steady himself. His head hit the stone floor and the candlesticks fell onto him, their flames setting light to the blanket, the altar cloth, and his threadbare garments, consuming the Hermit before the fire quickly blazed through the rest of the Chapel.

In The Stone Kitchen, they could hear shouts outside, and Will hurried out to see what all the commotion was about, with John following closely behind, worrying that the prisoner in the cage was already being moved and their opportunity had slipped from their grasp. Will watched in disbelief as the Chapel burned before their eyes. The soldiers hurried under the Constable's orders to stop the fire from spreading as they tried to contain it. The Tower men and women ran to save the storehouses adjacent to the burning building, desperate to protect the precious commodities that were housed there.

'John!' Will shook his son, who stood in a daze watching. 'We must act now. You must free the girl; there is no better time with everyone helping here. I will go and find Matthew. He must be in the Chapel. Quickly, find Abe the Smith before he joins the crowd, and he will help you. Run! Now!' Will pushed his son in the direction of the cage and John ran.

Will hurried towards the Chapel, ignoring the orders of the men trying to stop him entering. The blaze was intense, and he held his arm up in front of his face as the smoke filled his eyes, coughing at the fumes.

'Matthew!' he cried, desperately searching for his son.

'Father!' His voice was faint, and Will could vaguely make out his son; he was by the side door, trapped by the flames, which were licking at the rood screen, at the timber-framed ceiling, hunting their prey.

'I can't get to you! You must run!' Will shouted.

Matthew stumbled, struggling to breathe from the cloying smoke, but tentatively he left the doorway, trying to get around the burning altar and to the aisle where he might be able to run to safety, the stone floor a haven from the flames.

A creak. A moment of stillness as father and son paused in terror, looking upwards as the suspended wooden cross was caught by the flames, the rope which held it snapped, and the burning cross fell. A scream. A shout of 'No!' and the cross found

Tower of Vengeance

its victim. Crashing down on Matthew, it consumed him in a fury of fire and light. Rough hands grabbed Will and pulled him away from the burning Chapel, out into the cold night air. His son gone. His God had not saved him.

And as the Chapel continued to burn, a raven left the Tower and flew over the Tower's hill, circling the eighteen Jews as they danced with death on eighteen hanging trees.

Embers

The smell of acrid smoke was heavy in the air, and embers glowed in the remains of the King's Chapel as the snow began to fall. The fire had been contained so it had not spread, but the Chapel had been destroyed. There was disbelief on the faces of all those who surveyed it, in shock at the tragedy but grateful that the damage to their homes and livelihoods wasn't worse. The air was fraught with the sobs of Brother Anthony, who had arrived too late and now wept bitterly for his two friends and the sight of his holy place of worship reduced to ashes.

The Constable, Hugh Despenser, glowered as he walked through the groups of soldiers, workmen, and the rest of the Tower inhabitants, checking all were accounted for, that the prisons had not been compromised. He felt some relief that the damage had not been too great, although he would have to compose a letter to the King who he despised, reporting the incident and damages.

Will stood wordlessly at the sight of the burnt-out Chapel, now a pile of ashes and rubble. It seemed cruel that his son had been killed inside the place which had given him such solace in his short, troubled life. Will felt Simeon place a comforting hand on his shoulder, steering him back to The Stone Kitchen, where Will sank into a chair as Simeon placed a mug of ale in front of him. Simeon reluctantly left Will alone, not wanting to intrude on his grief.

Tower of Vengeance

Will buried his face into his hands, 'What have I done, Emma? I should have saved our son at least,' he muttered, his guilt overwhelming him. If he hadn't wanted to save the girl in some poor attempt at appeasing his mother's own death, perhaps Matthew wouldn't have stormed off to the Chapel and would still be alive. He could not understand how the fire had started, as it had been a bitterly cold night. He stared into the shadows, and he could smell the sweet scent of roses. Fear rose as he felt his mother's power growing and, not for the first time, he worried what role Maude had played in his life. 'When will you be done, Mother? Why can't you rest? You will destroy us all,' he whispered.

He heard the outer door open, and John and Joan hurried over to him.

'Matthew is dead,' Will said, his voice cracking.

'Oh, my days,' Joan said, collapsing onto the chair.

John sat down and reached for Joan's hand in comfort.

'I did as you asked and the girl is safe,' John said flatly. 'Abe was at the workshops ensuring the remaining fires were put out. He grumbled but cut the lock. The girl was half-frozen, but I wrapped the cloak around her to hide her face and then helped her across the Bailey. At the gate it was chaos, as they tried to prevent anyone entering to stop further confusion, but I saw Ralph and he let us through. She's safe for now just like we planned. I just can't believe Matthew is gone.' He rested his head on his arms, grief washing over him in great waves, especially because the last words he'd spoken to his brother had been ones of anger.

'Oh, Joan! I hoped you would be here!' Simeon said, rushing in. 'Will you come? I think Ruth is about to give birth.'

'Aye, Simeon.' Joan hauled herself to her feet. 'Let's go and see if we can at least let life into this world tonight. Now, have you sent for the midwife?' she asked him, as she followed him out.

Will reached for John's hand but, lifting his head, he pulled it away.

'It's my fault he's dead,' John said, distraught. 'I wished him dead when he said he would betray us and the girl. I couldn't understand why he would want another human being to suffer. I was so angry at him.'

'You can't blame yourself, John. We both colluded to save the girl. It was the right thing to do and if Matthew hadn't overheard us, perhaps this wouldn't have happened. Who knows why the Chapel caught fire. Matthew was just unlucky to be there when it did,' Will soothed, putting to the back of his mind his own fears as to who was really to blame.

'I just can't forget the things I said to him when we parted. I will never be able to forget how he looked at me when he left. Why did we have to dislike each other so much?' John was not to be comforted.

Tower of Vengeance

'John, please listen to me, you cannot spend the rest of your life burdened by grief and guilt. I know all too well what that is like and how it affects you every day.' Will knew he may now have to finally reveal some of his own story, if only to relieve his son's own guilt.

'What do you mean? I know you feel sadness over Mother's death but that was an accident. You didn't send her to her death like we did Matthew. She died knowing we loved her, didn't she?' John stopped as he suddenly realised his father was trying to tell him something, but part of him didn't want to hear it. The grief and horror they had gone through that night was surely enough.

But Will did not want their lives built on falsehoods any longer, not now that Matthew was dead, and he feared his mother's potency. He told John his own story, of his real identity, of his mother's fate all those years earlier, and then finally the tragedy of his relationship with Emma.

'Your mother and I were such close friends, and she got me through my early days at the Tower when I was so scared of being discovered. But another woman arrived who turned my head; I will not reveal who she was as it's not important now.' It was too dangerous to tell his son that he had had an affair with a member of the royal family, as much as he wanted to tell John the whole truth. He need only know that he cheated on Emma. 'But I broke your mother's heart, and she left with the Empress after her marriage, as you know. I knew I was to blame for her departure, and your grandmother, Jane, was mad at me.' He paused, contemplating what a fool he had been back then. 'When your mother came back with you, my precious son, I thought I had a second chance. I felt such joy. I loved you both so much, and then when Matthew was born, I loved him too. My family is what I now realise has been the most important love of all.' But he did not tell him how he tried to leave, how it was only his grandfather's death that had prevented him. He could not bring himself to tell his son that the earldom had always come first with him and that even now he wanted it, that he still resented his own fate, and continued even now to lie.

Will slumped back exhausted in his chair. John was horrified at his father's words. There had been so many secrets, so many lies, and he could barely process it all.

'How can you say your family is more important when all that you have done is destroy it this night with your very words? Everything I ever believed in, loved even, has gone and I have nothing left. You couldn't even love my mother enough.' His memories of Emma were vague, but he did remember the overwhelming love she had given to both him and Matthew. 'And you couldn't even tell us about your own mother even though you knew we sensed her. She scared Matthew, and you didn't once think to ease his fears. All these years you denied her to us. You could have at least trusted us with that. I don't care about your wretched title or the life we could have had. I don't even believe in God anymore – He didn't save Matthew, did He? If you expect sympathy, I have none to give to you. I don't even know what love is anymore.' And with that, he slowly climbed the stairs, struggling to come to terms with what had happened and what he had been told, leaving Will alone in the darkened room.

'What now, Mother?' he asked the shadows, as he listened to his son in the room above. 'Is this what you wanted?'

Nothing stirred. No smell of roses. No comfort. Only the dying flames of the kitchen fire, sparking gently in the hearth. And the ghost of despair.

Tower of Vengeance

Maude

When one is a child, the old priests always tell you that the Devil can't enter a church, that it is God's sanctuary on earth, safe for all God's children. But you see that is wrong, for the earth is the Devil's kingdom with all its earthly temptations. Nowhere is safe from the Devil's work, not even when you fall on your knees and pray for your God. He won't save you. After all, He didn't save His own son, did He?

Will the Hermit go to Heaven, all sins absolved? Perhaps. He was a trifling price to pay in my eyes. Because Matthew was intent on betraying and destroying my family, I was left with no other choice, and the Hermit was my conduit. Easy to fool a mind deprived of food, of warmth, of all comfort – I know that all too well – and starting a fire was easily done and can look like such a tragic accident. Matthew, my own grandson, could not live. If Matthew had not tried to block me when I tried to connect with him, perhaps things would have turned out differently. I did not want to do this, but sometimes we have to take paths we would rather avoid. I could not risk my son – all I have done is for him.

But John's blood still mocks me, and I cannot see who he really is even with all my magic. I recognise those dark eyes; they haunt me even in my shadowland. Have I sacrificed my own grandson for Earl Richard's bastard? But I feel such a connection with the boy, such love as I feel for my own son.

Tower of Vengeance

How can I not know? It was why I held back from John. The Devil will not tell me however much I beg.

Even though I can feel that my soul has darkened, I still love my family with what is left of it. They are the only light I have, and the Devil knows how my family drives me and our vengeful pact.

I'm amongst the embers of the Chapel now, watching the Hierophant dissolve into ashes. The Devil walks beside me. 'Such beautiful destruction,' he whispers, 'of God's own house, of God's own servants. How clever you have become. This delights me so much that perhaps at some point I will pay you back the debt.'

I watch as a card smoulders in the ashes – The Hermit – and the Devil laughs at how I have used him for my own gain.

The High Priestess flutters before me. The Devil smiles. 'She comes to save your son.'

The Magician sneers.

Renewal

Six Months Later

John woke in a tangle of blankets, his body soaked with sweat, and his heart racing. It was the dream which woke him – reliving that awful night when Death had taken his brother. Matthew's empty bed seemed a recrimination to the brother that lived, who had saved a stranger while his brother burned. He could hear his father leaving his room next door, so mercifully it must be morning, the weak May light not yet penetrating the room's wooden shutters. He got up, relieved he didn't have to try and sleep anymore, and opened the shutters to let in some light. He noticed Matthew's old cloak hanging on the door still as it was something that John couldn't bear to part with yet, the only reminder he had of his brother.

Downstairs, he could hear Bess talking to Will as they got ready for the day ahead. Large numbers of prisoners arrived each day due to the growing strife within the country, so the alehouse would be busy with soldiers wanting to quench their thirst after a hard day.

John bade Bess good morning as he came down the stairs and gratefully accepted the ale and bread she had ready for him.

Tower of Vengeance

'There's been a message from Joan.' Will said, looking up at him. 'She is unwell and wants to see you.'

John's heart sank. He had rarely left the Tower in his time of mourning, unable to face London's lively streets which mocked him, so full of teeming life with its pleasures and pain. He had found he missed Matthew with an ache which surprised him considering their differences and how strained their relationship had been while he was alive. He remembered the rare occasions they had got on, wishing they had been more frequent, and that he had made more of an effort to understand his brother's troubled soul. He regretted that their last moments had been spent arguing over the girl he had saved. He had blocked her out of his memories and had forbidden Joan from telling him about her.

'We owe her, John,' Will reminded him.

'I know, I know!' His tone was sharp. Bess frowned at him, and he realised he was being churlish about a woman who was the one constant left in their lives. He didn't want to admit that he was struggling to cope with how things had changed.

'Go this morning. We can manage here,' Will suggested softly, conciliatory, trying as always to placate his son. John reluctantly nodded his agreement, his temper cooling already, knowing he had no real argument not to go. A debt was owed to Joan for that night, but he had avoided going to her house as he could not face the girl who had inadvertently caused his brother's death.

Tower of Vengeance

* * *

The sun was shining as he walked to her house, but the mood of the city was sullen and tense. For the dispute with the King and his barons was now getting closer to London and it was merely a matter of time before the tinder of revolt was set alight. There was a restlessness on the streets which even John noticed, and he was glad to arrive at Joan's with its busy courtyard, where he was greeted by her husband's workers with smiles of welcome as he made his way to her private rooms.

'The mistress is sleeping now – she has been awake most of the night with a wretched cough, but she left orders for you to wait in her solar for she desires to see you.' The maid ushered him into the pleasant room which he knew so well. Bess had brought him and Matthew here throughout their childhood, and they had loved to play with their great-aunt's wool and had eaten all the tasty treats she had readily on hand. He sat in one of the chairs where the sun was pooling through the windows, and he dozed off in the warmth as he remembered how even his brother had been happy here, away from the Tower, embraced in Joan's love.

The door opened and John jolted out of his reverie. He did not know how long he had closed his eyes for but instead of seeing his aunt, he saw her, the girl from the cage. She looked much different now of course, her hair no longer dirty and matted but long and dark. Her clothes were fine and clean, but her

Tower of Vengeance

eyes, those green eyes which had peered at him from the darkness, remained the same – as if they pierced his soul. He knew her at once and it seemed she also knew him. They stared at each other in shock as John scrambled to his feet, unsure whether to stay or leave. Conflicting emotions passed over both their faces as at last, they met after all this time.

'It's John, isn't it?' she spoke tentatively.

'Yes,' he whispered, rooted to the spot.

'I'm Hannah. I believe I owe you my life for saving me from that terrible cage.'

He could not speak, his mouth dry, and he realised he must seem like some mute fool.

'Will you sit with me a while so we can talk?' she asked, and she nodded for him to sit back in his chair, taking the one opposite him.

'I am sorry for your brother. It must have hit you and your father hard. Joan has told me of the sacrifice you both made for me. I never meant to cause you so much sorrow, and now I feel such guilt for what I cost you, and if I've kept you away from this house.' She leant towards him, her green eyes glistening with tears. Her voice had soothed him, placating his desire to run.

'You are right,' his voice cracked, and he swallowed, gulping at the air as he struggled to speak. 'I do feel guilt. My brother was a fanatic; he loved his God and hated Jews. We argued over saving you and I hate that the last words we spoke were ones of anger. Even with my guilt, I still believe we did the right thing, but how do I stop these feelings?'

'I'm not sure you can. That remorse will probably always be there, but you have to live, John, and make a good life. I too feel awful that I caused someone that you loved to die, and nothing I can do will change that.' She looked away from him.

'I didn't even like my brother.' John laughed bitterly. 'But I didn't wish him dead. My father and I just work; we breathe but we don't actually live anymore.'

'We are young, John, and we must think of a future to make a new way of living. I too have lost my family, and Joan is helping me to rebuild my own life. I too am changed, but we must decide how we make that change a good one rather than a lost opportunity to live better.' Tears trickled down her cheeks as she mourned all they had lost.

John reached over and held her hand. He remembered how she had trembled with fear when he had carried her across the Outer Bailey that night. They had a shared suffering, and the act of talking together was easing his own sorrow because she understood a little of what he had gone through herself.

'I do have a question for you, John,' she said, brushing way her tears, 'and you may think I am mad. When I was in that cage, I wanted to close my eyes and sleep, a sleep that in that cold would have been eternal, but every time I closed my eyes a woman would nudge me awake. Can I trust you to keep a secret?' she asked.

He nodded in reply, guessing what she was about to say.

'I saw her quite clearly and she was no living soul. I can see ghosts – it is a gift or perhaps a curse I have, and I knew she was one.'

'She is my grandmother, Maude de Mandeville.' And John told Hannah Maude's story, which he had struggled to accept these past few months. He trusted that she would keep the secret if he kept hers.

'What a horrible death she had. I could sense her pain yet felt a connection between us, probably because she had been imprisoned there too.'

'My father believes she has been responsible for certain things that have happened in the Tower as she avenges her death,' he confided in her.

'Do you think that knowing your brother was about to betray you both, she acted to save us?' She looked deep into his eyes.

'Yes, I think I do.' John sighed; he was stroking Hannah's hand now, the act calming him as he finally voiced his deepest fears. 'But even if she did act, it alters nothing of what we ourselves did and how we caused it all.'

'No, I agree. I am the reason it happened, am I not?' She went to withdraw her hand, but he stopped her.

'I would not change that. I would still save you.' And he meant every word as he looked into the green eyes that held his future.

They heard a cough, quickly dropping their clasped hands, as they saw Joan standing in the doorway.

'How are you, great-aunt?' John went to greet her.

'Better now I've had some sleep after the mixture Hannah made me.' She looked at the girl with kindness in her eyes. 'You put my old potions to shame – your knowledge is superior to mine!' she enthused.

John accepted a drink from Joan, talking a bit longer, before he realised he must have been there a good hour or so and needed to return to The Stone Kitchen to help with the midday service.

'Oh, I must go. I hadn't realised I had been so long.' He reluctantly rose from his seat.

'Well, you can come back and check on me tomorrow,' Joan told him, suspecting she would be seeing a lot more of her great-nephew now.

And Joan was right – over the next month, John was a constant visitor, solicitous over her health, and she ensured she always required a nap when he arrived, leaving Hannah to entertain their guest.

Will too noticed a change in his son, and his more frequent visits to Joan. After a few weeks, Will had himself gone to see Joan to see for himself how she was doing, but talk quickly turned to the blossoming romance between John and Hannah.

'I am pleased some good has come out of this, Joan. The past few months have not been easy.' Will sighed.

'Yes, John told me that you had told him the truth about your past and about Emma.' There was little Joan did not know, for Will had confided some of his story to her after Jane's death, which had felt yet another burden so soon after Emma's. Luckily for him, Joan had been sympathetic, although there had been plenty of recrimination over his treatment of Emma, her beloved niece.

'I never meant to hurt Emma – I did love her,' Will reiterated now.

'I know you did. But she changed when she returned from overseas. She loved her sons, but she was never the same girl. Such sadness, even though I could see she loved you just as she always had.'

'Do you think so? I hurt her so badly. She seemed so distant at times. It was as if she couldn't bear my touch anymore. And I couldn't blame her for that.'

'I know you hurt her, but do you know I noticed her flinch when anyone touched her unexpectantly. I am not sure it was only you.' Joan suddenly recalled a memory which had long been hidden after all these years. 'We were in the kitchen once; she was poking the fire, we were chatting, so she knew I was there, and as I went to pass her, I got a bit unsteady on my feet, so I put my hand on her arm. She leapt so high she almost fell into the flames. I also saw it happen a few times with the men as she served them. And she was used to the men before she left, and it never bothered her then.'

'Do you know, you are right; I hadn't realised that until you said it. I guess you always think it's just you. Of course, we had changed when she returned – she knew I had betrayed her. I had loved another woman more than I loved her.' Again, he omitted Isabella's identity because of her royal lineage. 'Emma had travelled, seen a different world, had our son, and brought him home. We couldn't not change, but yes, now I think of it, there was definitely more to it. I had always thought that she couldn't forgive me for what I did. We will never know now. But I want John to be happy; that's all that matters to me now. That he is happy.'

'Then you will have to accept Hannah. And that comes at a risk. You know of her family, her religion, and what marrying her could cost John.'

'Joan, I care not for her religion. If Hannah loves my son and they are happy, even if it's brief, surely it is worth the risk? After all our suffering, I just want my son's happiness.'

'Then perhaps you should tell him that. So he knows he has your blessing. I think it's holding him back.'

So, later that evening, after Bess and her daughter had gone home and the alehouse door was bolted against the world, Will poured himself and

John a mug of ale and they sat in front of the dying fire.

'I went to see Joan today, to see how she fared. You have been so diligent in your visits there these past few months I wondered if she was dying or if someone else had your attention there.' Will grinned.

'I love her. Hannah, I mean, not Joan!' John admitted, blushing a bright red.

'Aye, son, I can see that in your face every time you come home. I know you love Joan, but this is quite different. I've been in love too – I know how it feels.' Will grimaced.

'What should I do? She's Jewish; we are forbidden by law to marry.' John sighed helplessly.

Will took a long drink from his mug and looked his son in the eyes.

'That depends on you two. If you love each other and you believe it's worth it, then take that risk. You will have to marry in church though if you want it to be seen to be real.'

'She won't give up her own religion, but she has said she is willing to hide it. We could have a secret Jewish ceremony for her. I would be happy to do that and for her to continue in her own worship, as I no longer care for our so-called God.'

Will realised he had been resentful for so long over what he had lost that he had not appreciated what he had gained in life. He had learnt his true feelings for Emma too late, but he could at least help John to be happy.

'Will you help us, Father? We love each other so much; I want to ask Hannah to marry me, but I was worried you wouldn't want us to.'

'Of course I will. But you must act now. You must have heard that Despenser has just left the Tower to join Simon de Montfort, who it is rumoured marches on the King. If the King comes here, the Tower may well be locked down and then you will be cut off from Hannah. Be happy, John. Take the risk, otherwise you will always regret it.'

And the bond that had been tested that fateful night once again began to strengthen. Their fragile relationship began to heal, but storm clouds gathered across the land and the King looked towards the Tower, needing its strength and power to keep his crown upon his head.

The Proposal

A few days later, Hannah and John walked through the early morning streets of the city towards the Tower. John had wanted Hannah to meet his father, to show her the alehouse which would be their home and to face her own dark memories of her last visit there. Hannah clung to John as they made their way through the growing crowds. She still feared being recognised by her former neighbours, who might easily betray her for a reward. John had tried to reassure her as not only had Despenser left, but all the Jewish prisoners had since been released from the Tower and the threat to her people was currently low.

'I promise you; no one even thinks you are alive. Remember, my father bribed one of the soldiers to say that you had died. Everyone thinks you lie in a grave-pit by the Chapel.'

Hannah shuddered. 'But my family would still recognise me. My father may have converted and be living in that Domus Conversorum in New Street, but my Uncle Hagin is still in league with the Earl of Cornwall and no friend to me or my family. I just wish I had news on my brothers. They seem to have disappeared since they were set free,' she whispered, concerned they would be overheard, and she wondered if she would ever feel safe.

They approached the Tower and Hannah knew she had a choice to make. She could marry John but live within the walls of her old prison, or go abroad into exile, away from the man she loved.

Time, she knew, was against them, with news of the King's imminent arrival, and the sullen streets they had just walked through were testimony to the unrest this news brought with it.

The Tower's entrance was chaotic, as numerous supply wagons made their way across the causeway, and men jostled to get through desperate to find work within the safety of the castle's walls. John Lund was easily recognised, and they got through with no delay. As they entered the Outer Bailey, Hannah stopped. It was a glorious summer's day, and the White Tower dazzled in all its glory and strength. When she had arrived last time, it had been a cold winter's night and she had been full of terror, barely taking in her surroundings before being thrown into the cage. It looked different now, still menacing, but there was life around her, people smiling in greeting to John, who still held her hand tightly, and there was the alehouse ready to welcome her home. She took a deep breath and smiled at John.

'Ready to meet my father?' he asked.

They walked into the dimly lit alehouse, which was empty at that time. John had deliberately chosen the early morning to bring Hannah. Even Bess and her girls had not yet arrived, and Will was busy bringing up the ale from the cellar, where he and John had been brewing earlier. Hannah looked over to the bar where Will was standing, ready to greet her. *He is a handsome man*, she thought, *grey hair tinging dark curls which enhance his brooding looks*. Knowing his past, Hannah could make out the noble refinement in his face; his keen eyes were watchful and there was a restlessness about him that John did not have.

'Welcome to The Stone Kitchen, Hannah. It is a pleasure to meet you at last.' He smiled at her, and she felt the kindness in his voice, which eased the tension she had held in her body since leaving Joan's. 'Perhaps you would like John to show you around. It's not a patch on Joan's house but we have made it as comfortable as we can, and there is room for improvement.' His dark eyes twinkled, and she thought she glimpsed a resemblance to John.

John led Hannah through to the kitchen and she took in the functionality of the space, admiring its cleanliness rather than its comfort.

'This room here used to be a bedroom, but you could easily turn it into your stillroom. We just store things in here at the moment.' John eagerly showed her the useful space next to the kitchen and he looked for her approval, wanting her to be happy.

'It is a good space and would be the perfect stillroom,' she agreed, as his face lit up.

The two large bedrooms upstairs were adequate, but they definitely needed a woman's touch, and she wondered how they would cope with any additional family members, but that was a problem for the future.

Hannah could feel herself liking the place – there was a warmth to it, a gentleness amongst its memories, and she could picture herself here with John. They re-entered the bar and it was then she saw her. The ghostly form of Maude de Mandeville was watching her from one of the tables.

Such beauty, Hannah thought to herself.

Maude smiled and Hannah realised she had heard her thoughts.

'Hannah? Are you alright?' John broke into her trance and Maude disappeared.

'Yes, of course, my love. It's time now to go to the cage. I need to face it again to banish the past.' Hannah felt John squeeze her hand as they left the alehouse and made their way to the elephant's cage.

'What do you remember of that time?' John asked, as they surveyed the iron bars, the old straw long gone, and the door swinging in the faint summer breeze, its broken lock dangling. As they looked at it, a raven came and perched on its roof, watching them quizzically.

'I know I was hovering between life and death, and I really just wanted to sleep. I was so cold and so scared.' She shuddered. 'I had no idea why we had been taken. My father had been so sure of the King's patronage that it was a shock when the men came and dragged us here.'

'Do you know why Despenser decided to put you in here?' John had long been puzzled about the ex-Constable's decision, but the time had never felt right to ask.

'It was just so manic that night, but I do have a faint recollection of him saying something to my father about hidden money,' she recalled. 'I wonder if

Tower of Vengeance

he was hoping to get his hands on Father's treasure, and when he didn't reveal its whereabouts, Despenser threw me in here as punishment.'

'I guess it would make sense. I just remember my own shock at discovering someone in here.'

'You were my angel.' She smiled at his beloved face. The same face that had peered through the bars, urging her to eat, and promising to save her.

'Will you marry me, my own angel, who has healed me and shown me what love is? Will you place your trust in me again?' he whispered.

'We saved each other and now is the time to banish the past together. I will always be afraid, but I would rather be afraid with you by my side than have a life without you in it.' As she made her decision, she knew her choice was the right one; she was bound to him and his family.

John gathered her in his arms and kissed her, feeling the joy in his heart.

The raven unfurled its dark, tattered wings and flew up into the blue sky, circling the stone turret, ecstatic with its news of happiness at last.

The Bride

Three days later, in The Golden Chain across the Inner Bailey, there was laughter and joy as the alehouse toasted the new bride and groom. For that day, John had arrived back from the city announcing his marriage to Hannah, a young girl he had met at his great-aunt Joan's and whom he said he had been courting this past year.

'Well, that was a surprise,' Ruth remarked to Simeon.

'Aye, I didn't see that one coming. I never thought he would settle down so young.' He shook his head. They looked over to where John stood introducing his new wife to some of the Tower inhabitants.

'She is very beautiful. They make a striking couple,' Ruth mused.

Hannah glanced over to them with a smile, her vivid green eyes sparkling with joy as John wrapped his arm about her slender waist, hugging her towards him, love radiating from them both. Her long, glossy dark hair complemented the black-blue colour of John's. Her smile was tinged with weariness too, as if she had known suffering, giving her an aura of fragility.

She could feel the eyes of the alehouse girls upon her and sensed their envy at seeing her stood beside John as his wife. If only they knew that the road to John had been paved with sorrow and sacrifice. It had been a hard decision to accept his hand, as to do so was to leave her old life behind, knowing she would have to worship her own God in secret, and to live with the constant worry that the knock on her door would come and she would be arrested once again. And to return here to her place of imprisonment even now made her feel uneasy.

She shook off her fears because this was her wedding day after all. It should be a day of happiness as they began their new life together. Her eyes appraised the room as she sipped her ale – it was a good quality although she preferred wine, which her family had enjoyed at mealtimes. She could see the alehouses were a good business. The Stone Kitchen, although bigger than the Chain, needed more work, and her and John had plans for it to rival the taverns in the city. It was time to profiteer on the wealthier prisoners who needed provisioning and at present relied on the city taverns to provide their food rather than the Tower alehouses. She had been lucky to be looked after by Joan, for as an alderman her husband had connections with the best merchants in London, and it would not take much to implement the changes to improve the alehouses and make them into taverns.

Hannah also had money which had been secreted away with a good friend who had kept it safe for her during her imprisonment, so that it wasn't seized by Despenser and his men. Hannah had sensed her father's enemies circling, known the King was fickle, and had ensured her small fortune given to her by her mother just before she died had been safe.

Even her father had not known of this legacy. Her mother had wanted her daughter to have some insurance, and Hannah was determined to use it now, thinking up plans for her stillroom where she could carry on her love for healing and potions, and she was sure she would find patrons among the Tower's inhabitants.

She smiled again as someone congratulated her on her marriage and John squeezed her waist in support.

'Are you happy, my love?' he whispered in her ear. 'Not long until we are alone at last.'

She giggled, but as much as she longed to be alone with her husband, she knew how important it was to mix with these people, their neighbours, their customers, to make them their friends, never to underestimate anyone no matter their status in life. She knew that the family she had married into were not what they seemed and now she too held their lineage secret. Who knew what lay beneath a person and when that person might help you. After all, John and his father had helped her in her time of need.

And there in the corner, she spied Maude. It was a relief to be able to speak freely with John, as he too saw Maude and it had made their connection stronger. John had struggled with his grandmother's presence after his brother's death, and they had spoken of her need for revenge.

'She seems to like you at least.' John was thankful, still concerned over Maude's power.

Tower of Vengeance

'She sees me as an ally for some reason, therefore she approves our match. But yes, there is a lot of anger in her, a real thirst for revenge. She will not tell me how she has managed to stay beyond the veil of death.' Hannah was curious. It wasn't easy to deny Death his dues, which was why most ghosts were malevolent, and she had always avoided those spirits. The ghosts of children, she often found, were trapped, looking for parents who did not come, unable to leave their earthly homes as they searched in despair. It was hard to ignore them.

Hannah could sense even now that Maude was different to other ghosts she'd encountered and much more powerful. Maude shimmered in the shadows and smiled at her before she looked for her son. Hannah noticed that Maude was only ever truly happy when she saw Will, who stood now talking to Joan and her husband, Walter. There was a peace to the room and Hannah too felt contentment, but it was to be short-lived.

The door burst open. 'The King is here, and he's ordered an immediate lock down, so anyone who doesn't belong here needs to get out now,' the soldier ordered.

The joyous day was over, Joan and Walter hurried away, and Maude was gone in a flash of fury. Hannah's happiness dissolved into fear once more as storm clouds swirled around the Tower's grim walls.

The Uneasy Crown

The last days of summer. Corn and fruit had grown in abundance, but the country knew no rest. The King had been hiding inside the Tower for two months, away from the arguments, the fighting, and the bitter recriminations of his own council. He had tried to leave once but had been forced back by Simon de Montfort, the Earl of Leicester, and so he had ordered the city's gates to be reinforced, and outside London's walls waited for his son, Edward, and his army – ready this time, at least, to fight for him.

Will had been summoned to the Royal Apartments to provide ale for the King and his guests. The royal household's supplies had now dwindled, and they would have to rely on the Tower's own resources from now on. It had been a long time since Will had entered the Blundeville Tower where the King now lodged, and he felt a pang of nostalgia for his old friend. The room Thomas had designed was octagonal in shape; cosy recesses housed window seats which looked out onto the river. Henry's canopied bed dominated the vaulted room and, in one of the largest alcoves, stood his own private chapel brightening the room with its colour – the gold, bejewelled cross demonstrating his own devotion to God. His throne glowed in the dying light of the day. The room was getting darker now as the day faded into dusk, the stone walls permeating a coldness that even the thick, glorious tapestries could not hold at bay. The last of the light winked through the windows and Will could hear the river beyond, the

Tower of Vengeance

boats, the ferrymen, and the waves gently hitting the walls as the tide rose.

Will stood in the shadows passing the ale jugs to the King's usher. The usher had asked him to stay in case they required more ale. Will had never been this close to the King before and, with a jolt, he realised this was Isabella's brother. Henry had the same blond hair and slight stature of his sister, but there the similarity ended. He was not a good-looking man; there was a weakness about him, and there was no illusion of charm or allure around him that had come so easy to Will's former lover. He lacked Isabella's vitality and Will found it hard to believe they were related.

'What news do you bring me, Richard?' The King was finishing his breakfast as Richard, Duke of Cornwall, entered the confined room.

'Well, your wife, our devoted Queen, has taken to the river and means to escape to Windsor.'

'Surely you joke. She has hardly left her chamber these past weeks as she still mourns our dear daughter Catherine. Does Constable Mansell know of this, and why was I not told immediately?!' Henry jumped to his feet and hurried to the window, where he had a limited view of the river as it approached the bridge.

'We both tried to dissuade her, but the Queen is a stubborn woman, and I presume her loving family are at Windsor?' Richard joined his brother at the window. They could see the royal barge as it neared the bridge, and they watched in horror as it began to be pelted from above by the London peasants. The barge rocked precariously as the missiles of rotten fruit and stones hit their target and the oarsmen battled with the tide and the onslaught. The second barge filled with luggage and her servants was already turning back as the Tower's guards started to shout to the boats to return. A swifter boat left the gatehouse with a small band of soldiers, and the oarsman rowed rapidly towards the Queen's vessel. The royal barge turned and with its increased escort made its way back to the Tower, out of reach from the mob who brayed with laughter.

'Has it come to this? We cannot even leave this place?' Henry was anguished.

'My men and I were also attacked as we came through the streets. There's a lot of resentment in the city and we know Leicester is popular with the mob.'

'And Edward? What news of him and his men?'

'At present they are waiting outside the city gates, but they grow restless, and the priories grow fearful. As you are more than aware, your dear son recently plundered my own priory at Wallinghead. We need to act soon.'

'I should go to the Queen – make sure she is unharmed.'

'Henry! We need to act. We are stuck here all the time you lock yourself up in prayer. Let her ladies see to the Queen. Mansell will ensure all is well. I have other news which I need to tell you. And I need ale!'

The servant hurriedly poured the Earl some ale as Will watched the King. The hooded eyelid of Henry's right eye twitching with palpable distress. The King sat and motioned to his brother to tell him the news. Will listened as Richard informed the King of Leicester's latest gains.

'I cannot believe my own sister would allow her husband to rise against us. She cannot mean to wear the crown in my place?' The King was incredulous.

'She was always ambitious, even when she was encased in that nunnery after the Marshal's death, and of course Isabella becoming an empress made her furious at the time. She saw de Montfort as her way to gain power and prestige.' Richard sipped his ale.

'Much good it did poor Bella.' Henry gulped.

'I never did understand why you sent her here to all places, when she had done nothing wrong,' Richard mused.

'You know why,' Henry hissed, and Will – still hidden in his corner with the silent usher – held his breath at this talk of Isabella. 'That stupid man, Matthew Paris, implied we were in some sort of forbidden relationship, and I couldn't have that rumour tarnish my crown. She had to be gone; I could not bear to look at her any longer. I prayed for her soul, and I gave her a magnificent marriage. I was not to know how it would turn out,' Henry argued.

    Richard was about to say more but thought better of it, and he turned once more to discussing strategy just as the Constable entered the room to bring news of the Queen, who was safely back in her apartments, pride battered, temper blazing. John Mansell was the King's man and Will knew he held much influence. The Tower soldiers liked him, as he was a steadying hand.

    'Mansell, sit and drink,' ordered Richard, and he signalled to Will to bring the ale. Will noticed Richard look at him curiously for a moment before he carried on talking. 'We need more men to fight against Leicester. He draws ever closer. Can you issue an edict calling up all capable men and boys in the city – they want someone to pelt, they can pelt de Montfort's scum.' Will's heart sank at the words, as he knew it would affect both him and his newly married son.

    'Aye, I can do that. Not sure how popular it will be, but I'll get the proclamation out. Just had word from Essex. You remember how recently old Fitzwalter's grandson was made the ward of Peter de Mandeville?' Mansell did not notice Will's hand begin to shake as he poured the Constable's ale.

    'Geoffrey de Mandeville's brother? The man who married our father's first wife?' asked Richard.

    'And two of the Carta barons! Enemies of the Crown,' cried Henry.

'Well, the grandson has become betrothed to Dervorguilla de Burgh…Hubert's great granddaughter…I mean, they are babes now, but a worrying alliance all the same.' Mansell let the news seep in. Will sank back against the cold stone wall listening intently.

'De Mandeville hasn't got an heir, has he?' Richard poured himself more ale.

'There was a boy. His nephew. The son of Geoffrey. He had been hidden in some priory when he was young, and I gave orders for him to be captured and brought to court. But he eluded my men,' Henry remembered, frowning. 'Richard, do you recall that story about the boy's mother? Geoffrey's first wife?'

'Yes, I do. The doomed Maude who was brought here and died here.' Richard shuddered. Will held his breath. He could smell the sickly, cloying scent of roses and wondered if the men also noticed.

'Well, the boy must be long dead. No threat to us. We don't need any more issues right now. And two babes barely betrothed can't do much now. We have enough trouble with our own family.'

'I better go and issue that edict if you want men,' Mansell said, and stood up.

'Yes, I mean to leave for Dover soon,' announced the King. 'We need to force de Montfort's hand and engage him in battle.'

'Is that wise?' Mansell looked at the two brothers.

'We can't stay here much longer. Edward's men get restless, as does the Queen. I think we need to get her away safely to her family in France.' Henry was adamant.

'And the Prince? Where will you send him?' Mansell asked.

'Back to Wales. We need their crops and livestock to fuel our army.'

'And their men? Will they fight for you?' Mansell was sceptical.

'They will die if they don't. Edward will take no prisoners.'

'I pray that you are victorious, my lord. These are troubling times. I am as ever here to serve.' The Constable bowed.

'I thank you, Mansell, and my orders are for you to hold the Tower. It is key to my success.' The King dismissed him with a wave of his hand.

'Then hold it I will.'

Mansell left the room and hurried down the stairs. The usher asked Will to fetch more ale, and he was glad to be gone. It had been so many years since he had heard news of his other family, and he felt the familiar urge to claim what was rightfully his. He had thought it pushed aside with his newly found contentment with his son and new daughter-in-law,

Tower of Vengeance

but his old resentment had risen up inside him as soon as the Earl and the King had mentioned the earldom once again. It had been strange to hear the King talk about him, evoking memories of those days on the road as Will had been hunted as a traitor. But for now, his priority was to get to the alehouse and warn them about the edict. They would not be able to refuse to fight for the King, but to do so meant Will and John might die in battle.

As Will entered the alehouse, the room was busy with the Tower's inhabitants having their mid-morning ale, and he scoured the room for John.

'Orders are about to go out from the King. All men of a certain age must fight for his army,' Will told his shocked son.

The room went quiet as word spread and Hannah, coming in from the kitchen with Bess, felt a dread wash over her. She gripped John's hand; surely she could not lose him, not so soon after they had wed, and on the cusp of building a future together.

'All of us?' John gulped.

'I was in the Blundeville Tower serving the King, along with his brother and the Constable, and that's what he said. All men.' Will could see the fear in the faces around him as they digested the news.

'Things must be serious if the Earl of Cornwall is here too, and did you hear about the commotion with the Queen on the river? The mob were throwing things at her from the old bridge! They won't like that in the Royal Apartments,' Bess said.

Tower of Vengeance

At the mention of the royal family, Hannah felt nauseous. Just when she had started to feel safe, or as safe as she could with John's protection, she found out that the very people that hunted her kind were here and now trying to take away her husband. The Earl of Cornwall had never been a friend to her father, and now she felt even more fearful when she heard his name. It was as if he represented a danger to her new family which she couldn't quite understand.

'It will be fine,' John whispered in her ear, squeezing her hand to reassure her, sensing the tension in her body. 'Nothing will happen to you.'

'I can't do this without you,' she said softly.

Amid the noise and confusion that now arose within the room, the door opened again, and the room fell silent as a soldier entered.

'All men are to report to the Outer Bailey immediately for inspection and the King's orders,' the man barked at them, and then turned on his heels and left.

For Hannah, it was reminiscent of a previous time when the soldiers had knocked on the doors in her old street, calling for the Jews to leave, dragging entire families from their beds and into this place of imprisonment. Such irony now that her man, her new family, could be taken from the same place to fight for a king who had already destroyed so much of her life. But now she needed to be strong for her husband, and as much as she hated being part of a crowd and close to the King's guards, she had to push aside her own fear and accompany John and Will outside to learn their fate.

The men had no choice but to obey. All the Tower residents were registered in the Constable's book, and no one could escape the King's orders. Reluctantly, they all trundled out of The Stone Kitchen and made their way out into the Outer Bailey into the sunshine. The place was eerily silent, as no tools were in use as the smiths, the bakers, the butchers, the storemen, the workmen, and the alehouse men stood in front of the Tower guards reporting for duty. John Mansell strode towards them, orders in hand, and he stepped onto an upturned crate so he could address them all. Hannah held her breath, dreading the thought of losing John.

'On the King's orders, I pronounce the convocation of all male citizens in London and within these walls. Men from the ages of sixteen to thirty years are forthwith ordered to join the King's army as it prepares to leave for Dover. Exceptions are the Tower guards and the Tower smiths. The rest of you are to report to the Tower armoury to be given a suitable weapon, and you must bring whatever provisions you can carry.' There was an audible gasp from the crowd and Hannah felt herself grow faint as her worst dreams came true. John had to fight, and he may not return.

As he was speaking, the Earl of Cornwall entered the Bailey and approached Mansell, who bent down to hear him. Mansell scowled as the Earl whispered in his ear but nodded his head to show he understood.

'And a further exception is the alehouse men,' he added. 'That's it. Be ready to leave at first light when you hear the muster bell ring.'

Hannah felt giddy with relief and fought back her tears. John was safe and would not be fighting after all. She hugged her incredulous husband to her, not wanting to let him go, and smiled at Will, who himself could not believe the reprieve they had been given.

The raven, perched on one of the Outer Bailey walls, felt a foreboding. The Plantagenet lions had spared the alehouse men, but their unsheathed claws were waiting to snare them, and she screeched a cry of warning, drowned out by the clamour of men going off to fight a bloody war.

Tower of Vengeance

Maude

My raven returns to me with persistent cries. She too is unsettled by these Plantagenet sons. I am thankful that my son and grandson are safe, but Erin is right – why did Richard save them? It does not make sense, and I feel the darkness in his soul.

However, I watch as the Wheel of Fortune spins again and today at least it turns in my favour.

I had laughed at the Queen being driven back by London's peasants, cheering every piece of rotten food which had hit its mark, the odd splat spraying the Queen herself, the revulsion plain on her haughty face.

I had scoffed at Henry's unease within his secluded tower – he thinks he is alone there, but he does not notice me reclining on his gilded throne, mocking his crown. I can sense his unrest; his mind is mainly closed off to me, but I get glimpses when he is particularly weak. For instance, when he remembers the whore that was Isabella I can see his pain, his misdirected feelings, and my heart rejoices.

King John's children deserve their unhappy lives and now they even fight each other. Henry at least feels the true cost of wearing the crown, and he pities his sister Eleanor and her husband, the Jew hater, their desire for it. But we always crave what we cannot have. My curse on all their marriages has been a strong one.

Tower of Vengeance

But I feel such anger at the news of the betrothal of a Fitzwalter and a de Burgh. I could see it unsettled Will, and we both want what is his by right. So once again, I curse a marriage. The de Burghs are ever an enemy of mine and if they were to set foot within these walls, I would strike them dead for taking what was my son's. It rankles that my power diminishes the further it travels. Even now some of my curses prove futile, but once my enemies step within my kingdom, my power is strong.

But now the Tower watches as King Henry breaks open the treasure house and begins to waste the Kingdom's fortune, and we wait the next act in this increasingly hostile world. The Wheel turns slightly.

Richard of Cornwall continues with his own games, dancing as always to his own tune. The reversed Magician, the trickster of the cards. He has spared my grandson a certain death on a bloody battlefield, but I wonder what he knows. I fear John is his bastard and a cuckoo in my family's nest.

My one solace is Hannah – the High Priestess. To once again have a kindred spirit to communicate with since Maria's absence, and to watch her bring love and happiness back to my boys. She has such strength and the love she shares with John reminds me of the love I lost. She must be our salvation.

The Judgement card flutters to the ground. I look around for the Devil, who is conspicuous in his absence. He does not come. The Wheel creaks and slowly tips towards de Montfort's banner. Will he overthrow the monarchy, thus giving me some revenge? The death of the Plantagenet lions is what I crave. That family gone whilst mine prosper. It is all I desire. But if de Montfort wins, his wife, John's daughter, will triumph and sit on the cursed throne – I had forgotten that in my glee. And de Montfort is no friend to Hannah. Can I ever win?

    The Wheel falters.

The Confession

Four Months Later

A comet blazed again as the King was defeated on Lewes battlefield, left to lick his wounds, as his son escaped to regroup his army and attempt to regain his father's power. London breathed once more as it welcomed back the victor, Simon de Montfort, its man of the people. But with him too, came the wounded, a straggling, wretched company of maimed men returning to the city. The absence of those who did not return felt keenly in its many streets, where children starved without fathers, mothers wept over sons, and survivors struggled to regain old lives. Across the country a decimated landscape yielded only death and sorrow.

Inside The Stone Kitchen, there was an underlying tension as de Montfort took over the Tower with his right-hand man, Hugh Despenser, once more Constable of the Tower. Will, John, and Hannah were wary around de Montfort's men, as they displayed the arrogance of the winner. The Tower's residents were also uneasy in their company and Will was constantly concerned that things might turn nasty. That evening was no exception, as the de Montfort men positively crowed with delight over the Tower's latest prisoner.

'Hidden in a windmill!' one soldier exclaimed with a laugh. 'The great Earl of Cornwall himself, defeated at Lewes and now here as a prisoner, shackled as well when they brought him in. How the mighty have fallen.'

'How long will he be here?' asked one of the Tower guards tentatively.

'A few days at least, while they decide what to do with him. Though I hear he will probably be sent to his sister in Leicester.'

'Isn't she de Montfort's wife?'

'Yes, you ignorant idiot,' the soldier sneered. 'But for now, the great man resides in one of the White Tower's turrets with just as much comfort as he deserves. I would have chained him to the walls of the Black Hall if it were me.' He smacked his lips with gusto as he swigged his ale.

Will and John glanced at each other, noting the latest news and watching the men to make sure the atmosphere stayed calm. They knew Hannah would stay out of sight as much as she could whilst de Montfort remained at the Tower.

The next morning, one of Despenser's men came to the alehouse and ordered John to take the Earl his morning ale. John thought it lucky that Richard was not kept in the circular turret which was haunted by his grandmother, but in one of the square ones overlooking the Inner Bailey. The room was sparsely furnished with a bed, a table, and a chair. Richard sat by the window, his clothes full of dirt and dust, his face grubby and worn, but his dark eyes were still alert as he turned to look at John.

'Your name?' Richard demanded, as the man set the ale jug on the table.

'John Lund, sir. I come from the alehouse with your provisions, as ordered by the Constable.'

'The alehouse down there?' Richard pointed through the window down into the Outer Bailey.

'Aye, sir, The Stone Kitchen.'

'Just you, is it, in this alehouse?' he enquired.

'I live there with my father, Will Lund.' John omitted his wife's name.

'Will Lund?' He paused for a moment as if remembering the name. 'How long has he been there, and is your mother dead?'

'I believe my father has lived here for over twenty years, my lord, and my mother died in the wall collapse of 1241,' he replied, although he couldn't help but wonder why this man, the Earl of Cornwall, was so interested in his family. He longed to be gone from the cold room and back in the warmth of his home as he felt the Earl study him intently. He wanted no attention brought to his family, especially Hannah, whose uncle was so embroiled with this man.

Richard continued to stare at him, sensing the man's unease. So intent was he on looking at John Lund's resemblance to his own family. He thought it a strange coincidence that the girl's death on the collapsing wall was the fateful day he had learnt of Isabella's death. With a wave of his hand, Richard abruptly dismissed him. There was nothing he could do about the Lunds now and he did not want his brother-in-law to know anything about their existence. When the time was right, Richard would be ready to use the information he had gained from a dying woman.

Richard thought back to the convent which he had made time to visit just before the latest battle. The Queen had been insistent that he went to see his sister Isabella's old servant. She had received urgent letters from the prioress saying that Margaret Bisset could not be at peace until she spoke to Isabella's brother for a last act of service and love for her long-dead mistress. And so, he had gone for Isabella's sake, his favourite sister whose death he had never got over. He missed her still. The nun's cell had been too warm and fetid even on the autumn day, and he could smell death upon the aged crone who lay propped up on damp pillows. When he had entered the cell, she fluttered open her beady eyes and stretched out a withered arm to pull him closer.

'You came, my lord! Thanks be to God, for I need to do this last service for my Empress,' she said faintly.

'It took you long enough! Why wait so long?' He winced at her foul breath.

'My mistress insisted I wait until the boy was an adult or I was about to die. I know I should have done it sooner. She told me to return it only to the boy, but I never found the time, and as I know my life is shortening, you are my only hope at getting it to him. You must hear me out.'

And she croaked out a tale of lust and secrets that only his sister would have been part of, Richard mused. He had known of his sister's appetites, of her desires, and he had vaguely remembered the alehouse boy; and of course he remembered the girl he had fucked on that wedding voyage. How strange that their lusts had entwined like that. His sister was even more like him than he knew, hunting for sport. He could not blame her that last act of pleasure, knowing now the unhappy marriage she had endured despite the comforts of being Empress.

'There in my trunk you will find a pouch with the Imperial crest on it. Inside is a letter for her son, a ring she had made, and an old rosary chain Will Lund gave to her. She wanted them given to the boy,' Margaret explained.

He retrieved the pouch and looked inside. The letter did not interest him except to prove the boy's birthright. The ring was beautiful, with a relief of John the Baptist – a clever deception to remember her son under a religious guise – and then he looked at the rosary chain.

'Did Isabella ever examine this?' he asked the old servant, his breath catching in astonishment.

'No,' she said feebly. 'I remember her laughing at such a tawdry trinket. He said it was his mother's, and it was a love token for my mistress from him. She had so many jewels then and we forgot she had it until it fell out of a cloak pocket one day.'

Tower of Vengeance

She paused for a moment to gather her strength before continuing. 'We hid it and when she lay dying, she told me to return it to her son with the letter and the ring.' She was now rasping for breath.

Richard looked once again at the rosary and at the inscription on the red ruby cross – *What is hidden, will be found* – it was the de Mandeville motto.

'Well, well, well,' he said with a smile. 'Not merely an alehouse boy after all, but a de Mandeville heir with a royal bastard. What I can do with these two!' He smirked, pleased to have found new allies to do his bidding at a point when he worried his family's hold was weakening.

Seeing the boy John today had left him in no doubt that the servant had been right. Years ago, when he saw the alehouse woman with her young son, he thought he recognised those dark eyes as his own and had believed the child was his bastard. But now Richard had confirmation the boy was in fact Isabella's child, not his.

The door to his turret opened again and Hugh Despenser's ugly face appeared.

'Your stay with us is to be short, it would seem. Tomorrow, you join your sister at her manor in Leicester. You will have a nicer prison at least.' Despenser smirked as he told him the plan, before leaving Richard to mull over his fate. He was grateful to leave this infernal place, as he had never much cared for the Tower and hated that their brother had locked Isabella away here before her marriage. But if he were to leave, that didn't give him much time to see more of the two men who could yet shape his own destiny. For the de Mandeville heir could be a useful pawn, dislodging the uncle who sided with the King's enemies, and he also had some claim to the Fitzwalter estates through his mother. His sister's bastard could be used in Sicily – that turbulent country with a history for giving illegitimate heirs thrones. Yes, Richard could use some leverage there and Frederick's own bastard son, the current incumbent, could easily be replaced with another, which would give him the powerful overseas ally he needed to make him stronger again.

All Richard could hope now is that the Queen and Prince Edward would be able to rally the royal forces behind the King and regain control of the country. Then they could free him from de Montfort so he could regain his own power again. For his two new players would be unknown to anyone but him, giving him a useful advantage. He looked out of the narrow window towards The Stone Kitchen, smoke curling out of its chimney. He just needed to wait for his opportunity. He smiled, enjoying the look of disconcertment on Despenser's face.

The Garden

Hannah was alone in the King's garden, collecting the last of the autumn's herbs for her stillroom before the coming frosts destroyed the less hardy of them. The garden was a pleasant, quiet space within the Tower, tended by an old man who lived above the stables and, although its main purpose was to support the royal kitchens, it was also allowed to be used by the alehouses. The old man knew Hannah and left her to her own devices as a regular visitor. She often came here early in the day when the dew was present on the plants, the bees were starting to gather around the flowers, and the birds were singing in the fruit trees. It was a relatively young garden, but the trees had been there for many years and produced a good crop, which was useful for her remedies.

In the garden, Hannah could always feel Maude's presence, and today her spirit was restless and angry. She suspected the cause being the Earl of Cornwall languishing in the turret above them. Hannah too felt anxious by his appearance within the walls of her home. Not for the first time she wondered how Will had coped all these years hiding in plain sight of his enemies. Hannah believed her own feelings of dread would never leave her – she was worried that someone would identify her as a Jew, after all unlike Will, she had grown up in a community that knew who she was. Her father, she had heard, had now returned to his faith and was once again a marked man; therefore, she dare not make contact with him even if she wanted to. Her uncle

Hagin worked secretly for Earl Richard and would gladly give her up for more favours once the Earl was a free man. And now Hugh Despenser had returned to the Tower with Simon de Montfort himself, who had murdered so many of her community. Despenser was of course the man who had thrown her into the cage and now she lived in constant anxiety that he would recognise her even after these passing years.

Her eyes hovered over the beautiful belladonna plant growing in a secluded corner of the garden, hardy even in this cruel cold air. The belladonna was hidden away from most, luckily, but she knew its power, and she wondered if this was the answer to her problems. A small concoction mixed in her stillroom and added to Despenser's wine. There had recently been a spate of unexplained deaths amongst some of the nobility – talked about in the alehouse as poisonings by foreigners keen to stir up trouble. She quickly dismissed the thought, or rather it felt like Maude had penetrated her thoughts to stop her from making a foolish mistake.

'Will you do it then?' Hannah challenged Maude. 'I know what you are capable of!'

Maude laughed at her. 'Maybe I could, but we have to use Death wisely, and I don't feel he is an immediate threat to us. We will be rid of him soon enough,' she assured Hannah.

'I've been calling to you from the gate,' whispered John, wrapping his arms around her and startling her. 'You were lost in your own thoughts.'

Tower of Vengeance

'You fool, John! I thought you were one of Despenser's men come to drag me away, back to that cage!'

'I'm sorry, my love,' he said meekly, chiding himself for a silly jest. 'I didn't think. Are you alright?' He hugged his wife close.

'It's not just me you need to be careful of now,' she said, and placed a protective hand on her stomach where new life was growing. Their daughter.

'And how is our babe today?'

'Kicking good and proper,' Hannah said with a smile, as the babe responded to her mother's voice. 'I am so scared now that man is back, John. What if he recognises me?' she said in a hushed voice.

'You hardly look the same as that poor girl who was thrown in the cage. It's been a few years, and I doubt he would expect to see you here of all places.'

'That's what your father says. If you hide in such a place as this no one expects to see you.' She remembered Will's words and the wisdom he had gained from living his life the same way as hers in the shadow of the Tower.

'Well, he should know. And Despenser and these other men have enough to deal with fighting the King to worry about the likes of us at the moment. We are of no importance to anyone right now, are we?' he argued.

She nodded, knowing he made a good point as there were bigger battles to be fought from what they had heard the night before in the alehouse. 'Maude is worried though, I feel it. She senses something bad is coming.'

John shuddered, knowing that Maude was unstable and could unleash her power at any given moment. They could all sense her frustrations against the royal family and they wondered how it would and could end for all of them, knowing what she was capable of.

'Come, let us return home. It's time to breakfast and get ready for the day. Father will wonder where we are. He worries about you and the babe so much.' John laughed, amused by this new side to his father.

John took his wife's hand, and they left the stillness of the garden to return to The Stone Kitchen with its noise and bustle.

The raven found herself alone and called to her mate, who was circling the White Tower. He responded in turn, and she flew up to meet him. Together they glided on the gentle breeze, dancing in the air, no troubles for them, merely the sheer joy of the flight until their thoughts turned to food and they set off towards London's busy streets to scavenge what they could. But they too would return to this nest of kings and watch as the Wheel of Fortune turned once again towards Henry's banner.

The Bastard

Five Years Later

Will was alone in the bar of The Stone Kitchen, now officially a tavern as it had begun to serve food other than pottage a few years ago, the ale-stake replaced by a creaking sign over the door. He could hear Hannah and the children in the kitchen. She was chiding them for getting under Bess' feet and he could hear the laughter of the serving girls in the cellar below as they brewed the Tower's famous ale.

John was over at The Golden Chain overseeing the wine delivery from the All Hallows Priory. The Chain too was a tavern now and both businesses were profitable. The taverns were clean, spacious, and provided both good food and drink plus a warm welcome. They supplied not only the Royal Apartments with ale and wine, but also provided victuals to those prisoners who could afford it, and the crown continued to pay them to supply the workmen with a daily allowance. The soldiers and guards were ever their regulars.

Will sat by the fire resting his tired body. He was feeling his age, and the mornings were hard now as his joints stiffened overnight. But life was good – his two grandchildren, with another on the way, provided him with joy and were such happy children. Hannah and John had turned all their lives around, creating a contented family at last. He only wished that Emma had lived to see what Hannah and John had done, making The Stone Kitchen a proper home with a real family within it. The only sadness was the death of Joan, his dearest, closest friend, but the years had finally caught up with her and they all missed her kindness and love.

Five years had passed since Evesham battlefield, where Prince Edward's army had finally prevailed and returned his father, the King, to his rightful place at the seat of power. Simon de Montfort had been killed at last and falling with him were Hugh Despenser and the last of the de Mandevilles. There had been mixed emotions in The Stone Kitchen as Hannah had experienced relief that de Montfort was no longer a threat to her or the Jewish community, but Will had felt some resentment over the loss of the de Mandeville name and the earldom. He knew that there was no chance of gaining it now.

The Tower was not required by the royal family in times of peace, and it held such unhappy memories for the King. Maude remained a constant presence in their lives. However, she too seemed to have a period of stillness, but Will knew this would not last long with his mother, as the royal family prospered and that could not please her. Hannah spoke of unfinished business, of some form of doubt, and now he could sense Maude growing restless again, as if waiting for something or someone. It reminded Will of that time just before Isabella had arrived and it made him uneasy too.

He was dozing now, enjoying the warmth of the fire, his breakfast taken and a mug of ale by his side. The tavern door opened, bringing a gust of cold morning air. Will forced his eyes open and grunted, 'We are closed!'

'I'm looking for Will Lund, or should I say William de Mandeville?' The stranger entered the room, certain this was the man he had been dispatched to find.

Will froze. The years fell away, and he was that young boy running scared on the London road worried he would be captured. He recovered himself, because this man in front of him was no soldier. He was well dressed – of good breeding, it would seem – and he was also alone, which would be unlikely if Will were to be arrested.

'Who are you?' Will asked him.

'I am Philip of Cornwall, bastard son of Earl Richard.'

The Earl was Isabella's brother. Will felt the shadows dance behind him, the malevolence of Maude within the room. And so, it had finally come. The day of reckoning.

Philip sat himself down on the chair opposite.

'In this bag I have orders from my father for you and your son to return with me to his household,' he explained.

'How do you know I am William de Mandeville?' Will demanded.

Philip reached into his bag and pulled out a pouch plus the written orders of his father, and he placed them on the table.

'This rosary chain you gave the Princess Isabella was your mother's, and proof that you are the rightful de Mandeville heir. My father requires your fealty to his banner. He means no harm to you and only demands your loyalty.'

Will was stunned. He had waited so many years to recover his birthright, but after the passing of Fitzwalter, he had given up all hope of it coming to pass.

'Why now after all this time?' Will demanded.

'You must know the rest of the de Mandevilles are dead and the earldom is vacant? My father needs a strong ally, and if he helps you regain what is rightfully yours, he would expect loyalty in return. He is a powerful man and has re-established his own wealth, but like all great men, he desires more, and you have a son who could be very useful to his cause.'

'Why do you need my son? I will accompany you alone,' Will countered.

Philip continued, 'Also in this pouch is proof that your son, John Lund, is the son of Isabella of England and nephew to the Earl. Your son therefore has a claim on the crown of Sicily and my father has use of him there. After all, bastards have successfully held the throne there, so why not your son? My father aims to extend his power base and, although to me it seems a long shot, my father grows older, and this is perhaps his last throw of the dice.'

Will was no longer listening to the man's words. He did not care why Richard wanted his son. Right now, it seemed as if the world had stopped. All he could think was that it could not be true. John was his and Emma's son. Emma had returned home from Italy so they could be a family. But as Will thought about the man's claims, it began to make sense. The dark taunting eyes, the way John tilted his head, the slight smile when he was being persuasive and oh yes, he had his mother's charm and grace. How had he not seen it before?

Noting the confusion on the man's face, Philip realised he had not known the truth until now. He handed him a letter and a ring.

'My father says this will explain and should be given to your son along with this token.'

Reading the letter, Will felt a range of emotions as the room grew darker and the atmosphere changed.

Hannah came through from the kitchen carrying ale jugs and stopped as she saw the stranger with Will.

'Oh, I am sorry. I didn't realise you had a visitor.' She was curious as to who the finely dressed man was, as he was not their usual patron, and also wondered why she could see Maude glowering in the corner of the room.

Will quickly folded up the letter.

'Could you give us a moment alone, Hannah. We won't be long,' Will said calmly.

'Of course.' She nodded and left them.

'I need time to think this through,' Will told him. 'This news comes as a great shock. We have a life here, and my son has a wife and children. We can't just leave them, but then I can't deny them their birthright,' he reasoned.

'I can only delay a little while. We need to leave tomorrow,' Philip insisted.

'Come back tonight after the curfew bell. The guards will of course let you in, being the Earl's man. Meet me here and we can talk it over after the day is done. First, I need to speak to my son alone. The Earl owes me that,' Will was insistent.

Philip's father had given orders that the Tower Constable must not know of his visit. It was imperative that the true identities of the Lunds was kept secret until the men were under Richard's roof, his control, his banner if he were to gain the advantage he desired from his scheming.

'That seems sensible, but you must realise you have no choice. If you don't come willingly, these orders from the Earl give me the power to raise the Tower's Constable and guards to make you yield to me,' Philip bluffed, as he put the precious orders back in his bag. Both men knew it was inevitable that

Tower of Vengeance

the de Mandeville men would have to go with him – the Earl brooked no dissent.

Will sank back in his chair as Philip left. He tucked the pouch into his tunic, hiding it away from prying eyes. At the mention of Isabella's name, he realised the power she still had over his heart after all. But for now, all his thoughts were on finally gaining what was rightfully his. At last, he could become the man he should always have been. And John would have the chance for such riches – such a life they could have at court! No more hiding his own identity. He could claim the de Mandeville title and return to his home, which would satisfy Maude who had wanted this for so long. He would need to persuade his son and Hannah that this would be a good thing for their family, but he was not sure that Hannah would agree.

Slowly the tavern sprang into life around him as they prepared for morning service. The girls brought up the ale and John returned from his errand at the Chain. The first of the day's customers arrived with the soldiers, the workmen and women, the guards, the bakers, the smiths, amongst those seeking the morning repast. As they took their places around him, Will suddenly felt like a stranger in his own life. The pouch and the truths it held weighed heavy in his pocket and left Will with an important decision to make. He could reclaim his identity and reveal his son's birthright, which would mean he and John would become Richard's pawns in a power game he did not understand. But to defy the Earl of Cornwall, King John's own son, could bring more dire consequences for his family. Either way, Will now realised he could lose all that he had gained over these past few years.

In the circular turret, a storm is raging. A maelstrom of hatred as the smell of belladonna fills the air. The Wheel of Fortune is spinning frantically, not knowing which way to turn. Plantagenet lions with their blue tongues and slashing claws circle the ravens eerily. The ravens screech in defiance but their dark, merciless eyes dart in agitation, as all could be about to be lost.

The Poppet

When the afternoon rush was over, John had hurriedly left for a meeting with a wine merchant in the city, leaving Bessie to mind the children in front of the fire. Hannah was busy in her stillroom preparing her tinctures for her customers. Will came through to the kitchen with some more of the empty jugs, still working as usual but his mind elsewhere on the news that he was about to be finally acknowledged as the Earl of Essex. He would no longer be Will Lund, the tavern keeper, within the Tower of London. He decided he would talk with John on his return. There was a nudge at his elbow, and he looked down at his granddaughter. Eliza, the eldest, had dark straight hair which reminded him of his mother, and her left webbed foot was a secret mark of her heritage. It was strange how the webbing must have bypassed John. Nature has its own tricks and perhaps, he now wondered, John's royal blood had something to do with it.

'Hello, sweetheart. How's my favourite girl?' He smiled.

'This is for you, Grandpa.' And she held out her hand. Will could not believe what he saw. Eliza thrust the poppet into his unwilling hand and trundled back to the fire, oblivious to what she had done. He went to call her back, to question her on where she had found the hideous doll, but he could not speak. Instead, he stumbled through to the storeroom, where he found Hannah mixing a healing lotion for one of the smiths who had burnt his arm quite badly. At first, she didn't even acknowledge Will's presence in the stillroom. But when he didn't speak, she looked up to see who had entered the room without a greeting.

'Will, are you alright? Do you need to sit down?' His face was pale and haggard, and she feared he was unwell with a fever taking root.

'Do you know where this came from?' He held out the poppet and Hannah gently took it from him, slowly looking at it. 'Eliza just gave it to me, and I had thought it long gone.' The shock was evident on his face.

'The children had it? Where could they have got it from?' she murmured. 'I haven't seen it before. This is no ordinary toy. It is full of enchantment. How do you know it?' she asked him, and then listened intently as Will retold the story of Jane's sister and how they had all believed it was Alice's childhood toy, given to him by Maria all those years earlier to help prove his claim as Jane's nephew.

'You all saw what you wanted to see,' Hannah explained. 'It is not Alice's, yet Jane believed it was. Its purpose was to bring you here. To save you from the road, to save Jane from destitution, for she would never have been able to keep The Stone Kitchen going alone, and it was to bind you and Emma together. It contains deep, powerful magic,' she explained. 'But the poppet has not returned by chance. What was that man's business this morning?'

Tower of Vengeance

Will reluctantly told Hannah what Philip had told him; it was in some way a relief to unburden himself and to discover what she thought of this new life ahead of them. He could have told John first, but he had turned to her knowing that she had a power of her own, especially with Maude. Hannah listened in astonishment as she absorbed the revelations of Richard's man. Her body started to tremble with fear. She clenched her fists to stop her shaking hands.

'I fear how John will react to the news of his lineage, especially when he had no idea that I had betrayed Emma with a princess whose brother is the King. He has had so much to deal with in his life, and now there will be the upheaval of leaving here and going to Court…'

'How can we though?' Hannah interrupted. 'Someone will recognise me; my Uncle Hagin is Richard's moneylender. We will all be in danger if he sees me, so I cannot go to Court. Yet even if I stay here, John will be sent to Sicily – never to return.' She gripped Will's arm, as if to shake him back to reality. 'Richard's son, Henry, is already dead – we heard the news only the other night about how he was murdered whilst taking mass in the church at Viterbo by Guy de Montfort avenging his own father's death. These people stop at nothing to kill, and there will be more than enough people who will want John dead too. We are finally happy, so how can you risk all of this to return to a life you never knew?' Hannah questioned him.

'My whole life has been a lie, and now I have the chance to tell the truth.' He shook himself free of her grasp, not willing to believe her. This was what he had wanted, and he suspected why his mother had stood watch all these years to see justice being done and his birthright restored. Hannah looked him squarely in the eyes, undeterred.

'We have made a life that matters. Do not let this news change this and make you think once again that it is not enough. This poppet is a warning and controlled your choice then as you fled your life as a de Mandeville. You gave that life up to become a Lund, and now you must choose your own destiny. You can stay here, be content and loved with the family you have made; or go, become the Earl of Essex, be controlled by Richard, or even killed by the King, who thinks of you as a traitor to be hunted down. And if not Henry, then his son Edward, whose reputation goes before him and who hates Jews with such a passion, he seeks to wipe us from this world.'

'I am sorry, Hannah, for putting you in this position,' Will apologised. 'Naively, I hoped that the title would make you safe and it would make life better. Now I am not so sure.'

Hannah could feel a presence lurking on the shadows as the familiar smell of roses filled the air.

'No, Maude! This is his choice. You chose revenge and that is your fate, but he is alive, he can be free. You cannot control him,' Hannah defended, not caring if she risked Maude's ire. For once it was out of Maude's hands and Hannah only hoped Will would make the right decision by them.

'But what can I do? There is no choice.' Will sighed helplessly. 'I am expected to leave with Philip. I am not free. Isabella's confession changed it all and we are discovered. There is proof confirming our identities,' Will argued.

'Know that if you leave willingly like a fool, you will likely never be able to return. You or John. We all lose you. Maude can't leave and neither can I. I will not go into the lion's den, and I will not allow my children to either.'

'John won't leave without you,' Will realised, not wanting to break the family apart.

'The news that Isabella is his mother will put us at more risk when it is revealed,' Hannah said, her voice catching in her throat. 'It's fine to be a bastard of a prince but not of a princess, and the King could kill you for that alone! You will have more enemies as William de Mandeville than as plain Will Lund. You are only alive while you are useful to Richard, while he lives. He is an old man, and a new age is almost upon us. They already say the King is dying. Edward will not need you and he will sooner kill us all than have you inherit your birthright and pose a threat to his reign.'

As Hannah spoke, it brought to mind Emma's words long ago when she told him how her father had warned her not to trust kings. Hannah was right – he was about to place his entire family at risk by trusting the royal family. Everything came down to this moment. He looked at Hannah, so indignant in her rage; he felt Maude's anger; and he suddenly saw clearly the waste of his own life stretched out behind him, spent craving a life he had never known – a life that was now on offer but could mean the end of all of them.

The poppet lay on the work bench, reproachful in its malevolence, and Will found it odd that such an inconsequential thing had led him here, controlling his own destiny. Hannah saw him gazing at it. 'We must destroy it,' she told him. 'And Philip's orders too, to delay while we can, for if you accept, we will all be destroyed. We are all in danger from that man and his plots. We must fight for our family now. King John's family cannot destroy us any more than they already have.'

But for Will, it was hard to think about letting go of his long-held dream of returning to his childhood home. Yet Hannah was right because it was not home, and he would never be able to go back to what he had briefly known there. His mother wouldn't be there, in her own stillroom, to welcome him back, and the house would be a stranger to him. His memories were here, his family were here, and the life he had lived was here. As he grew older, that was all that he needed. Soon the curfew bell would ring, and a choice would have to be made. Life or death.

'Have I wasted my life wanting to be someone else?' he whispered.

'Is your family a waste? Your son? Your grandchildren?' Hannah wrapped her arms around him. 'It's what you have now that counts. Will you be happier without us? With a title? To leave this all behind – all you have achieved.'

    Will thought of Isabella. When he had known her, she had wanted her new life as Empress, coveting the riches and jewels that her marriage would bring her, measuring her own happiness by status and wealth. But her letter had told a different story, and she wanted her son to be free. Did he not owe it to her and to Hannah to ensure John lived a life away from the schemes of a corrupt and devious Court? John represented everything good in Will's life, his greatest achievement, and he would do everything to protect his son.

    He kissed Hannah on the cheek, pulled himself free from her warm embrace, and picked up the poppet. Hannah watched wordlessly as he left the room, knowing this was Will's tale and his to end.

Maude

You would think I would be happy. All that I ever desired for my son – his title and his home – are finally to be returned to him. But, like Hannah, I do not trust Richard. He wants my son for his own schemes, his own power, and I fear that nothing good can come of this.

I always thought my grandson to be Richard's, which was bad enough, but I cannot bear the news that he is the whore's son. Emma put herself at risk trying to protect that woman's son and the girl was too good for us. I dismissed her as an alewife's daughter, but she was the strongest of us all and she possessed a capacity for love that none of us can match. The Devil tried to tell me with his wretched tarot card – Strength. I thought it signified my own strength when in fact it was Emma's all along. And I killed her. I regret that now.

At the time I thought Will would be destroyed if it was revealed John was not his son. Yet John was his son, and Emma had a heart big enough to love a boy that was in fact her rival's. What courage she must have had. She who was treated badly by me and Will, and by Isabella and Richard too – we are the same after all. Each death has a consequence, and the Devil warned me. But the Lunds were the only people who ever showed us real love and I have destroyed them. Her father tried to help me, her mother gave my boy a home, and Emma gave her heart. Now there are no Lunds left and we have taken it all. I can never put that right and it will torment me in my own hell. I cannot regret Matthew though…that would push me too far. He was a worthy death. He really would have destroyed my family.

      For once I am powerless. I cannot kill Philip as he has royal blood. I rage at the injustice, the irony of it all that Richard will take my boys to be used for his own means. King John's son offers us all we ever wanted but it's poisoned once again. We are at the mercy of that wretched family. I hear the curfew bell chime, and I am about to lose my son once again. I summon the Devil. He owes me after all, for a burnt chapel, and he promised to honour the debt. Perhaps there is another bargain to be made.

The Reckoning

The bells of All Hallows chimed midnight as Philip approached the Tower's entrance. The curfew had rung long before but as Earl Richard's son he had the authority to come and go as he pleased. He approached the lone sentry on guard. The soldier, bored and tired, glanced at his papers and unlocked the gate to let him through with little thought. London was peaceful now as the city held its breath waiting for the death of the King who lay dying at Westminster.

Philip walked along the causeway towards the second gatehouse, where another sentry and another locked gate awaited him. A mist had settled, shrouding the Tower like death's winding sheet, and he could barely see beyond his own feet. Strange. The night had been so clear just a moment ago. He shivered as he pulled his cloak around him, checking his bag was secure with its precious orders. He needed to get to The Stone Kitchen to meet with the two men who could shape the destiny of two crowns. What a find they were for their cause here and in Sicily – something to stir up the barons again and threaten Prince Edward's soon-to-be throne.

The shriek stopped him. It sounded like his mother calling his name, but she was long dead. He could make out a gap where the causeway's wall had somehow crumbled away. He could hear the lapping of the moat against the Tower walls, but instead of the usual noxious smell, he thought he could smell

Tower of Vengeance

roses. A dread settled on him, and the mist held him in a chilling embrace. Philip, panicked now, went to turn away from the wall's breach – to get to the safety of the gatehouse, to summon the soldier from the guard room – but as he did so, he felt a shove on his back. In his terror, he lost his balance, and now he was tumbling through the breach, and within seconds the moat appeared to come up to meet him, sucking him into its murky depths. Philip struggled against the sludge and shit, his arms flaying around as he tried to save himself, but the moat dragged him further down as if devouring its prey. As the life drained out of him, the bag around his waist worked free and the Earl of Cornwall's final orders were lost, falling downwards to the bottom of the moat.

In the guard room, Godric the night watchman thought he heard a noise, and he reluctantly left the warm room. He opened the gate and walked a little way down the causeway. The night was now clear. Nothing stirred. As he went to return, he glanced behind him into the Tower's Outer Bailey, and he saw a woman walking toward the White Tower, her dark cloak swinging around her as a raven flew beside her. He turned back to lock the gate, and then he looked for her again, ready to call out to her, but she was gone, only the raven flying up to the Tower's circular turret. Godric shrugged – the night played tricks in this place, and he longed for his warm bed in the room above the guard house. Instead, he returned to his watch and hoped the morning would come soon.

Tower of Vengeance

As the clock struck one, Will banked down the fire before finally going to bed. He turned over the golden chain in his hand and a memory of Isabella came into his mind. John was his son, and his heart filled with joy. He had always loved John; he had been the best of sons, and fortunately he had none of the deceit of King John's family. John must have inherited all the goodness of Will and Isabella. He had proved this with his love of Hannah, the risks he had taken for her and the life they had built together. Will longed to protect them from Richard, for them to be safe there in the Tower; together, they had built the taverns into a thriving business which would provide for their children in future too. Still holding the chain, he climbed the stairs to his room and once again felt the emptiness of the bed, the absence of Emma, and he dreamed of her, filled with love and longing for her after learning the sacrifices she had made for him. He dreamt of grey-green eyes rather than the dark eyes that had constantly haunted him.

* * *

When the morning bells rang out across the city, one of the soldiers waking in the upstairs room of the gatehouse looked out of one of the arrow slits. Glancing down towards the causeway, he noticed the breach in the wall.

'Oy, Ned, come and look at this,' he called back to his companion. Ned came over to him and looked at what he was pointing at. 'Was that hole in the wall there yesterday?'

'Not that I remember! Bloody hell, how could that have happened? The Constable's not going to be happy.'

As they looked, something seemed to move in the moat.

'What in God's name is that?' exclaimed Ned, pointing in horror to the hand sticking out of the murky water.

The men raised the alarm and the Constable, Walter de Gray, ordered that the body be retrieved and identified if possible. It was not easy to remove the body from the moat as they dragged it out, using their spears to hook the body; the chain of men steadying each other were fearful of a slip that could send them tumbling to the same fate.

'Where is the night watch? Did they see anything? And when did this breach appear?' Walter was not best pleased with having to attend to this matter before he'd even broken his fast.

The night watch was brought before him, and the sentry testified that Philip of Cornwall had entered at midnight, but no one had yet to see him leave. The other sentry, Godric, denied seeing Philip, and that the man had not requested entrance at the second gatehouse. He did not mention the woman he thought he had seen for fear of seeming a fool.

Tower of Vengeance

Walter turned pale at the thought of the body being that of Earl Richard's son – bastard or not, the man was still royal, and this had happened on his watch, so there would be consequences.

By now quite a crowd had gathered at the causeway. Will had left the tavern to get some air and, noticing the commotion by the gatehouse, he had joined the rest of the spectators as they watched the body emerge from the water. Even now with the dirt which encased him, Will could see it was Philip. He pushed forward to see if the bag Philip had worn yesterday was on his body, for in it had been the Earl's orders which could yet destroy his family.

'Nothing on him, sir, apart from this ring with what looks like the Cornwall crest on it,' one of them informed the Constable, who sighed in dismay as Will slumped against one of the walls, relief coursing through his body. The bag must have sunk into the moat. A reprieve at least, and he could easily hide the letter, the ring, and the chain that Philip had left with him. Without that evidence, what could Richard prove? They were free at last.

He watched as the body was taken for immediate burial in the Tower's graveyard, which stood beside the newly built Chapel. The body stank so much from the filth of the moat that the Constable could not possibly send it back to his family. The crest on the ring would have to be identification enough. Walter sent a messenger to Earl Richard and would have to wait anxiously for what came next.

Tower of Vengeance

Will slipped away from the crowd to return to The Stone Kitchen and open it to its first customers of the day. Godric the night watch entered, in need of a strong ale, which Will was quick to pour, always ready with a jug of well-brewed ale and a reassuring manner that meant patrons confided in him.

'I thought I heard a noise,' Godric recounted, relieved to talk to a man he could trust. 'But it didn't sound like a splash, more like one of those ravens making an ungodly sound like they do. I looked out and it was clear along the causeway when a few moments before it had been so dark. And now I think on it, the gate was unlocked, and I dare not tell the Constable that. There was something else too.' He took a gulp of ale as he recalled in hushed tones something about seeing a lady and the raven.

'It must have been the raven you heard, and as for the woman, it was most likely a trick of the light, a mere shadow. There could not have been a woman at that hour,' Will assured him. 'You were overtired but did nothing wrong. If you saw nothing else, it would be wise not to speak on it any further. Just drink your ale and get to bed. You need sleep, my boy.' Will patted him reassuringly on the back and sent him on his way.

Will looked round for his son. It would be easy enough to burn the letter, but he had promised John there would be no more lies after Matthew's death and he needed to tell him the truth. John knew his father had been unfaithful to Emma but not that it had been with such a woman as Isabella, but to find out he was also her son would be a huge shock. But

Richard knew and once he found out Philip was dead, he would surely send another man, another order for John to be brought to him. The bag had disappeared, but it had only delayed things for a time until Richard sent more orders. John would know the truth then – better for it to come from him now and for him to be forewarned.

'You alright, Pa?' John, walking by with the ale jugs, saw his father hesitate as he saw him.

'I need to give you something, but better we do it later when the tavern is quiet.' Decision made; the truth was best.

'Oh, I forgot to tell you the latest news, Pa. A messenger just arrived. Earl Richard died a few days ago, and now the Constable is unsure who to send news to regarding his son's death.' After departing his news, John walked away to serve the men.

Will closed his eyes, listening to the tavern around him. The mugs clanking, the dice rolling, and the laughter of the soldiers as they broke their day's fast on the bread Hannah was giving them. They were safe. No more threat from Richard. Was it over? He felt the pouch tied to his waist, where it had remained since he had been given it. He could easily cast the letter into the fire, throw the ring into the moat, and hide his mother's chain. He doubted his son would remember his earlier comment; he had been so distracted by the message, the customers in the tavern, and always his eyes searching out his beautiful wife. The letter could destroy his happiness and make him like his own father – a victim to his own identity, unable to be satisfied with the life he had. Because that had always been Will's problem – he recognised that now. That endless dissatisfaction with everything he had. But John was so much stronger than him, and the love he had with Hannah would surely see him through. And of course, Hannah already knew they had no secrets from each other, and Will could not ask her to keep one so big as this. She would want her husband to know the truth.

And finally, Isabella had loved her son and wanted him to know she had loved him. Did he want to deny her that? Will had loved her once and they had made this wonderful boy. Their son. Will was getting older; he felt the weariness in his bones, the aches that would not go away. Soon he would no longer be here to protect his boy, and if someone else knew of his birth, there would be more enemies to come. John should know. Again, the decision was made. Time to face the consequences of the past.

Revelations

When the tavern slumbered from the morning's rush, Will sat down with John by the dying fire as Hannah saw to the children. Will looked serious and John was immediately concerned for his father's health. He was no longer young, and the years had been hard on him with all the turmoil in the Tower. John also knew that both Will and Hannah worried about being discovered, and he wondered if they would ever feel peace.

'Are you alright, Pa? Shall I fetch Hannah?' he asked.

'I'm fine, John, but I once promised you no more secrets, no more lies,' Will began, and John noticed his father's hands were trembling. 'I did keep one piece of information from you regarding the identity of the woman I had the affair with all those years ago. She was Princess Isabella of England, once a prisoner here and the woman I thought I loved,' John gasped. 'There is more to tell, I am afraid. I have this ring to give you and a letter which I will let you read on your own. But I want you to know that what it reveals was news to me too. But I could not keep this from you, although I am scared that you may not forgive me. I will just say this – you are still the same man. You are loved.' Before John could react, Will got up and left him holding a letter faded with time. John carefully unfolded it.

Tower of Vengeance

Foggia 1241

My son,

I am writing this in the hope that one day this reaches you and you will know how much I love you. It's evening here in Foggia. Margaret is lighting the lamps as we await the arrival of my unborn child. Tonight, I have such strange thoughts, and it seems I cannot shake off the past. It's been five years since you left with Emma, and in that time, life has changed so much. When I think back on my old life, I see how much I have changed. I was so proud, so arrogant, so cruel but so happy. I thought I was in prison in that great Stone Tower, and I wanted to get away to my dazzling life as an empress. I dismissed my family and my lover thinking I was so much better than them.

But what did I gain?

A glittering, triumphant wedding journey. To Cologne, where the ladies of the town applauded my beauty and envied my gilded life.

An emperor for a husband. A husband who loved his mistress more than he loved his wives.

Two children who could never replace the ache and loss I felt for you.

Palaces and castles such as the Castel del Monte, which are bathed in light, furnished in luxurious silk, but stand on isolated hills where sparrow hawks hang balancing in the air.

Tower of Vengeance

Isolation. That is what my life has become. Secluded in Frederick's harem. Surrounded by eunuchs – watchful, vicious, nasty spies who control your every move, what you wear, what you eat, and where you sleep.

How I miss the Stone Tower. All its dreariness, its coldness – the heat here exhausts your very soul – and its teeming life. I miss talking with Thomas, laughing with my ladies, plotting with Margaret, and later my friendship with Emma, the woman you will probably know as your mother for yes, we became good friends even after I broke her heart. Your father? Do I miss him?

I can close my eyes when I feel sad and allow myself the indulgence of memory. For no one can control thoughts and memories. I see Will's face; I remember the way he looked at me and how he loved me.

Did I love him? I want to be truthful with you, my son, for truth is such a rare thing. No, is the answer. I was such a damaged soul like all my father's children. We were incapable of love. To us, people were possessions, there to please us and to obey us. We were royal, golden immortals around which the world revolved.

And now I have become such a possession. No longer seen unless my husband wants me to play a part on his Imperial stage. No longer golden. No longer loved. It seems I was cursed when I left that Stone Tower. Tonight, the shadows close in on me, the child inside me no longer kicks, and I feel so

Tower of Vengeance

weary. I have little time left before the eunuchs come to take me into my confinement, for this child is due soon. So, this may be my last chance to write to you, to tell you my story – our story.

We left England in the May of 1234. Emma will have told you perhaps of how she came to travel with me, so I will waste no time on that. By the time we reached Cologne, we realised the seasickness we had both suffered on our journey was in fact due to our pregnancies. I had noticed a change in Emma during the voyage – there was already a sadness about her, but she began to flinch at the slightest noise, and she was scared to be alone. I admit that I was a selfish creature and did not give that the thought I should have. But then the discovery of my pregnancy gave way to such fear of my own and she recognised my predicament, it mirroring her own. She was kind, forgiving even, and suddenly we clung to each other. I admit we tried to rid ourselves of both our babies, but Margaret's foul potions did not work for me at least. But with her help we managed to keep our pregnancies a secret. Somehow, I managed to pass you off as Frederick's after our marriage – thankfully we consummated it the night after the wedding. Fortunately for me, his astrologers predicted that night was auspicious! Oh, the irony. And whether I tricked him into believing I was a virgin I think we both cared not.

Frederick then announced that all my retinue was to return home – that was the first sign that my life was changed forever. I could do nothing to stop this, as I did not have the power I had presumed I would have. He allowed me to keep Margaret and my embroideress, for he liked her work. As Emma by then was too sick to travel, we concocted a story of a dead husband to allow for her pregnancy and Frederick allowed her, and Agnes and Magedla – two maids from my retinue – to reside in Foggia at least until her child was born.

And then I was sent into seclusion and Frederick left. I am never told when he leaves or when he arrives. He tolerates me as his wife, and I believe he finds me pleasing like a pretty jewel he owns. We share a love of falconry, although it is ravens who haunt my dreams.

We had no plan of what to do with you when you arrived. We lived day to day pretending you were Frederick's, who was pleased at such fertility. By luck, Emma was with me that day. She had been allowed to see Margaret because she was still sick. Her baby had not moved or kicked. As Margaret examined her, I felt the pains of labour. Margaret quickly locked the doors, declaring no one should assist the Empress except herself. Frederick was away, and the eunuchs were unprepared and had received no orders as to my confinement, as you, of course in their eyes, were early.

Sadly, Margaret told Emma her baby had no heartbeat, and in that moment our lie was conceived. Margaret gave Emma a herbal concoction to induce her labour. It was easier to swap you with Emma's dead son. We knew there had always been a risk in case you grew up to look like dark-haired Will. Frederick has such red fiery hair to drown out my

Tower of Vengeance

blonde golden locks, so people might have guessed you were not the Emperor's son.

For once in my life, I loved someone unconditionally. You changed me but I couldn't keep you. Even then, you looked like Will with a dark mass of hair, and you were so strong, so lusty. You screamed in Emma's arms as I held that other poor lifeless child with his dull brown hair, swapping our babies.

Frederick didn't care that our child had not survived; he had heirs already and I was young enough to bear more. A year later, I gave him a daughter, Margaret, and the following year, Henry. I love them both dearly, my one joy in this sad, lonely life, and I will love this little one inside me, but my heart aches for you.

I hope you are happy. I know Emma and Will will have loved you as much as I do. I think of you daily. I imagine you in the Tower, not yet brewing ale with Will for you are still so young; perhaps you are chasing the ravens! I laugh at the thought of a royal bastard being brought up under the noses of his own family, perhaps one day running the alehouse and making your own family there. Be careful not to be discovered – my family are not to be trusted, and they see everyone as a threat to their own power or as a pawn in their games.

This letter I will give to Margaret, who is warning me that time is running out. I fear it truly is for me. I look out to the gardens here and the roses smell so strong tonight. Their smell always makes me fearful, I know not why – such beautiful flowers.

I will also return Will's rosary – now I am a mother, I can understand what it meant for him to give that to me, and I am sorry for my cruelty. There is also a ring I always wear – my husband thinks it symbolises John the Baptist, but it is my own personal memento of you. It keeps you near.

Know that you are the beloved son of Isabella of England and of William Lund. Be happy. Be loved. Be free.

Your mother

Isabella

Will had left his son reading a letter that would change his life as much as Prior Thomas had changed Will's all those years ago. He walked out of the tavern into the sun that seemed to light up the White Tower with all its memories and finally he felt peace. The road to the Tower had given him a home, a thriving business, and a family he loved. What more could he want?

He felt a touch on his arm, and he turned to look at his son. He went to speak but John stopped him, his tearful eyes looking into his.

'It's going to be alright, Pa. It changes nothing. Emma was my mother as you are my father. I am proud of Emma, of what she did for us, and I just wish her life had been happier. She lost a son, your son, and still she brought me home. We owe it to her and to Isabella, both of whom risked so much for me, to live and be content with what we have,' John insisted. 'I am just plain John Lund married to Hannah with two growing children. They are all I need, all I want. I know you have struggled with your own identity but that's not me. Everything I love is here. I am happy.'

'I would have told you about Isabella, but I didn't want to endanger this family without reason. I had no idea you were our child,' Will insisted, tears falling down his face.

'Pa, I understand. Of course, I was shocked over the letter and the fact the woman you betrayed my mother with was in fact royal, but it was a long time ago. Hannah has taught me that we can't change the past, we can only move forward.' He looked at the letter in his hand. 'Isabella is dead. I am grateful to her for letting me come here where I am truly loved. She made sure I came home to you and with someone she knew would love me as her own. The Tower is where we belong, is it not?' But he slipped the ring onto his little finger, a tribute to the mother he had never known.

Will smiled at his clever, sensible son, who would have a happier, more contented life than he had known.

'There's ale to be readied for later.' John laughed and they walked back into The Stone Kitchen, where Hannah greeted them, and the children demanded their attention. There was an absence of roses.

Outside the bells started pealing out across the city, mourning bells. The ravens screeched, flying upwards into the sky. A cloud passed in front of the sun and the day was now grey and bleak. But the smell of roses permeated the air as a messenger galloped into the Outer Bailey shouting furiously:

'The King is dead!'

Tower of Vengeance

Maude

The Devil had laughed when I had asked him to change the pact. 'You dare to bargain with me? I decide when the debt is repaid, not you and not yet. The pact cannot be broken, have you not realised this?' I was furious but he continued. 'This is your son's choice, but you can of course help him in some small way – just use your power, my pretty one.'

So, I watched as my son left the tavern after the curfew bell rang. I followed him as he made his way to the gatehouse and hid himself within the shadows. Richard's bastard was on his way, and I knew my son's heart. His choice had been made. The poppet destroyed in a hiss of flames. My beloved son wanted to give up his birthright and not become a pawn of that evil family. It was I who unlocked the gate and caused the breach that gave Will a means. I who created a mist that kept him hidden, as my raven spooked the bastard, and we played some tricks on his mind, but it was Will that shoved him into the moat.

Just like all those years ago when Will had to kill the monk to survive, he killed again for his family. We are all killers if we need to be. Will was no longer The Fool but the Tarot's Magician, taking Richard's reversed card and making it his own. Richard was the trickster, but Will has inherited my alchemy to show a resourcefulness hidden within him. It seems he had to make his own choice over his fate, and I realise now that he could only be happy if it was his decision. He chose The World. The card we all strive for – completion, fulfilment, and ultimately happiness. He has finished his game.

The Wheel of Fortune stops.

'Ah, such happiness for your son,' the Devil says sarcastically. 'His tale is almost over, but what of his son, his children? It's not over for them. I can see more tests to come, but the High Priestess has a daughter with such potential I am almost giddy with excitement.'

A card appears and I watch as the Tower's walls stop falling and instead begin to rise, and I sense yet another threat ahead; but as quickly as I feel it, the card disappears, and I am interrupted by the Devil.

'And you? How goes your revenge tale?' asks the Devil, changing the subject. 'What have you achieved in all this time?'

'I have learnt that Death is too easy a revenge. Death would be too quick, too simple.' The Devil nods, encouraging me to continue. 'Better to curse a life so that they suffer. To lose all that they hold dear – that is a better punishment than a physical death, to be consigned to a living one instead.' The Devil hands me The Hanged Man – such an appropriate card as I turn it in my palm.

'Yes, poor Isabella. Such a lovely curse you made for her.' He chuckled. 'The one thing she most desired was a glittering marriage where she had power and was worshipped. Instead, she gained a

Tower of Vengeance

husband who consigned her to a harem where she became a nobody, a queen in name only, a mother to an emperor's spare heirs.'

'No longer loved, no longer lusted after. All that beauty hidden away. Such a shame she died so soon,' I muse.

'I see you have had a lot of fun with royal marriages. All those Eleanors with their lost children, dissatisfied husbands, and their own unhappy, restless lives. I did wonder though why you didn't kill Simon de Montfort? He was not royal, and you had the opportunity whilst he was here.'

'Is it not better to have him fight his wife's own brother? I made them lust for a crown that brought him to a painful, ignoble death on a dirty battlefield, humiliated and unshriven; and brought Eleanor de Montfort a lifetime of regret and misery in a nunnery.' I was particularly pleased with that curse. 'Though of course, part of me wanted him to destroy those Plantagenet lions, but I feared for Hannah, and I know she binds our fate.'

'You have learnt well, my dear. I almost admire you.' The Devil looks at me with his red, burning eyes – where once I saw kindness, I now see mischief.

I knew my pact with the Devil would come with consequences, for there is always a price to pay. I have paid the ultimate price, as I have become what I most hated – a murderer. Yet it was so easy to succumb to the Devil's charms. He is no monster from the priests' tales, as how else could he seduce

Tower of Vengeance

you? He represents your heart's desire, your lust, your pride, and your revenge.

The Devil laughs, that wicked, sinister sound. 'Don't you find you enjoy it now? After all, it's not a bad way to spend eternity, is it, and there's so much more to do. The King is dead, but long live the King. Time to spin the Wheel again and watch the lions roar once more.'

I feel a frisson of fear, but now he's shuffling his pack, as the Wheel begins to slowly turn once again, and I have to follow his lead. After all, I am more than ready to avenge my death; there is no completion for me, and I feel the new magic within my family beginning to grow. I look eagerly now for the card as he slowly turns it.

The Devil is shown in all his horned splendour, dancing on his victims.

He smiles.

He always wins.

There is no end to this game, just a beginning.

Tower of Vengeance

Historical Note

In researching the book, I have used many historical facts, but for plot purposes some have been changed. This is a summary of the main facts and fiction.

From 1214, there is an entry in *The Tower of London Prisoner Book* for a Maude or Matilda Fitzwalter, for repulsing King John's romantic advances. She was placed in the North East turret of the White Tower in an effort to break her resolve. She refused to yield so she was poisoned by an egg and, in seeking revenge her father, Robert Fitzwalter, led the barons' uprising in 1215 that resulted in the King signing the Magna Carta. There are many theories regarding the truth about Maude – including the story that she was in fact Maid Marion! She was indeed married to Geoffrey de Mandeville, Earl of Essex, and she is buried in Little Dunmow in Essex. There were no surviving children. However, there are stories of her ghost within the White Tower…

Both Robert Fitzwalter and Geoffrey de Mandeville were Magna Carta barons and spent time abroad in exile from John's court prior to Runnymede. Bizarrely, at the start of 1214, Geoffrey married John's first wife, Isabella, Countess of Gloucester, whose marriage with the King had been annulled after he was crowned. Geoffrey paid 20,000 marks for the privilege, but the marriage did not stop him and Isabella joining the baronial rebellion against her former husband. In 1216, Geoffrey died of wounds received in a joust, and in another twist,

Tower of Vengeance

Isabella married Hubert de Burgh, although this union was short-lived when she died shortly afterwards. Geoffrey's brother William succeeded him to the title of Earl of Essex, and he was also married to one of Fitzwalter's daughters, Christina. William died in 1227 without heirs and the earldom became extinct. The motto I have used in the book is of my own invention.

Robert Fitzwalter was patron of Binham Priory in Norfolk and his friend Thomas was the Prior until he was ousted at some point. Robert died in 1235 (for plot purposes I allow him to live a lot longer!) and he was also buried in Little Dunmow Priory. Fitzwalter's grandson, also Robert, was married to Dervorguilla de Burgh, great-granddaughter of Hubert, in 1274.

Hubert de Burgh was a significant figure in the court of both King John and his son King Henry, but he fell from grace under Henry in 1232 and was taken to the Tower. According to the *Prisoner* book, he was bound in chains but was shortly transferred to Devizes. He was pardoned in 1234. In 1236, the knowledge of a secret marriage between his daughter Magota to Richard of Clare became public – King Henry revived the treason charges against de Burgh and the marriage was annulled. Although the charges were dropped, Matthew Paris, the chronicler, records that Magota died of a broken heart.

King John had five children with his second wife, Isabella of Angoulême. After his death she left England, abandoning her children and marrying

Hugues, Count of Marche, the son of her former fiancé!

Henry III came to the throne in 1216 and married Eleanor of Provence in 1236. They had five children: the future Edward I; Margaret, who married Alexander III of Scotland; Beatrice, who married the son of the Duke of Brittany; Edmund, Earl of Lancaster; and Katherine, who was born disabled and died in 1257 to the grief of both her parents. Eleanor was a strongly protective mother and was also known for the influence of her Savoyard uncles, who were greatly resented at court. In 1261, Henry and his wife were besieged in the Tower and when she attempted to reach Windsor by river, she was halted at London Bridge, pelted with stones by an excited mob of Londoners. Henry died in 1272.

Richard, Earl of Cornwall, was one of the richest men in Europe, who had a tempestuous relationship with his brother, the King. He was married several times: first to Isabella Marshall, daughter of William Marshal, 1st Earl of Pembroke, and they had four children. In 1271, their son, Henry of Cornwall, was murdered by Guy de Montfort in Viterbo in revenge for the death of his father Simon at the Battle of Evesham. Richard's second wife was Sanchia of Provence, younger sister of Henry's wife Eleanor, and they had two sons, one of which died in infancy. His third wife was Beatrice de Falkenburg – she was fifteen and he was sixty-one. He had several illegitimate children – one of which was Philip of Cornwall. Richard went on crusade in 1240 and on his return journey in 1241 he visited his sister,

Tower of Vengeance

Isabella, and her husband Emperor Frederick at their court. He was elected King of Germany in 1257. He fought with Henry against Simon de Montfort and was captured after the Battle of Lewes in 1264 after he was discovered hiding in a windmill. He was taken to the Tower for a brief period before being moved to his sister Eleanor's residence, and he was kept prisoner until 1265. He died in 1272.

Isabella of England is also an entry in the *Prisoner* book. She is recorded as being 'held comfortably pending her wedding to Emperor Frederick II of Naples and Sicily'. She was apparently held from 1233 to 1236 and released to marry. There is no obvious reason why she was held in such secure surroundings and three years seems doubtful. Matthew Paris, a monk who chronicled much of the comings and goings of the royal family in his thirteenth-century work *Chronica Majora*, tells us she was brought there in 1235 so that Frederick's ambassadors can interview her, but whether she remained there until her wedding is uncertain. Paris does indeed make a slip by describing Isabella as Henry's wife at one of the Easter feasts where they wore matching clothes, so I have taken the liberty of using this fear of Henry's to be one of the reasons for him sending her away, i.e., he has an incestuous love for his sister and it appals him. I have shortened the period of time she spent at the Tower.

Isabella became Empress on 11th June 1235. Her trousseau is described in King Henry's wardrobe accounts held in the National Archive. The rolls not only mention all the wonderful clothes (at least 122 items), jewels, and that beautiful crown, but all the people who Henry assigned to attend her – sixty-eight men and five women. Where possible, I have used their actual names – in particular: William de Derneford was her serjeant; Alfred Aloet her usher; Jordan her cook; and the unfortunate Ysend who was 'of the chamber'. Her cloak, which Emma is given, is mentioned in the rolls. Margaret Bisset was seen as one of the most important ladies in Isabella's household, although she does seem to have returned in 1238 as she became a long-serving member of Queen Eleanor's household.

Matthew Paris also describes Isabella's wedding procession through Cologne, where she was made to wait for Frederick for six weeks. Frederick was twice her age (she was twenty-one at the time of their marriage – quite late for a royal bride) and he had been married twice before and already had heirs. He also had a long-standing mistress, Bianca Lancia, with whom he had a son, Manfred. All his illegitimate children were educated at court and there were rumours of an Eastern-style hareem. It was said that after her marriage was celebrated, Isabella was handed over to eunuchs and placed in seclusion. All her attendants and servants were sent away apart from Margaret and Kathrein, a renowned embroiderer. There were also two English maids, Agnes and Magedla, who were allowed to reside in Foggia. Isabella had four children: a son named Jordan born in 1236 who died at birth; a daughter Margaret in 1237; Henry in 1238; and her final unnamed child dying at birth in 1241 when Isabella herself died. When her brother Richard saw her at court just before her death, she was pregnant, and he was not granted immediate access – she was rarely permitted to appear in public, although she travelled extensively with Frederick. Isabella died at Foggia on 1st December 1241 - there were rumours of poisoning and ill treatment, rumours which had dogged the death of the Emperor's second wife, Isabella-Yolanda, and she was buried alongside her at Andria. Her son Henry died in 1254 without issue. However, her daughter Margaret married the landgrave of Thuringia, and in a more fruitful union became an ancestor of Prince Albert and Edward VII of England.

The ring Isabella leaves John is of course fictional, but I did base it on a ring that can be found in the Victoria and Albert Museum, Jewellery, Room 91. It dates to the thirteenth century and is a gold signet ring set with a sard intaglio. The intaglio is of a man's head in profile and inscribed round the edge are the words *IOHANNES:EST:NOMEN:EVIS* (John is his name), referring to the naming of John the Baptist.

Eleanor, unlike her sister, was married at a young age (she was nine) in 1224 to the powerful William (II) Marshal, Earl of Pembroke, who was fifteen years older than her. Marshal died in 1231 at the wedding celebrations of her brother Richard, and Eleanor took a vow of chastity and retired from public life. However, she secretly married Simon de Montfort in 1238. They had five children – one of which, Guy, killed her brother Richard's son. After her husband's death at the Battle of Evesham in 1265, she retired to the Dominican convent of Montargis.

Tower of Vengeance

She died in 1275.

The Constables of the Tower are listed in the *Prisoner* book, and I have used the names recorded there but not necessarily in the right order or timeline. I have tried to keep to the thirteenth century. This is the correct timeline for those I have used:

1225–1226 Thomas de Blundeville – nephew of Hubert de Burgh

1231–1232 Hubert de Burgh

1234–1235 Hugh Giffard

1241 Walter de Gray, Archbishop of York

?   Bertram de Crioyl

1257–1258 Imbert de Pugeys

1261 John Mansel – he was the King's man and was also with Henry in the Tower in 1263.

1262 Hugh Despenser – he was de Montfort's man and was killed at the Battle of Evesham.

The Tower described in the book is different to the one we see today, and I have tried to be as accurate as possible with its thirteenth-century layout with reference to the *Kings Works* and the help of the White Tower staff. The White Tower was whitewashed in 1241 by Henry III as was his fashion at the time. The walls did collapse in 1241, and the visions and dreams regarding Thomas Becket were recorded in Paris' chronicle. Maude's prison in the circular turret of the White Tower is not open to the public but I was fortunate enough to be allowed to see it and describe it as it is. Much of the buildings described within the Inner Bailey no longer exist, including the Great Hall and Coldharbour Gate. The White Tower's foreclosure is also gone but an example of what it would have looked like can be seen at Rochester Castle. The Tower's entrance was probably roughly where the Beauchamp Tower is now – the outer curtain wall was not added until Edward I's reign, when he put another line of defence around the fortress – also moving the moat. The Wakefield Tower which was built by Henry as his new royal apartment was originally called the Blundeville Tower after Thomas de Blundeville, who was Constable at the Tower at the time of its construction. It was named the Wakefield Tower in 1344.

The Chapel of St Peter ad Vincula which we see today was rebuilt in 1519. However, there has been a place of worship on this site for over a thousand years. Henry III repaired the building, which was there in 1240, adding the enclosed cell for an anchorite. He supported three recluses: Brother William; Idonee de Bocland (a female); and Geoffrey the Hermit. Henry and his son granted the Tower chaplains a yearly sum of fifty shillings and their role was to conduct divine services for the officers and servants residing in the Tower. Edward I demolished this church in 1286 and had it rebuilt, only for it to be damaged by fire in 1512.

The royal menagerie was supplemented by Frederick, Isabella's husband, who sent the King three leopards (they may well have been lions) to mark his marriage to the King's sister. The elephant was a gift from the King of France in 1255 and it did die from a diet of wine. Recorded in the *Prisoner* book in 1257 is the imprisonment of an unnamed Jewess in the empty elephant's cage.

    Abraham the Jew was imprisoned in 1247 for murdering his wife after he defecated on a Christian statue. And in 1255, the ninety-two Lincoln Jews were imprisoned in the Tower for the alleged murder of Hugh, an eight-year-old boy – eighteen were hung for 'refusing to plea'. The remaining Jews were released in 1256. A detailed research project has been carried out at the Tower regarding the records of over 1,000 Jewish prisoners and it signifies the huge issues Jews had in the country at this time. Henry and Richard both used Jews to their advantage and historically Jews belonged to the Crown – the Evesque family in particular were close to both. Elias le Evesque did convert to Christianity but converted back in 1266. His brother Hagin was an agent of Richard. Domus Conversorum were homes for converted Jews and were set up by the King. Christians were banned from eating and drinking with them and sex between Jew and Christian had a charge of bestiality.

    There were probably areas in the Tower in this period where ale was served and produced. The Tower has an interesting history of taverns within its walls and by the Tudor period the following taverns were recorded: The Stone Kitchen; The Bunch of Grapes; and The Tavern in the Tower. By the time Wellington closed the taverns in 1846, there was also

Tower of Vengeance

The Tiger Tavern, The Warders Hall, and The Golden Chain. There is a watercolour by Thomas Hosmer Shepherd (1792–1864) that depicts a view of The Stone Kitchen, a tavern housed at the south end of Mint Street, between the Byward and the Bell Towers. The sign in the picture states, 'The Stone Kitchen, Calvert & co Intire by John Lund'. Today, there is one remaining tavern left inside the Tower – 'The Keys' run by the Yeoman Warders carrying on the long tradition.

Alehouses were originally run by alewives who brewed their own ale daily (very different to the modern process and as a result much thicker and cloudier – there were no hops at this time), an ale-stake or long pole with a bush at the end denoting that ale was sold there. The alewife declines in the fifteenth century, when it becomes a man's job and taverns and inns become the norm. Alehouses only served ale which was brewed on the premises, and it would only last one day. In 1189, the rules of London had ordered that all alehouses must be constructed in stone – as the brewing posed a fire hazard, hence my Stone Kitchen – and by 1285 Edward I issued a statute that stated only freemen were allowed to keep alehouses in the city. Day labourers did receive drink as part of their wages. Taverns served food and inns provided accommodation.

Matthew Paris and his *Chronica Major* is a rich source of information in regard to so many things, not just the politics of the day. He richly describes the weather, the numerous comets, and atmosphere in the country. Paris was said to be fed news by the royal family themselves, and so to some degree could be described as biased, but his work is astonishing in its detail and a gift for a fiction writer.

The last word goes to the ravens – for if the ravens leave the Tower, the Tower falls and so does the kingdom. A disputed legend, but the Tower still keeps at least six (as stipulated) plus a couple of spares. They would have been commonplace in Medieval London – natural waste disposers, they would have fed on all the filth, gore, and rubbish the city had to offer. Maude's raven is called Erin in memory of my favourite Tower raven.

Acknowledgements

So many people contributed to the writing of this book, and it may take me some time to acknowledge them all! But as it's my first book, indulge me...

Firstly, my lovely friend and publisher, Karen Stanley of Mabel and Stanley Publishing, who gave me the confidence to self-publish, and this leads me to thank in turn the fabulous Marnie Summerfield-Smith, who introduced us. You two are the best writing tribe I could possibly want.

A late addition to #teamMaude is Karen's wonderful daughter-in-law, Dani Butler, of Build the Buzz, who has provided a lot of the marketing for the book. She provided such great content to help this book fly.

I am also incredibly lucky to have found the most amazing editor, Katie Seaman, who really was the missing piece to my book. Katie pushed me to write a better story and working with her is a joy.

Also, a huge shout-out to my extraordinary proofreader, Mark Swift, who went above and beyond reading the book several times to spot all of my mistakes. I really do need to buy a bag of commas.

I could not have done this without my beta readers, who had to endure a lot! My everlasting thanks to Judith Hudson and Linda Grant, who read a lot of drafts, and listened to me over many a cocktail

Tower of Vengeance

as I tried to tweak out character and plot issues. (I should also thank the fifth-floor bar and the long-suffering staff at Waterstones Piccadilly for the two for one cocktails, otherwise we could have been a lot poorer!) Also, thanks to the rather gorgeous James Edward-Hughes and Josh Lunn, who read early drafts and gave such useful feedback.

When I started this writing journey, I enrolled on a lot of Curtis Brown Creative courses, and on my very first course I met the wonderful Julie Sullivan, and we have been partners in wine ever since. Her own book promises to be amazing. I should also thank Patrick Larsimont, also on the course, who challenged me to make my random witch a real historical person with a motive, and hence Maude stepped forward.

I found Maude and Isabella in *The Tower of London Prisoner Book* by Brian Harrison and although Brian is no longer with us, I thank him here for this real gem of a book which never leaves my desk. I know his family are proud that his work has helped me so much.

To the Tower of London, where so many people have helped me along the way. Huge thanks and appreciation go to the following: Christopher, Jaz, and Mickayla Skaife for everything you do for me; to my Tower Twin, Victoria Carrington; David Coleman for all the information on the Tower Taverns; Craig Joyce for the tour of Maude's turret – an incredible experience to really feel what that room would have been like as a prison; Ana Nohales for sharing with me her extensive knowledge of the

White Tower; and to all my other Tower friends for the adventures and support over the past twelve years – Holly and Nathan Bridgeman, Julie Ttoffali, Roy Booth, Andy Merry, Laura Farleigh, and Gary Leighton.

The following people tried to educate me over the years, and they deserve a lot of gratitude: my A Level history teacher way back when I really was a Goth, Barry Wellington – I apologise re Jean Plaidy! – Professor Susan Wiseman and Professor Alan Stewart, who got me through Birkbeck and my PhD – Sue did once tell me I would probably be a better historical fiction writer than an academic; let's see if she is proved right!

To my gang of friends: Kitty and Andy Cowan; Emma Rainbow and Ian Madgin; Alan Beeson; Hannah Berry and Simon Norton, and of course, Amelia, Rosie, and Socks; Hayley Turner; Darren Dadabhay and Colin Delvin; Lindsey Fitzharris and Adrian Teale. Every single one of you rocks!

Finally, to all my family who have no idea what I get up to half the time but always support my crazy ventures, especially my darling mum, Jackie, who is my constant star and definitely gives me the world. My sister and bro-in-law, Kathryn and David Stonier, provide a lot of laughter and fun. Love also to Carolyn, Graham, and Laura Relph; Emily Mildren and Toby Bolton; Harry and Astrid Mildren; Jo Wooding; Michael and Pat Hinrich.

Tower of Vengeance

I wish my lovely mad, bad, and dangerous-to-know uncle, Howard Bacon, had lived to see the book finished, but it's dedicated to his memory and I know he will be dancing in Heaven (the club, not the celestial place – I rather think Howie will be giving the Devil a run for his money).

And Erin, my familiar, my raven, soar high my beautiful, canny bird.

About the Author

Samantha Ward-Smith holds an MA in Renaissance Studies and a PhD in English from Birkbeck. She has volunteered at the Tower of London for over twelve years where she became haunted by a story that wouldn't leave her alone until she wrote it!

She lives in Whitstable with her two cats, Belle and Rudy. She loves ravens, cats, castles and travelling as long as she has a case full of books to read.

You can find out more about Samantha on her website…

www.samanthawardsmithwriter.com

Photo credit – Janice McGuinness

Tower of Vengeance

Printed in Great Britain
by Amazon